BLOOD BATTLE

Even Ben Raines was later forced to admit that most of the Rebels' attention had been focused on traversing the terrible highway. That changed in a hurry when lead started flying and whining off the vehicles.

"Get those tanks off the trailer!" Ben yelled into his mike.

The Dusters were the first to unleash their 40mm cannon fire at the muzzle flashes coming from the edge of the small town. The main battle tanks lowered their deadly snouts and blew everything in their path to hell with 105 HE rounds. Fifty caliber and 7.62 machine gun fire began raking the area. Ben let them rock and roll for several minutes and then picked up his mike.

"Cease fire! Tanks up and check it out. Rebels behind the tanks. Let's go in and do a little night hunting!"

DEATH
IN THE
ASHES

WILLIAM W. JOHNSTONE

PINNACLE BOOKS
Kensington Publishing Corp.
http://www.kensingtonbooks.com

PINNACLE BOOKS are published by

Kensington Publishing Corp.
850 Third Avenue
New York, NY 10022

All Kensington Titles, Imprints, and Distributed Lines are available at special quantity discounts for bulk purchases for sales promotions, premiums, fund-raising, and educational or institutional use. Special book excerpts or customized printings can also be created to fit specific needs. For details, write or phone the office of the Kensington special sales manager: Kensington Publishing Corp., 850 Third Avenue, New York, NY 10022, attn: Special Sales Department, Phone: 1-800-221-2647.

Pinnacle and the P logo Reg. U.S. Pat. & TM Off.

ISBN-13: 978-0-7860-1967-0
ISBN-10: 0-7860-1967-0

First Pinnacle Books Printing: December 1998

10 9 8 7 6 5

Printed in the United States of America

Dedicated to Linda Howington
If Ben Raines makes a mistake, she'll let me know about it.

BOOK ONE

I slept and dreamed that life was beauty.
I woke—and found that life was duty.
—Ellen Sturgis Hooper

1

Ben turned his head to gaze at the silence that was once Monroe, Louisiana. Buddy had cleared the small city of Night People some months back. Ben could only wonder if any of the cannibalistic people had returned. Probably so, he concluded. But that was now the problem of Ike and Cecil.

The long column rolled on westward and put the city in their rearview mirrors.

There was no conversation in the Blazer; that would come later on. For now, Ben and his personal team were silent with their own thoughts.

The Blazer hit a rough stretch of interstate and Ben grimaced. That was something else that the Rebels would have to start on, and do it pretty damned quick. The nation's highways were deteriorating rapidly; if something wasn't done to correct it, ground transportation would be slowed to no more than a crawl.

But Jesus God! Ben thought. There were thousands of miles of just interstate alone, and the Rebels were so few. He twisted in the seat and looked at Beth.

"Make a note, Beth. When I call Base Camp One this evening, remind me to tell Ike to put together a combat engineer crew and start working on the interstate system."

"Yes, sir."

"The Mississippi River bridge at Vicksburg is to be guarded at all times."

"Yes, sir."

"Ruston up ahead," Cooper said. "You want to stop, General?"

"No. All this sector is Ike's baby now. We'll start our inspection tours when we clear the Louisiana line." Ben lifted the mike from its hook and keyed it. "Eagle to Scout."

"Go, Eagle," Tina's voice came through the speaker.

"Give me your twenty."

"Coming up on Minden."

"Roll on through. Stop at Bossier City and wait for us."

"Ten-four, Eagle. It'll be slow going from our position on. The roads are not in good shape."

"Ten-four. Any detours to watch for?"

"Not yet. And no signs of life either."

"I was afraid of that. Eagle out." Ben opened a map case and studied the clear plastic enclosed map. Maps had become very precious articles; they were taken whenever they were found. And they were constantly being updated by a small section of Rebels working at Base Camp One. Whenever the forever wandering teams of Scouts found a bridge out, they would radio back to Base Camp One and alert the map section. The map crews would then change the maps and radio that information out to all field units.

And it was a job that seemed never to end as the nation's highway system continued to fall slowly but steadily into disrepair.

The long convoy was slowed to a crawl after passing the Minden exit.

"We'll be lucky to make it out of Louisiana by nightfall," Ben said. "And this used to be an easy three-hour run." He smiled. "Driving only slightly over the posted speed limit, that is."

"General Raines breaking the law," Jersey said sarcastically. "I just can't believe that."

Ben took the ribbing with a smile.

"I remember order and laws and policemen and TV and all that," Corrie spoke from the back seat. "But I didn't appreciate the safety of it, of course. Not until the whole world fell apart."

"That's the way it always is, Corrie," Ben said. "Now it's up to us to try to rebuild it back to some semblance of what it used to be."

"It seems an impossible task for so few of us," she countered.

"Castro started a revolution with only three or four people—and won."

"Who's Castro?" Jersey asked.

Ben halted the column at Bossier City, a couple of hours before dark. They needed that much time to seek safe shelter and set up guard posts and for the meals to be distributed.

Ben set up his CP in the Hilton Inn in Bossier, just off I-20. A team of Rebels began scouting out the hotel and reported back that they had found nothing, except a lot of litter. They declared the interior of the building secure.

Ben radioed back to Base Camp One and reported in. He instructed Ike to form an engineer team and get to work on the roads and bridges.

"None of us will ever live to see the highway system completely repaired," Ike told him.

"I know it. But it's a start. We can only hope that those who come after us will continue our work. Have you heard anything from Striganov?"

"Nothin' since you pulled out. I expect he's busy outfitting his people and then will move over to the Canadian line, to wait for you."

"Ten-four. Talk to you tomorrow. Eagle out."

Ben ate an early dinner and walked outside, joining Dan and Buddy and Tina in the parking lot.

"We'll stay on Interstate 20 to Dallas," he told them. "We'll spend a few days there checking the place out. From Dallas, we'll hook up with 287 to Wichita Falls. I want an outpost established in that area, so Dan, you start talking to the settlers with us. We'll spend a few days with them, helping them get settled in."

"Yes, sir."

"After that?" Tina asked.

"We'll play it by ear," Ben told his daughter.

Ben had heard the sounds of something alien to the night reach his ears. He let the others talk while he listened. He stepped back away from the others; they were deep in conversation and did not notice. He cradled his M14 and walked toward the hotel building, his eyes moving, searching the darkness. There it was! Something . . . no, several somethings were crouched in the darkness next to a line of rusting and long-abandoned vehicles. Ben could not make out what they were; he assumed they were humans, for the light breeze was coming from their direction and he could not detect the hideous scent of Night People, which he considered a subhuman species.

Ben stepped close to the building, putting himself out of sight of the hostiles, and he had to assume they were hostiles until they proved otherwise. He began working his way along the side of the building. Dan picked that time to glance at Ben. Ben pointed to the line of cars.

One second Dan and Tina and Buddy were standing up talking, the next instant they had vanished. Tina stayed where she was, flat on the parking lot, weapon ready, while Buddy and Dan circled the row of cars.

A figure darted from the darkness of the abandoned cars, a short-barreled Uzi in his hand. Ben knew it was a he because of the shaved head clearly visible in the darkness, and the way his jeans fit.

"Looking for me, punk!" Ben called.

The young man spun around, bringing up the Uzi and letting loose a stream of lead in Ben's direction.

But Ben had moved, shifting positions as soon as the words had left his mouth. The slugs hit concrete and glass and nothing else. Ben leveled the old Thunder Lizard, set on full rock and roll, and gave the skinhead a burst of .308s. Ben was using a twenty-round magazine; the thirty-round mags were too heavy and clumsy when the M14 was fired from the shoulder. Ben used them when the M14 was bipodded. The .308s lifted the skinhead off his boots and dropped him to the parking lot.

Dan and Buddy were firing from Ben's left, so Ben did the only sensible thing under the circumstances: he went belly-down on the concrete until the firing had ceased.

"General!" Dan called.

"I'm all right. What'd you have over there?"

"A pile of dead bodies No. Here's one left alive."

The area had filled with Rebels.

"Secure it," Ben told them, then walked over to stand with Dan and Buddy.

"They're all bald," Buddy said. "What happened to their hair?"

"They shaved it off," Dan told him, kneeling down beside the badly wounded young man.

"Yeah, man," the badly wounded skinhead said. "Just like our daddies done. It's groovy. So if you don't like it, screw you!" He groaned, both hands holding his bullet-torn belly.

One of Ling's medics appeared, medical kit in hand. He looked at the young man, then looked up at Ben and shook his head.

Ben knelt down. "You have anything you'd like to say, boy. You're hard hit."

"Yeah," he gasped. "Death to all niggers and wops and spics and slopes and Jews and . . ."

Ben tuned him out. He'd heard it all before . . . many times. He looked at Dan. The Englishman arched one eyebrow.

When the young man paused, gasping for breath, and sweating from the pain, Dan said, "Now that you have most profanely stated your opinion of what at one time comprised about ninety percent of the earth's population, perhaps you would be so kind as to enlighten us as to what you and your . . . cohorts were doing skulking about in the shadows?"

"Haw?"

Dan sighed. "What the hell were you doing here?"

"We come to kill Ben Raines."

Ben did not change expression. At least half the population left on earth—at least in North America —wanted to kill him. All that had started years back, when civilization—for wont of a better word—was still flourishing, and Ben had been a popular writer of fiction. Ben had called it like he saw it, on a great many subjects, until finally he was receiving several hundred hate letters a year. His home had been shot into and he had been shot at several times.

His position was that anyone who kills another person while drinking and driving should be put to death. Honky-tonks should be burned to the ground. Poachers should be imprisoned . . . for a long time. Domesticated animals have rights. Anyone who would poison a dog should be forced to eat the same poison. Most judges had shit for brains. You couldn't be a lawyer and be honest. And so on and so forth.

To say that Ben was opinioned was like saying an elephant was heavy; no need to dwell on the obvious.

"So what else is new?" Ben asked. "You're too young to have read any of my books—that can't be it. Besides, you're probably illiterate . . ." Ben looked down at the young man. He was wasting his breath. The man was dead.

Buddy was going through the pockets of the dead men.

"Find anything, son?" Ben asked.

Buddy put his flashlight beam on a piece of paper. The paper had been encased in plastic. He quickly scanned the typewritten words, holding it in a gloved hand. "They belong to some sort of survivalist group, Father. This was written by someone of very limited intelligence." He handed the paper to Ben.

Ben stood up. "Glove up and inspect these bodies," he ordered. "Then burn them." He walked back into the hotel and sat down, adjusting the light of the battery-powered lamp to better read.

It was a declaration of war from some group with the name of Help Americans Live, Fight, And Stay Strong.

Ben had to chuckle at first, then he burst out laughing when he shortened the title to the first letter of each word.

HALFASS

Tina and Dan looked at him, curious expressions on their faces.

The short document declared war on everybody not of the Aryan persuasion, and it did so profanely —with a number of misspelled words. But whoever had written it certainly managed to get their point across. Since the Rebels had people of all races and colors within its ranks, Ben Raines's Rebels were number one on the target list to be killed. Especially Ben Raines.

And Emil Hite and Thermopolis were also on the list.

"Tina?" Ben called. "Get on the horn and advise Base Camp to inform Emil that he and his followers are on a hit list from this bunch of nuts." He waved the paper. "And radio our people with Thermopolis that Therm and his bunch are also on the list. Advise them all to go to middle alert and stay there."

"What's the name of this bunch, Dad?" Tina asked.

Ben told her.

Tina looked startled. Dan said, "I beg your pardon, sir?"

Ben repeated it.

Dan walked away, muttering and shaking his head. Tina went to the communications truck to alert those on the hit list.

Buddy entered the lobby and walked to his father, sitting down. "They're well armed, Father. Uzis, and the weapons are in good shape. They might be a bunch of nuts, but they take good care of their arms."

"You find out anything else about them?"

"A Rebel patrol found their motorcycles." He paused. "And the women who came with them."

"Alive or dead?"

"Very much alive."

"Wonderful." Ben's reply was very drily offered. "Were they with the crash truck?"

"I beg your pardon, sir?"

Dan had returned, to stand by Ben's chair.

"I did a book on motorcycle gangs years back. The crash truck is a van or truck or sometimes a converted school bus that travels about a mile or so behind the main bunch of bikers. It's used to pick up broken-down bikes. It's also used to carry the weapons, ammo, supplies, and drugs. It's almost always driven by females. Send out patrols to locate it. It'll be around. Bet on it."

"Yes, sir. Sir?"

"Yes?"

"We found identical tattoos on the men."

"A 1% symbol?"

"Yes, sir. How did you know that?"

"That's an old symbol. Years back, the American Motorcycle Association stated that ninety-nine percent of the nation's motorcyclists belonged to the AMA and were law-abiding. The 1% symbol became the mark of the outlaw bikers. If these are the people who took out our patrols in the Northwest, they're well organized, strong in number, and dangerous as hell."

"There is one woman with them who says she is not a part of this group. The other females corroborate her statements. They say she is something called a Cutie—whatever that means."

"That means, son, that she was kidnapped, taken against her will, and probably raped and beaten into submission."

Buddy thought about that for a moment. "Why, Father, back when law and order was supposed to have prevailed, didn't society do something about these gangs?"

"What would you have done, son?"

"I would have eliminated them, Father."

Ben smiled. "Yes. I also advocated that, too, Buddy. Which is another reason why I'm still on somebody's hit list."

"You goddamn right you are, you son of a bitch!" the female voice shouted at Ben from the doorway.

"Motorcycle Mamas," Ben said. "My, what an interesting trip this is going to be."

2

The Mamas were not unattractive, in a rough sort of way. However, it appeared that none of them had taken time to bathe in what Ben guessed to be about a year and a half, approximately.

Without getting up from his chair, Ben said, "Take these . . . people to the shower tent and give them soap. After they have bathed, or you have been forced to bathe them, and if the latter is the case, find steel horse brushes to use on them, disinfect them, and bring them back to me. Burn their clothing."

The women were taken from the hotel, kicking and cussing and biting and behaving in a most unladylike fashion.

"Where is the, ah, Cutie?" Ben asked.

"She's being looked at by the medics. Doctor Ling is having her tested for diseases. She says she was kidnapped several days ago. She and her boyfriend were driving to join us at Base Camp One. The boyfriend was tortured and then killed."

"Name?"

"Meg Callahan."

Ben grinned. "I bet she's redheaded and has a temper."

"She most certainly does have a temper," Dan said. "She gave me a proper cursing, then apologized when she found I was part of the Rebels. And her hair is auburn. However, it is in her favor that her ancestors came from Southern Ireland. She did not spring from that damnable bunch in Northern Ireland."

The ex-British SAS officer had little good to say about Northern Ireland, having served several tours of duty there, fighting the IRA.

"Now, now, Dan," Ben kidded him, looking up as Tina once more entered the hotel lobby.

"All parties notified, Dad," she told him. "What's all that screaming about over at number three shower tent?"

"Some, ah, ladies are being forced to bathe."

"Ladies! If those broads are ladies," Tina declared, "I'm the Jolly Green Giant."

Ben laughed and rose from his chair, walking to the ever-present coffee pot and pouring himself a cup. He turned to face his daughter. "Had Thermopolis ever heard of this bunch of bikers?"

"No. It was news to him. And Base has absolutely no intel on the group."

"Well, I guess it's up to us to provide it." Ben walked back to his chair. "When the, ah, ladies return from their bath, have Ling let his interrogation people work on them. And I want to see Meg Callahan as soon as the medics are through with her."

Dr. Ling entered the hotel lobby and walked up to Ben, taking a seat. "I think," the doctor said, "Miss Callahan was a very fortunate young lady. The group that kidnapped her was in a hurry to get to us, you specifically, General. She was not raped. That was to come later; after you were killed—sort of a victory celebration, one might say."

Ben grunted. He lifted his eyes as Meg was escorted into the hotel lobby. Auburn hair, green eyes, a very lovely Irish lass. Ben guessed her at about five-five. Very shapely.

He stood up. "Miss Callahan. Won't you take a seat?"

Tina rolled her eyes at this unexpected gallantry from her father. That usually meant that he had something up his sleeve or was romantically interested in the woman—or both.

But in a way she was glad to see it. It meant that her dad had finally decided to put Jerre out of his mind forever. Or at least try. She cut her eyes to Buddy. He was smiling.

Meg put her green eyes on Ben and stared at him for a long moment. Six feet one or two, she guessed. Dark hair peppered with gray. Strange blue eyes. She guessed him to be around fifty. Maybe one hundred ninety pounds. Looked to be in excellent physical shape. Not a handsome man in the pretty boy vein, but . . . interesting-looking. Very interesting-looking.

"Thank you, General Raines."

"Somebody bring Miss Callahan a cup of what now passes for coffee." They had found a warehouse full of coffee in New York City, but that was carefully hoarded, and not for everyday use.

21

Coffee in hand, Meg sipped and sighed gratefully.

"Tell me what you can, if anything, about this bunch of bikers who, whether they knew it or not, have named themselves HALFASS."

The woman looked startled for a moment, and then burst out laughing. "HALFASS?" she finally managed to ask.

"Yes. Help Americans Live, Fight, And Stay Strong."

"I never put it together," she admitted. "Well, I probably know more about them than I ever cared to know. Where to start?"

"From the beginning, Miss Callahan."

"Call me Meg."

"Very well, Meg. Where was your home?"

"Originally?"

"Yes."

"Southern California. Los Angeles. My mother was an actress—mostly bit parts, but steady work nonetheless. My father was a writer. Paperbacks."

"Matt Callahan?"

She nodded.

"Hell, I knew him well. We met at a WWA convention three-four years before the balloon went up. Both of us had books up for Best Western that year."

"I know. You won. Dad said you deserved it."

"That would be just like him. Go on, please."

"I was visiting my mother on location the summer the bombs came. In Arizona. We became separated in all the confusion. I've never seen her since. Eventually I drifted up into Wyoming—that was after five or six years of drifting around—and found myself a little cabin, and stayed. Raised a garden in the summer and hunted for meat during the winter . . .''

Ben thought it odd that she had mentioned nothing about her father.

"About three years ago, Satan showed up."

"Who!"

"The biker who calls himself Satan."

"He's the head of this HALFASS business?"

"In a manner of speaking, yes. Anyway, he tried to come on to me. I told him to get the hell off my land. He left, but came back later that night. I shot him. Thought I'd killed him, but later found out he was only slightly wounded. It got really wearisome there for a time. I had to watch my back at all times."

"No man in your life?"

"There have been very few men in my life, General. I generally find I can get along without them very well."

Ben smiled. "Oh?"

"Yes. And no, I don't like girls—not in the way you were probably thinking."

"I wasn't thinking that at all, Meg."

She studied him for a moment. "Yes, you probably weren't thinking that. From all that I've been able to find out about you, you're an honorable man."

"I don't know about honorable, Meg. I swore off women about a year ago, that's all."

She arched one eyebrow.

"And no, I don't like boys, either!"

They shared a laugh, Meg saying, "Anyway, I pulled out. I hated to because I'd been there for a long time. I loved that little place. Satan found me. I moved again. He found me again. Then suddenly the harassment stopped. For a year I lived alone, and without being bothered. I couldn't figure it out. Then one day this young man showed up; he was five or six years younger than me. He'd been tortured by Satan and his group. Managed to escape. I hid him for the rest of that year."

She paused and Ben took it up. "How many people does Satan have?"

"Men and women?"

"Yes."

"Thirty-five hundred, I'd guess. Their headquarters is Sheridan. It was a . . . brutal takeover. The bikers are not nice people."

"The women play the same role as the men in Satan's army. By that, I mean . . ."

"I know what you mean." She frowned. "Not all of them are fighters. Although all can fight, if you know what I mean."

Ben nodded.

"I would guess that the Rattlesnake Kid . . ."

"The *who?*" Ben blurted.

Her smile was a mixture of humor and sadness. "The Rattlesnake Kid. He calls himself Snake. Anyway, I would guess that Snake has probably a thousand men; maybe fifteen hundred. So that means a force of over, oh, three thousand, combined. But that's just in Wyoming. He has other colonies—as he calls them—in Washington, Idaho, and Montana. He shares power with some survivalist up in Montana. They, well, don't really get along too well."

"Who in the hell is the Rattlesnake Kid, Meg?"

"The real brains behind Satan and his bikers."

"Nobody with any brains wrote this." Ben held up

24

the plastic-encased paper he'd taken from the dead skinhead.

Again, Meg laughed. "Oh, no. One of the outlaw bikers wrote that. I'm sure that Snake found it to be hysterically amusing."

"Have you ever met this Snake person?"

"One time, recently, that is," she said mysteriously, "and then only by chance, and for a very brief moment."

"I'm surprised he let you go free."

"Oh, Snake wouldn't hurt me!" Meg's green eyes widened. "You see, the Rattlesnake Kid is my father."

Ben learned that Matt Callahan had apparently gone over the edge after the Great War. Gone so far over he had joined some racist group and rapidly became the head of the fool thing.

Then he tipped way over, and became, as Ben recalled, one of the characters Matt had created in a Western written years back: the Rattlesnake Kid.

Meg said that her father now dressed in Western garb, wore two six-shooters, and rode around on a black horse. Ben guessed that he and Matt—or Snake—were about the same age.

Meg had told him that her father had pulled together all the extreme right-wing groups left and set them up in a three-state area—at least three states, she guessed. Probably more.

Snake used the bikers as enforcers, and was the brains behind the entire operation. She wasn't sure where her father lived.

Meg was heading west to link up with Ben and his

Rebels, and to warn him of the powerful force that now controlled much of the northwest.

The bikers sent to ambush Ben had probably monitored Rebel radio transmissions and waited in Bossier. They had taken Meg and killed the young man with her several days before arriving in Bossier.

Dr. Ling approached Ben as he stood in the darkness outside the hotel. "We have broken those foul-mouthed female bikers. Their stories seem to corroborate what Miss Callahan told us. She does not know that we were monitoring her conversations and answers to our questions with a PSE machine. We believe she was truthful in all her statements."

"The biker women?"

"One died. The problem is, what do we do with those remaining?"

Ben sighed. "We can't turn them loose, that's for sure." He motioned for Corrie to join them. "Bump Cecil, Corrie. Tell him to send a detail over here to get these . . . ladies. Get them started right now. They should be here by daylight. We'll pull out as soon as we turn over the prisoners to them."

"Yes, sir."

"Get some sleep, Doctor. I'll see you in the morning."

Ben walked the perimeter of the hotel, chatting briefly with each sentry. Then he turned in. His last thought before sleep took him was that this journey was certainly not going to be uneventful.

The column pulled out at midmorning, having transferred the female bikers to the detail Cecil sent out. The biker mamas were less than happy about it, and voiced their dissatisfaction loudly and profanely, heaping dire threats upon Ben's head.

"What a lovely bunch of girls," Corrie said as the detail of Rebels pulled out, heading back to Base Camp One.

"Just darling," Beth said. "But at least they're clean. Probably for the first time in months."

"Drive, Cooper," Ben said.

Meg had declined Ben's offer to return to Base Camp One, instead, asking for and receiving permission to accompany the column westward. She was outfitted and assigned to the office staff until she could prove herself in a combat situation.

The Rebels rolled through Shreveport and then crossed over into Texas. The Interstate system was only slightly better in the Friendship State.

"Eagle to Scout," Ben radioed.

"Go, Eagle."

"Tina, check out Marshall and get back to me."

"Ten-four. I'm on the outskirts now."

Ben halted the convoy just before the exit sign leading off to Marshall and waited for Tina's report. He had checked his map—an old one—and found the town had once had a population of twenty-five thousand. There would be some survivors, but how many and in what kind of shape was unknown.

"Got some people here, Dad," Tina reported. "About five hundred, I'd guess . . ."

That was just about right. Ben had found during his wanderings that approximately one in fifty had survived the Great War. That computed to a population of about five million now living in what was once the United States. Give or take a couple of hundred thousand.

But they were a damned elusive bunch, spread out all over slightly more than three and a half million square miles of territory. And there was no way of determining how many had fled the U.S. borders for Canada or Mexico.

"If I could get them together," Ben murmured, "we could rebuild this country. And make it work."

"Beg pardon, sir?" Jersey asked from the back seat.

"Talking to myself, Jersey." He keyed his mike. "Their condition, Scout?"

"They're in good shape. But they want no part of us."

And had happened before, that made Ben hot. And as usual, he calmed himself quickly. He had no right to impose his own views on someone who did not wish it; not as long as they were living in peace with others and more or less abiding by some rules of law that were acceptable to the majority in the community.

"Would I be wasting my time coming in and talking with them?" Bed radioed.

"Probably," his daughter told him. "I have encountered friendlier folks."

"Hell with them," Ben replied. "Move out and check the next town." He glanced at Cooper. "Roll, Coop." He glanced back at Beth. "Make sure Cecil gets the message that this town is to receive no help from us, in any way, shape, or fashion, at any time. They want to stand alone, they can sink alone."

"Yes, sir."

Hard words from a hard man. But Ben had learned throughout the years that progressive, forward-thinking people were almost always eager for the Rebels to move in. To eagerly receive the help that

28

only the Rebels could provide. Those who wished to remain stagnant usually didn't last too long.

He had a hunch that the next town down the seemingly never-ending highway would be filled with people—a lot of them from towns nearby—who had banded together to reopen schools and clinics and were looking toward the future, living under laws and rules and regulations.

The miles rolled by. Tina called in.

"Go, Tina."

"Longview is deserted, Dad. Except for a few people that look as though time forgot them. They're a pretty sorry bunch. They say that those who reoccupied Tylor ran them out. This bunch is a complaining and whining lot."

"Pull out and head for Tyler. That seems like a good spot for an outpost, if the people want it."

They did. Ben found a clean town, with a population of about fifteen hundred, all working together toward a better and safer future. They welcomed the Rebels.

The elected officials of the town readily agreed to a meeting with Ben. They listened to Ben's ideas and agreed to become part of the network of outposts Ben was setting up around the country.

One more step toward pulling the land out of the ashes of destruction.

Ben radioed back to Cecil and informed him of the new outpost. Cecil would dispatch equipment and a small team of Rebels immediately, and yet another rung was climbed on the tall, tall ladder toward rebuilding a shattered nation.

The Rebels stayed one night in Tyler and pulled

out at dawn the following morning.

The spokesperson at Tyler had told Ben that between Tyler and Dallas, there was nothing. And no, they did not know where the people had gone. Just that they were gone; north or south or west of there. But just gone.

And Dallas was a haven for thugs and punks and hoodlums and outlaws and the like. Nobody, but *nobody* ever went into Dallas.

Ben had smiled.

The spokesperson asked why he was smiling.

"Sounds like a lovely place to visit," Ben told her.

"Roads are a mess," Tina radioed back. "And getting worse. Some of the cars abandoned have bullet holes in them."

Ben glanced at his watch. One o'clock in the afternoon. "What's your twenty, Tina?"

"About thirty-five miles east of Dallas."

"Hold what you've got."

"It must be slow going up where she is," Cooper said. "We're just a few miles behind her."

Ben glanced out the window at the brush and weeds along the interstate. "Dandy place for an ambush," he muttered.

A second later a bullet whanged off the side of the armor-plated Blazer.

"We're under attack!" his radio blared Tina's voice.

Ben jerked up the mike. "So are we, kid. Just hang on."

3

Either their attackers were awfully stupid, or they just did not realize who they were attacking.

Every truck had a Big Thumper. The high-firepower 40mm machine gun launched grenades at rapid-fire, with a one hundred percent kill-radius of ten yards per grenade. And could launch four different types of rounds.

Each platoon had at least one .50 caliber machine gun and at least one 5.56 Minimi machine gun, which was capable of spitting out 750 rounds a minute.

The attackers which swarmed out of the brush and tall grass died almost instantly after revealing themselves.

"Two tanks up to Tina's position," Ben radioed. "Dan, take a team and go."

"On my way, General."

Ben stepped out of the truck and a frightened little dog ran up to him, shivering with fear as it sat between Ben's boots. Ben knelt down and picked up the animal, knowing damn well he was going to have fleas all over him. He held the dog close to his chest and it calmed quickly.

"What'd you got there, General?" Tony asked. The young captain was the CO of D Company.

Ben held the dog out while his Rebels were going through the carnage they had just wreaked. The wounded were being looked after . . . in a manner of speaking.

"Pure mutt," Ben announced. "With a bad back leg. How about a mascot, gang?"

Those around him agreed to that and Tony named the mutt Chester. Ben handed Chester to a Rebel and got on the horn to Tina.

"How's it looking up there, kid?"

"Oh, just wonderful, Pops! Thank God I can hear the tanks coming. You?"

"I just found a little dog. Or rather, he found me. We named him Chester."

There was a long pause. "Well, I think that's just marvelous, Dad. You need a companion. God-damnit!" she yelled. "Are you sending help up here?"

Ben chuckled and looked down at his hand. It was covered with fleas. "Somebody bathe that mutt," he yelled, keying the mike. "Dan's on the way. Are you being overrun by a pack of punks, daughter?"

"No! We just beat them back. You all right?"

"I have fleas." Ben scratched his chest.

"Say again."

"Never mind. Pull back and join us. It's too dangerous a run from here on in."

"Ten-four, Dad."

Ben began walking among the dead attackers, piled up like tornado-tossed debris. He scratched as he strolled amid the torn bodies. Chester was a four-footed walking flea factory. Cute little fellow though. Ben stopped and knelt down beside one man, who appeared to still be breathing. Carefully, Ben tossed the man's weapons out of reach and then placed the muzzle of his M14 against the man's cheek.

"If you're thinking of going for a hideout gun or a knife, partner, I'd think again."

The man opened his eyes. Hate shone like burning coals at Ben. "Raines! We pulled the wrong cards this time, didn't we?"

"I would certainly say so." Ben glanced at the man's bullet-shattered belly. "If you have anything to say, you'd better say it quick."

"You a hard bastard, ain't you, Raines?"

"Yep."

"You don't remember me, do you?"

"Fortunately, no."

"I was with Hartline back when you was named President. Right before them rats come with the disease."

"Hartline is dead."

"Yeah, I heard you kilt him. I'm a-gettin' cold."

"You want me to set you on fire?"

The man cursed Ben. "I never met a human being as hard as you, Raines," he gasped. "I seen you with that stupid-lookin' dog over yonder. You act like you cared what happened to him, but it don't bother you none to squat there and watch me die." He moaned in pain, hands clutching at his bloody belly.

"The dog can't help being what he is, mister.

That's the difference."

"What's the difference."

"You had a choice."

The man died cursing Ben.

Ben stood up and walked around, finding no more wounded. He paused and watched as Tina and Dan returned. They walked over to him. "Who are they, General?" Dan asked.

"Trash. Probably trash before the Great War."

"We got the fleas off Chester," Cooper's voice drifted to them. "Now who's gonna get the fleas off me?"

Ben scratched his arm.

"You have a rash, General?" Dan asked, his eyes following the scratching.

"I have fleas."

Dan immediately started scratching.

"Let's roll on," Ben said. "We'll stop at the next town we come to and decide what we're going to do about Dallas."

"What about the bodies?" Corrie asked.

"Leave them for the carrion birds and the coyotes and the other animals. They have to eat too."

Hard words from a hard man. But nations aren't rebuilt by any other type of person.

"My people have worked in close enough to the city to see lots of torchlights," Dan told Ben.

"Estimates, Dan?"

"Hundred, at least. Perhaps as many as several thousand. My Scouts have only approached from the east side."

"Tell them to back off, Dan. No point in risking their lives needlessly. We need to know if those in the city are holding hostages . . . and they probably are. We're just going to have to play it by ear in the morning."

Ben stood on an overpass and looked at the sprawling city. For a time, he had believed the Twin Cities to be destroyed; that was the rumor. And like so many rumors, it had been disproven.

Ben shifted his M14 into a more comfortable position. He had stopped carrying his Thompson because a great many people—including some in his own command—were beginning to think the old Chicago Piano had some magical power, and that Ben was some sort of God.

Ben had done his best to dispell those rumors.

Meg Callahan walked up with Jersey and Cooper to stand by Ben's side in the middle of the westbound lanes.

"I certainly remember the TV program," she said.

"Old J.R.," Ben said with a smile. "He wouldn't like Dallas much now."

"Are we going in?" Meg asked.

Ben nodded. "We'll approach the city—or what is left of it," he added, looking at the smoke that hung low over Dallas. The city appeared ravaged, and probably a lot of it had been. With no way, or will, to fight fires, he was certain a lot of buildings had been destroyed, mainly because of neglect and carelessness.

"Dan?" Ben called, and the Englishman walked over to him. "Take your Scouts to here." He pointed to the map. "I'm sending a tank in with you. Check the area out carefully but don't advance unless you receive orders from me."

"Right, sir." Dan walked off, yelling for his Scouts. They began pulling out almost immediately, the main battle tank leading the way, its 105mm lowered and ready for a fight. In addition to the 105, the tank had one .50 caliber machine gun and had been modified for two 7.62 machine guns. The big V-12 engine could move it along at 40 mph.

The tank clanked to a halt a block east of Buckner Blvd. Dan and his people, in APCs, waited behind it. Rifle fire came from a building north of the tank, the bullets whining off the heavily armored tank. The commander shifted the 105 and the early morning was shattered as a HEP—high-explosive plastic round—knocked a huge smoking hole in the building.

Men could be seen running from the smoking structure. The .50 caliber started yammering. The men were hurled spinning and sprawling as the heavy slugs impacted with flesh.

The area became very quiet except for the moaning of the wounded men to the north of the tank and Dan's Scouts.

The tank commander swung the big 105 and gave the closest building to the south a round of HEP. The impacting round knocked a man screaming from the top floor. He hit the ground and lay still, his rifle beside him. The TC put a round of Willie Peter into the building.

Lifting 7x50 binoculars, Ben could see men running out the back of the smoking structure. Ben turned to Corrie. "Tell Dan to check it out."

The orders were relayed.

It did not take Dan long to determine that the immediate area around his position had been deserted.

"Another tank up," Ben ordered. "Tell Dan to split his people when the support tank arrives. Clear north and south for two blocks."

Another main battle tank rumbled past Ben and moved into position. Scouts scrambled from APCs to walk along the safe side of the tank as the tanks moved north and south.

Ben looked at Meg. "Meg, find Dr. Ling and ask him if he has any rabies innoculations with him."

"Sir?" she appeared startled.

"For Chester," Ben explained with a smile.

"Right." She walked away, thinking that the man's mind sure worked in curious angles.

"You want to interrogate any of the wounded, General?" Corrie asked. "Colonel Gray is on the horn."

"Yes. Bring them to me."

Ben hand-rolled a cigarette while he waited. He looked up as Meg approached.

"Dr. Ling says he wasn't aware that he was running a school of veterinary medicine, General Raines. But he would certainly radio back to base and have some vaccine dropped by air."

"We're going to be here all day, Meg. Tell Ling to have that done. It's just a short hop from base to here. Let's get Chester all fixed up. No need to take any chances."

"Right, sir."

Several of the less severely wounded men were brought to Ben. They smelled as though they had forgotten that water was used for things other than drinking. They appeared defiant, but fear was clear in their eyes.

"You know who I am?" Ben asked.

They knew.

"We can do this easy or hard," Ben told them. "It's up to you. You can answer my questions now, or I can turn you over to an interrogation team. They'll pump you full of drugs and learn the truth that way. You have about a sixty-forty chance of surviving it. It's up to you."

"And if we tell you what you want to know right now?" a burly lout asked. "What then?"

"You walk free. But not back to the city; at least not so I can see you do it."

"What do you want to know?"

"How many men in the city?"

"I ain't got no way of tellin' that, General Raines. The city's all cut up into zones. They's probably fifty or sixty different warlords controllin' different parts of Dallas and Fort Worth. You go a half a dozen blocks in any direction, they's someone else in charge."

"And it's always changin'," another added. "Mac-Nally's got this area today. Lopez and his bunch might have it next week. Next month, Pete Jones might control it."

"What's left in the city?"

The man shrugged. "To be honest, nothin'. It's been looted so many times . . . it's just a shell."

Ben could believe that. He'd seen it many times before, in other cities and towns. "How many prisoners—slaves, if you will—are being held inside the city?"

"Bunches," the first man said. "There agin, I ain't got no way of knowin'."

"How many are you holding and where are they?"

"I ain't holdin' none personal. But MacNally's got about . . . thirty, I reckon. He lives over yonder about four blocks from Buckner." He pointed the way. "It's a warehouse."

"Heavily guarded?"

"Oh, yes, sir. Plenty of men around it all the time."

"This Lopez and Jones . . . what can you tell me about them?"

"They bad. But I don't now where they're livin'. Everything changes all the time. One gang will move out to go on a raid, another gang will move into their territory and then they'll be a big fight when the first gang comes back. That's the way it's been for years."

The other prisoners agreed.

Ben told the Rebels who'd brought the men to him to take them to Ling's aid station. He looked at the men. "If I ever see any of you again, and you're armed, I'll kill you where you stand. Get out of here."

They got out quickly, prodded by the muzzle of an M16. Dan returned, to tell him it was clear for Ben to enter.

"We going to clear the city, General?"

Ben was thoughtful for a moment, then turned to face the hazy city. "We'll spend a few days here," he finally said with a sigh, putting his back to the haze of the Twin Cities. "But God knows I don't want to." He lifted a map. "We're close enough to Base Camp One to be reinforced within a few hours' time—by

39

air. Dan, have Captain Tony's company swing wide around the city. I wouldn't even suggest using 635. I'd backtrack, to avoid unnecessary confrontations, up through Garland, Richardson, Carrollton, and Coppell, then drop down into the Dallas-Fort Worth Airport. Start clearing it. Tell him to take two tanks with him."

"Yes, sir."

"How have these crud managed to keep the creepies out? I should have asked those scumbags."

"There hasn't been a sign or smell of them, General. Not as far in as we pushed."

"Well, the creepies do seem to like airports. Advise Tony to be very careful. Tell him to push off as soon as possible. And have your people past Buckner hold what they've got."

"Right, sir."

"Corrie, advise Base Camp One that I am preparing to clean out Dallas-Fort Worth—or at least sections of it—and to be ready to airlift supplies to me starting yesterday."

"Yes, sir," she said with a smile.

He turned to Meg. "You ready for a little taste of combat, Meg? The Rebel way?"

"I'm with you, General Raines."

She had been armed with the weapon of her preference, and that happened to be an AR15; said she'd owned a Colt AR15 for years, had used it against outlaws and trash several times, and certainly knew the nomenclature of the weapon.

The Rebel philosophy was: whatever you're comfortable with. It kept the armorers and the reloading factory busy, and the Rebels happy.

"All right, Meg. You'll stay with the support people for the time being. Don't worry. Before this is over, you'll get to see more combat than you ever dreamt of seeing. And that's just in this area."

Ben waved his people to the Blazer. "Let's go, Cooper."

"To Buckner, General?"

"Right up to the lines, Coop. I want to personally see what these yahoos are made of."

"Here we go again," Jersey said.

"General, you reckon these people are in cahoots with the creepies?" Cooper asked.

He shook his head. "I don't think so, Coop. And that puzzles me. One thought I have is that the outlaws were strong enough to drive them back, or out. The next batch of prisoners we take, we might get some answers."

A tank pulled across the intersection, preventing the Blazer from going any farther. "Nothing clear from this point on, General," the voice came out of the speaker.

Ben opened the door and got out. "Let's go, gang. Looks like we hoof it for a time."

4

The tank commander was frantically radioing Dan Gray, telling him of Ben's going into bogie country with only a small team.

Ben had crossed over into no-man's land and approached a warehouse, waving his people down and spread apart. He had caught motion from behind a very dirty window. The window suddenly shattered and a gun barrel was shoved out, spitting lead in the Rebels' general direction.

Ben lobbed a grenade toward the window, and luck was with him: it sailed through the broken glass. A few seconds later, it blew, and all was silent.

"Good toss," Beth said.

"Pure luck," Ben replied as the sounds of running boots from behind them reached Ben's ears.

"Goddamnit, General!" Dan was shouting and swearing as he ran toward the warehouse.

With a laugh, Ben ran the short distance to the warehouse, hit the door with his shoulder, and rolled in. Lead started zinging and whining all around him as he rolled toward the dubious protection of packing crates; he hoped they were full of something that might stop a slug.

Ben tossed another Fire-Frag toward the direction of the unfriendly fire and hit the door as it blew.

Screaming filled the close air of the warehouse. "We yield, we yield!" a man yelled, just as windows were knocked out with Rebel gun butts and muzzles of weapons set on full auto were poked through the holes.

Ben stood up and looked at a red-faced and very angry Dan Gray. Ben beat him to conversation before the Englishman could rebuke him for taking unnecessary risks . . . which Ben knew Dan was just about to do.

"Get the prisoners outside, Dan. And secure this area. I want to talk to these so-called outlaws and warlords." Ben reached up and plucked a grenade off Dan's battle harness. "I only brought two with me," he said with a smile. "I used them."

The newest batch of prisoners were just as scummy-looking as the last bunch Ben had spoken with. Sullen and shifty-eyed as they stood before Ben in the lobby of an office building just cleared moments before.

"One of you MacNally?" Ben asked.

"Haw!" a man snorted. "You come up agin MacNally and he'll skin you alive and hang your hide up to dry."

Ben's smile was not pleasant. "Lots of people have tried that over the years, trash. I'm still here and they're rotting in the grave. If I took the time to bury them," he added.

"You say!" the man sneered.

"Yeah, he says," another outlaw spoke up. "And he done it, too. Don't get too damn lippy, Hal."

"I'll get as lippy as I want to with this tin soldier boy," Hal replied. "He ain't nothin' to me."

"Dan!" Ben called. "Take Hal outside and shoot him."

Dan stepped forward and Hal paled under the dirt on his face. "Now, wait a minute! Lookie here . . ."

"Shut up!" Ben yelled. "I'm losing patience with the lot of you. Just answer my questions and I'll cut you loose. Get smart-assed with me just one more time and I'll have the lot of you shot! Is that understood?"

It was amply understood. One outlaw almost broke his neck shaking his head in the affirmative, his Adam's apple bobbing up and down with fear-swallows.

"Fine. I am so pleased that we now understand each other. Where is this MacNally person?"

Hal was very eager to talk and please the General. "He's done gone into hidin', I reckon, Ben Raines. He tooken his army and is hidin' out."

"You'll show me where his home was after we talk." It was not a question.

"Oh, yes, sir. Be right proud to do that, Ben Raines."

"Dallas seems to be free of what we call Night People. Why is that?"

"They tried to come in here, General," another man spoke. "They tried bunches of times. The warlords finally struck a deal with them. We give them women and kids after we's done havin' our way with them. That way everybody is happy."

"Good God in Heaven!" Dan exclaimed.

The man shrugged. "I figure we're all gonna be shot anyways. Might as well level with you people."

"You don't seem afraid of dying," Ben remarked.

"I got the cancer."

"All right." Ben stood up. "Let's go see where this MacNally lived."

Squalor was the single word that sprang into Ben's mind as he stood in the building where the warlord, MacNally, lived. The place was a filthy, rat-infested, cavelike dwelling. A dozen men, women, and children were chained like wild animals to a wall. They were naked and cowering at Ben's approach.

"I reckon MacNally was done with them folks," Hal told Ben in a matter-of-fact tone. "Probably going to give them to the Night People next time they showed up."

"And when was that going to be?" Ben asked, watching as his Rebels, using bolt cutters, freed the frightened people from their chains. They were led outside, to be transported to Rebel aid stations.

"Sometime this week was all I know," Hal said.

"Where does the exchange take place?"

"South of the city. On the old county line 'tween Dallas and Ellis County. I can show you, Ben Raines."

"Thank you. I'll take you up on that offer." Ben looked at the outlaws. "You men will be our . . . guests for a time. You will not be mistreated, but you will be confined." He motioned for the men to be taken away. When they had gone, he turned to Dan.

"Order all advancing parties to hunt a hiding spot

and keep their heads down. Pull all vehicles and tanks into cover. I want the creepies—if they have scouts out—to find the city they are accustomed to seeing. We make no contact with the warlords, and fire only if fired upon. Let's see if we can pull this thing off."

"We get rid of a lot of creepies and then sweep the city," Dan stated.

"That's it."

"Dad," Tina said. "The thought has come to me that we may just have to destroy every city and town we come to. The only towns remaining will be the ones our people occupy. That way we can force the creepies out into the countryside where we can deal with them."

Ben sighed heavily. "I'm afraid you may be right, Tina. Rebels everywhere may have to go on search-and-destroy missions—nationwide."

Ben, traveling with only a small team of handpicked Rebels, personally viewed the area where the warlords handed over prisoners to the creepies. It was located between two small towns on the county line. Ben took the exact coordinates of the area and radioed back to Cecil, briefing the man.

Talking to him on the scramble frequency, and using translators, Ben said, "Our prisoners say the creepies always come up from the south, Cec. And always on Interstate 35. So I'm betting they've occupied Waco. The exchange takes place at midnight. Always at midnight, always on a Friday. They've been doing it that way for several years. No reason why they should change it now. We're constantly monitoring frequencies, and have picked up nothing that would indicate MacNally has alerted the creepies to our presence. I don't think these outlaws even have long-range radio hookups. Most of what I've seen is CB equipment, and it's in bad shape. So here is what I want . . .''

For several days the Rebels maintained a very low profile, with not one shot being fired from either side. Many of the warlords felt the Rebels had left the area, moving on to wherever they were originally headed. Captain Tony had reached the airport and found it deserted. He dug his people in tight and stayed out of sight.

Ben quietly moved a handpicked team of Rebels close to the exchange point; he personally led that team.

Back at Base Camp One, Cecil and Ike had readied the equipment Ben had requested and were standing by.

"Want to see a show tonight, Meg?" Ben asked the woman.

"You mean like a movie?"

Ben smiled. "Better. This won't be play-acting."

"Sure."

"Be ready to go in an hour."

Quietly, without attracting any attention—he hoped—Ben moved his teams into position near the exchange point. He climbed to the top floor of a building where nightvision equipment was set up. He glanced at his watch. Nine o'clock.

"What's all that stuff?" Meg asked.

"So we can see this evening. Ever seen a creepie, Meg?"

"No, but I've heard of the disgusting things they do. Even Satan is scared of those people."

At Base Camp One, several PUFFs were taking off. The PUFFs were flying instruments of death. Each PUFF carried four 20mm Vulcan cannons, six-barreled Gatling guns, four pairs of 7.62 machines and Bofors cannons, all side and bottom-mounted. When the PUFFs got into position, flying in a slow circle, they were the most destructive flying machines ever built.

"How many creepies did the prisoners say usually met the outlaws?" Tina asked.

"They weren't sure. Only that it was quite a bunch. MacNally and the others usually handed over hundreds of captives."

"For the slaughter," Meg said softly.

"That is correct—literally for the slaughter."

At eleven-thirty, Rebels drove hastily repaired old bob trucks they had found outside the city up to the exchange point. The drivers quietly and very quickly got the hell out of that area.

"Won't be long now," Ben murmured.

"What won't be long?" Meg asked.

"A show like none you have ever seen before," Ben told her. "I can promise you that."

The minutes ticked by in silence. Once again, Ben glanced at his watch. "Corrie, contact the PUFFs."

"They're in position, General," she told him. "Flying without lights as ordered."

"Here they come, General!" a Rebel said, peering

through the night scope. "Must be fifty or sixty trucks. And they're running without lights."

"It worked," Ben whispered. "Come on, you creepie bastards. I have a present for you."

"Closer," the Rebel watching the convoy announced.

"PUFFs in," Ben ordered.

Within seconds, the howl of props reached the Rebels.

"Creepie convoy stopping within coordinated area," Ben was informed.

"PUFFs in position and circle completed," another Rebel announced.

"Commence firing," Ben ordered.

The night sky was shattered as the crew chiefs and gun mechanics opened fire. The PUFFs trembled and shook as they released their lethal loads. An area the size of several football fields was instantly turned into a deathtrap. Gas tanks on the creepie trucks exploded as hot lead tore into them.

There was no place for the creeps to run; practically every square foot was being mauled from the air. Sixteen thousand rounds of death was hurled into the coordinated area in only a few minutes. The fires set by the impacting incendiary rounds lit up the sky so all could see the carnage.

"Cease firing," Ben ordered.

The night became still except for the crackling of flames.

"Return to base," Ben said. "Good job, people."

Meg was standing by the window, her mouth hanging open, still in a mild form of shock at what she had just witnessed.

She finally shook her head and said, "Are you going to use these against Satan?"

"I don't know. A lot depends on the terrain and whether innocents might be harmed. Then there is your father to think of."

"My father is nuts," Meg said flatly. "He'd be better off dead. There is no telling how much human suffering and degradation he has caused . . . indirectly and directly. I resigned myself to my father's fate months ago. I'll keep the good memories of him; back when conditions were normal. More or less," she added.

Ben nodded. "All right, gang. Let's get back and get some sleep. Tomorrow we start destroying a city."

Ben was up long before dawn, as usual. He dressed, pulling on body armor and slipping into his battle harness. He picked up his M14 and stepped outside his quarters to stand beside the sentry.

"Everything's been quiet, General," he was informed. "Last night's show probably gave the outlaws some second thoughts."

"It might have," Ben replied. "But they've got nowhere else to go. They'll fight, I'm thinking. Unless they have some other tricks up their sleeves. We'll know just after dawn."

After breakfast—S.O.S., nothing ever changes in any army, but at least it was hot and filling—Ben was enjoying an early morning smoke when Dan walked up, a city map in his hand.

"The outlaws have pulled back, General. To this

point." He held up the map. "And they are flying a white flag. They don't look like they're surrendering, so I can but assume they wish to talk."

"You're probably right. Has Captain Tony radioed in?"

"Affirmative. He said they'll start clearing a runway for the birds at first light. No creepies."

"All right, Dan. Find out what the scum have on their minds."

"A deal," Dan reported back in a few minutes.

Ben leaned back, smiling. "Let me guess: they would be willing to trade whatever prisoners they hold in return for their safety?"

"My, my, General," Dan said with a smile. "What an astute fellow you are."

"Why, of course, we'll make a deal with them!"

Meg had walked up with Corrie. "You'd deal with outlaws?" Meg asked. "I always heard that Ben Raines didn't make deals with anybody."

Ben put a hand over his heart and hung his head. "How in the world do you suppose such a terrible rumor ever got started? What a horrible thing to have said about a man like me. A heart as big as all outdoors."

Then he and Dan burst out laughing.

Meg and Corrie looked at one another and shook their heads. Tina and Buddy had walked up to catch part of what was taking place.

"Pay absoutely no attention to either of them," Tina told the women. "My father wouldn't deal with scum like those in the city if that was Buddy and me being held."

Now Meg looked more confused than ever.

"I . . . don't understand."

Buddy explained. "General Raines is going to get the prisoners freed, and then he will declare war on the outlaws and probably kill them all . . . or as many as don't run away."

"Can you believe this, Dan?" Ben tried his best to look terribly hurt. "My own children speaking about me in such a manner. Oh, the shame of it all. What did I do wrong?"

"Our father," Tina said, "also has a lot of B.S. in him. You'll get used to him . . . in time."

Ben stood up from the steps where he'd been relaxing and thinking, enjoying the spring weather. "Dan, get the main battle tanks in position, also the Dusters and the 81mm mortar crews. We don't have enough people to box them in, so this is going to be a frontal assault."

"Right, sir."

Ben smiled thinly. "Now we'll see if MacNally and those others of his odious ilk have a sense of humor about them."

"In other words, Father," Buddy said, "we are going to see if they can die well."

"Precisely."

5

"I ain't buyin' this atall," MacNally said. "Ben Raines don't give up this easy. He's a-pullin' something. Bet on it."

"Scared, Mac?" Pete Jones sneered at him. The huge black man hated MacNally and had never made any attempt to hide that hatred.

"Yeah, and so are you, you ugly coon. But I got sense enough to admit it. You're just stupid!"

Pete faced his white outlaw counterpart. "I think, MacNally, when this . . . situation has been resolved, I shall kill you!"

"I doubt it. Now git your ugly face outta mine."

"Knock it off!" Lopez told them. "We have enough to worry about without fighting among ourselves. Now are we going to take General Raines's offer, or not?"

Pete was the first to speak. "I don't see that we have a choice. But we're no match for Raines and his Rebels. Not with this rabble around us."

"Nigger, you shore talk funny," Mac told him.

"You know 'at?"

Pete sighed with his race's centuries-old, built-in patience when dealing with white trash and rednecks. He had educated himself during his second hitch in prison. For rape and murder. He'd killed a dozen men and women before finally getting caught and sentenced. Pete was very literate, but still just as much trash and just as worthless as those around him.

"Then what do you have in mind, Pete?" the Mexican asked.

He looked first at Lopez, then at Mac. "I really don't like you, Mac, but you can fight and you've got some good men with you—even though they are a motley crew of white trash . . ."

"Git to the point, coon," Mac told him. "You just bumpin' your gums to hear your head rattle."

Pete grunted in disgust. "Mac, you and Lopez and your people. Me and mine. Young, Morgan, Bass, Hardy, and maybe a few more. Yeah. Pipes and Howard. We cut our prisoners loose like all the rest and then get the hell out of this city. I think Raines is going to throw some heavy artillery in on us as soon as the prisoners are clear."

"Why not take the prisoners with us?" Lopez asked. "For trade down the line."

"Because we're going to have to be traveling fast," Pete explained. "And the prisoners are a drag."

Lopez nodded. "Makes sense to me. OK. I'm in." He looked at MacNally. "You?"

Mac shrugged. "Why not?"

"Let's get busy."

*　　*　　*

56

"Where is the exchange point to be?" Ben asked.

"This bridge right here on 175," Dan said, pointing it out. "Noon."

"Everybody in position?"

"Setting on ready."

"Corrie, bump the base and alert Cecil that we're going to need lots of trucks and some medical people over here. We can fly the seriously injured out. And we're going to need to be resupplied."

"Yes, sir."

"It never ends," Beth said. "It just never ends. There is no light at the end of the tunnel."

Ben knew how she felt. He'd been fighting for a decade, ever since the world was torn apart by nuclear and germ warfare.

"It's there, Beth. It's a very faint light. But it's there. We have to keep believing that. If we, of all people, can't have that faith, then civilization is doomed."

"I know," she said. "I just get so discouraged at times."

"So do I," Ben told her.

"What do you do to shake the mood?" Beth asked.

"Why," Ben said with a straight face, "I just sit right down and have myself a good cry!"

The laugher at the thought of General Raines sitting down on the curb and bawling broke the somber mood.

"Let's go get in place, gang," Ben told them, walking toward the Blazer. He looked around. "Where the hell is Cooper?"

"Probably trying to put the make on some unsuspecting female," Jersey said.

"Around him," Beth said, "there are no unsuspecting females. I cringe every time he crosses his legs for fear he'll damage his brain."

Ben watched the activity on the other side of White Rock Creek through binoculars from the top floor of a building just off Hawn Freeway. It was getting close to the exchange time and the outlaws were working feverishly to get their prisoners to the bridge.

"How will we know we won't be dropping rounds in on innocents the outlaws have held back?" Meg asked, standing beside Ben.

"We can't be one hundred percent sure. But we won't fire until we've spoken with some of the exchange prisoners. If we can get the majority out . . . I have to think it'll be worth it."

"Hal and the other men we're holding are getting a little bit edgy as to their fate," Buddy told his father.

"I intend to cut them loose," Ben replied. "They've cooperated with us right down the line. I told them their best bet would be to go far away from what we leave of Dallas-Fort Worth, and take up gardening. I think they got the message."

Meg was sure they did. She was learning that Ben Raines could be a compassionate man on one hand, and totally ruthless on the other. To say Ben was a complex man would be understating him.

"Captain Tony said they have a runway cleared, General," Corrie told him. "They'll mark it with flare pots."

"Inform Base Camp One of that news, please." He glanced at her, smiling. "And how is Chester doing these days?"

"Vaccinated and clean and getting fat. Colonel Gray is his biggest fan. Chester sleeps on the front seat of the Colonel's Jeep. The two are practically inseparable."

Corrie spoke to communications back at the base camp, smiled, and said, "General? Dr. Chase has a message for you."

"I just bet he does. What is it?"

"He says the next time you capture biker women, don't send them to him. Just shoot them."

"Ask the old goat where is all that compassion he's supposed to possess?"

After a brief exchange, Corrie said, "Dr. Chase said something in French, General. I don't speak French."

"It's just as well, Corrie. I have a pretty good idea what he said. Did it sound like *mon cul?*"

"Yes, sir."

"He just told me to kiss his ass."

"Yes, sir. And the trucks to take the prisoners back left Base Camp One several hours ago, sir."

"Good." Ben lifted his binoculars. "Heads up, people. Here they come." Ben lowered the field glasses and handed them to Corrie. "And the prisoners are in pitiful shape. I'm going to enjoy destroying those bastards," Ben said grimly.

"Those children look . . . defeated," Corrie said.

"We've found that a percentage of those we've rescued will never come all the way back, Corrie. They've been too badly abused and used. But most of them make it after a time."

"How about the ones who don't respond?"

"They're placed with loving, caring families. We

do the best with what we have."

They stood, mostly in silence, as the bands of prisoners were handed over to the Rebels. As soon as they were across the bridge, as many as possible were quickly questioned.

Corrie listened to her headset. "Colonel Gray says he believes all the prisoners were handed over, General. He also says that advance Scouts on the south end of the airport report a large number of men leaving the city on Interstate 30. Heading west. Looks to be several hundred."

"The smart ones are bugging out. I expected some to do that. Tell Dan as soon as the last prisoners are across . . . open fire."

"With pleasure, sir," Corrie said.

There were many outlaws who took Ben at his word. They stood on the bridge and just directly across from the exchange point, grinning foolishly, totally unaware they were looking down the barrels of hundreds of weapons.

The first volley of rifle fire took the gawking, grinning, arrogant outlaws by surprise, knocking them screaming and spinning and sprawling. Then the tanks started lobbing in 105 rounds, HEP, Willie Peter, Incendiary, in that order. With a range of 3300 meters, the main battle tanks started dealing out misery.

The 81mm mortars opened up, tossing in one round every twenty seconds. Ben had beefed up his initial request for the self-propelled 81s. Each company had three of the mortar carriers, and with a range of nearly 3700 meters, the 81s could reach out and touch someone two and a half miles away.

Forty-millimeter Big Thumpers began yowling out their lethal loads in rapid-fire. On the west side of the bridge, chaos became king as the outlaws found themselves with no place to run.

"That son of a bitch!" Pete Jones cursed Ben Raines. "You just can't trust anybody nowadays."

He was tooling his Cadillac through the rubble and waste of Fort Worth.

Pete's main man, Sam, sat in the front seat and, like his boss, cussed Ben Raines. When he wound down, he asked, "Where we headin', Pete?"

Pete shook his head. "I haven't make up my mind, Sam. I don't know where Ben Raines is heading, for one thing."

"What difference does that make?"

A pained look passed Pete's face. "Because, Sam, I would really rather avoid the good General and his Rebel army, if at all possible."

Sam thought about that for a moment. "Oh! Right, Pete. Sure."

Ben and his Rebels rolled on through the bloody and destructive afternoon. By midafternoon they had hammered their way to the convention center, leaving behind them streets filled with dead and dying outlaws.

Ben called a halt to the advance. "Scouts out," he ordered. "Let's see what's out there."

The reports began coming back in sooner than even Ben had expected. "They've bugged out, General. We can't find a sign of life anywhere."

Other Scout teams who had fanned out in all directions reported the same thing.

"Stand down," Ben ordered his people. "Maintain

middle alert. Tomorrow is going to be a very long day."

"What's on the agenda for tomorrow, Father?" Buddy asked.

Ben looked at his son. "We destroy the city."

When Ben finished speaking with Base Camp One, he leaned back in the chair and accepted a cup of coffee with thanks. He was tired. Not so much physically, but emotionally. He had taken the first step toward doing something that he had known for years must be done.

He was about to destroy the remains of a society, in order to rebuild what he hoped would be a better one.

"Cecil is sending in enough explosives to blow up the world—his words. The first planes will be landing in the morning. Dan, start scouting around and find some Lo-Boy trailers. Then set our mechanics to working on bulldozers. Find out where the county kept their equipment." He smiled. "If we didn't steal it ten years ago and take it up to the Tri-States, there'll probably be plenty of equipment still around."

"Right, sir. We have found several huge underground gasoline storage tanks. The gas tested out to be free of water. I've ordered all available tanker trucks to start sucking it up."

"Good move. What we can't haul with us, we'll send back to Cecil and Ike. Corrie, might as well get Cecil back on the horn and tell him to get some tanker rigs on the way over here." He looked at his watch. Almost midnight. He stood up and stretched.

62

"Are we certain that all innocents are clear of the city?"

"I believe so, Dad," Tina told him. "Are we going to fire the city by sections?"

"Yes. It's not the suburbs that attract the scum and the creepies, it's the cities themselves. An attraction that I have yet to understand. So the cities and the larger towns go down under the torch, so to speak."

"The scorched earth policy of the colonies' civil war," Dan said with a slight smile.

"Yes. And I didn't agree with it after I studied about it in school," Ben said. "And I'm not happy with myself for ordering it done now. But the cities and probably seventy-five percent of the smaller communities are not reinhabitable, nor is it feasible to think about doing so. It will be a century, or longer, before cities once more become the vogue—if they ever do. I'm sure that future generations will curse me for destroying them, and then after they do that, they can settle down and rebuild. But for now, the cities are containers of the scum. So they have to go."

"Over how many campfires have we discussed this down through the years, General?" Dan asked.

"Too many for me to count, Dan. I probably should have started with this policy right after the plague hit us. I've toyed with the idea for several years." He drained his coffee cup. "Well, to bed. We'll have the taste of ashes in our mouths for days to come."

6

Ben was at the airport when the birds started arriving at first light. The twin-engine cargo planes were packed with C4 and C5 explosives and timers and detonators. When the explosives were off-loaded, some of the more seriously injured—both body and mind—of those freed prisoners were placed on board for the flight back to the base camp.

Corrie had looked at the sprawling airport with wonder in her eyes. "The highway runs right through the airport!" she exclaimed. "I never saw such a thing!"

"Yes," Ben said drily, remembering his mixed feelings about DFW. Especially when he landed at gate 3 and had twelve minutes to get to gate 62. Same airline. "It was a . . . wonder, to be sure."

"You flew the big jets out of here, General?" Jersey asked.

"Many times, Jersey. From where I lived, if you flew east, you changed at Atlanta. If you flew west, you changed at Dallas. With very few exceptions."

"That must have been exciting," Jersey said.

Ben looked at her and smiled. Jersey had been in hundreds of fire-fights during her tenure with the Rebels. And she was excited about a plane ride. It was true that even war became blasé after a time.

"Let's go to work," Ben said.

The Rebels began blowing up and burning the city block by block. And the rats came out by the hundreds of thousands, in brown filthy racing hordes. Dr. Ling put in an urgent request for rabies vaccine and anyone who was bitten, and there were several Rebels who were bitten, was immediately inoculated against the dread disease.

"There was a study done some years ago," Ben mentioned casually, "by some university, back when those things were done, that concluded that someday we would all be dining on rat meat. It's supposed to be full of protein. Good for you." He spooned some lunch into his mouth.

Meg looked at the goop on her plate and suddenly lost her appetite. "Rat meat! Are you serious?"

"That's what I read. What's the matter, Meg, lose your appetite?"

"Have you ever eaten a rat, General?"

"Can't say as I have. One of the guys involved in the Watergate mess did, though. Said he did."

"What's a Watergate?" Corrie asked.

Ben sighed as he felt the years press just a little bit harder on him. "Pass the hot sauce, please."

*   *   *

Nothing was spared in the Rebel's plan of destruction. At first Ben tried to inspect each building before bringing it down. But after a few forays, he discovered that anything of value had long been looted. After that, he gave his people carte blanche and the work went swiftly.

The Rebels became accustomed to the smoke smell that settled in their nostrils and seemed to permeate their clothing.

Where once a great city stood, now there was nothing but smoke and rubble.

The Rebels left the destruction behind them and moved the few miles westward to Fort Worth. They found a dead and deserted city. As the first really warming days of full spring settled over the nation, the Rebels began destroying Fort Worth. As had happened in Dallas, many of the fires spread into the suburbs. The Rebels made no attempt to check the flames. They used bulldozers and explosives to cut fire lines at the outer edges of the suburbs, and that was all they did to contain the often-times out-of-control and wind-whipped inferno that raged from county line to county line.

Ben had sent teams up to Wichita Falls even before the destruction of Dallas began, and with those teams went more than fifty settler families—pioneers, they were called. A few more families willing to face the unknown in an attempt to rebuild a shattered nation.

Ben and his Rebels left the smoking ruins of the Twin Cities behind them and pulled out, taking Highway 287 up to Wichita Falls. There, the Rebels found a neat little city, governed by a forward-looking group of people, who had reopened schools and had a staffed and adequately equipped hospital.

At Ben's request, a platoon of Rebels was flown in from the base camp to settle in Wichita Falls. Another outpost was firmly a fixture in the offices of central planning at Base Camp One.

One more step.

The Rebels relaxed for a time, resting, eating something other than field rations, and going over equipment, and they finally got a chance to wash the stink of smoke and destruction from their BDUs.

As soon as Ben saw the first signs of restlessness among the men and women of the Rebels, he ordered a pullout. They stayed on 287, heading for Amarillo, and driving straight into the unknown. The elected officials of Wichita Falls had advised Ben to disregard any rumors he might have heard about Amarillo being a dead and destroyed city. It was very much alive and crawling with outlaw scum, including a group of Night People, who had worked out a peace treaty with the outlaws.

"The outlaws raid outside Amarillo, take prisoners, and give the creepies human beings in return for their safety," Ben stated flatly.

"Yes, sir."

"Here we go," Jersey summed it up.

The Rebels drove the hundred-odd miles to Childress without seeing even one sign of human habitation. It was as if they had landed on a deserted planet.

In the main communications truck, specially built and bullet-proofed, the operators were constantly scanning the frequencies, picking up only static.

Ben halted the convoy just outside of Childress. "This place used to have about six thousand people in it," he said, glancing at a map. "Now it appears to be a ghost town."

"Scouts going in," Corrie informed him.

"I can just about tell you what they'll find," Ben said.

"Nothing," Dan said, walking back to the Blazer. "There is no one in the town."

"Let's look it over, Cooper."

Ben walked through a looted hardware store, then a department store filled with dust and very little else. The dead giveaway came when he inspected a drugstore. Drugs to make a person high or low, depending on the individual's choice, had been looted. Valuable antibiotics, now mostly out of date, had been left behind.

"Scum and trash hit the town," Ben said. "Pleasure seekers with not a thought in their heads concerning the future, living only for now. All right, Dan. Middle alert for tonight. Let's get settled in for a very brief stay."

Ben cut his eyes to Meg. She had picked up a small bottle of perfume. She met his gaze. "My mother used to wear this fragrance. I haven't seen it in a long time. It just . . . surprised me to find it here. It used to be very expensive."

Ben watched her carefully dust off the bottle and place it on the counter. "You're not going to keep it?"

Meg shook her head. "Too many memories attached." She smiled. "What was your favorite fragrance on ladies?"

"Shalimar."

"I'll wear some for you . . . if I ever find a bottle, that is."

"That would be nice." He stepped to her and took her arm. "Let's get out of here before memories overwhelm us."

As dawn lightened the area, the Rebels were pulling out. Dan had sent a team of Scouts toward Amarillo hours before. They had reported back that the inhabitants of the small city seemed braced for a fight.

"All right," Ben said, climbing into the Blazer. "We'll damn sure give them one."

The little Texas towns faded into their rearview mirrors as the column made its way toward yet another showdown. They were mere shells of what they had once been. Empty shells, looted and left to crumble as time relentlessly passed.

"Scout to Eagle One." Ben's speaker rattled the words.

"Go, Scout."

"They're bugging out of Amarillo. Heading north, south, and west."

"Ten-four, Scout. Hold what you have. We're about an hour away. Do not enter the city."

"Ten-four, Eagle."

"What do you make of it, General?" Dan radioed from his Jeep.

"No stomach for a fight. I'm thinking some of those outlaws and warlords who skipped out of Dallas early headed for Amarillo. They've warned their buddies off."

"Do we destroy it?"

"Right down to the ground."

Ben inspected the college first. It had been looted and vandalized and very nearly destroyed by packs of punks and other crud who were scared to death of education. But they had enough sense to know that with education came civilization. And that was the last thing they wanted.

Next to the college was the airport. "Clear a runway," Ben ordered. "We might have to be resupplied. Come on, gang. Let's go see what's left of the town."

Filth littered the streets and the stench of Night People hung like a stinking shroud over the city.

The Rebels searched for prisoners and found more than two hundred men, women, and children.

"The outlaws and creepies assumed that we'd be too busy dealing with the prisoners to pursue them," Dan observed.

"They assumed right," Ben said. "Corrie, give the base camp a bump and tell them to start getting the birds in here. Medical teams on board. Advise base that we'll need to be resupplied with explosives. Let's give the city another search to see if we missed anybody. Then we start bringing it down."

The crash and thunder of demolition began that afternoon as yet another haven for the lawless was destroyed. The planes landed the next day and began taking the newly freed prisoners back to safety and, hopefully, some sort of rehabilitation to piece their shattered lives back together.

The Rebels were becoming experts in demolition, and the work was going faster with each city they entered. Block by block, the city of Amarillo was coming down, to lie in piles of sometimes smoking but always useless rubble. They set fires and let them burn.

"The dirty bastards!" MacNally cussed the Rebels from his safe spot in a small town some thirty miles south of Amarillo.

Pete Jones didn't curse Ben Raines. Not because he didn't feel like it, but simply because it wouldn't accomplish anything. He sat outside a long-abandoned service station and watched the black and gray and greasy smoke pouring into the sky, coming from what had once been Amarillo.

"He's smart," Pete finally said.

"Who?" Lopez asked.

"Ben Raines."

"Ben Raines is a no-good, sorry, bully, son of a bitch who won't mind his own business!" the warlord Bass loudly proclaimed.

Pete chuckled at the man. "I never heard Ben referred to as a bully before now. Interesting word coming from you, Bass."

"Ain't he bullying his way all over the friggin' country?" Bass demanded.

"That's one way of lookin' at it, I suppose."

"Just another damn cop!" Young summed it up. "With a funny hat."

The Rebels all wore berets.

"But Ben Raines is honest, you have to give him that much. Unlike many of the cops we knew."

"I guess," Young reluctantly agreed. "But how

come you say he's so smart?"

"The cities have always been our sanctuaries. Ever since the Great War, and we've always controlled them. All that is about to change, I'm thinking."

"You mean"—the outlaw Pipes looked at him—"that that dirty no-count Ben Raines is goin' to blow up and burn ever' damn city he comes to?"

"Probably."

"Hell, that don't matter all that much," another outlaw said. "We still got thousands of small towns to hide out in."

"That can be destroyed by long-range artillery or bombed by the planes that Raines has."

"But first Raines would have to find us, right?" Mac asked.

"He'd find us. Raines is merciless, ruthless, when it comes to people like us. One of his ambitions is to wipe us from the face of the earth. I studied the man through his books, while I was in prison. Wrote a thesis on him . . ."

"Wrote a what?" Mac asked.

"A paper, if you will. Raines basically is a savage. A man much similar to those witch burners back several centuries ago in Salem."

"Jones," Mac said with a sigh, "I think you are as full of shit as that Christmas goose! You rattle on about the damndest things I ever heard of. Now you tell me this: if you so damn smart, what the hell are we gonna do about Ben Raines and them Rebels of hisn."

"We're going to defeat him," Pete said simply.

"Oh, we is, is we?" Mac sneered at him. "Now just how in the hell do you think we gonna do that?"

"By gathering an army that is bigger than the Rebels and outthinking and outfighting him. That's how."

"And where do we find an army that size?" Morgan asked.

"Up north. In Wyoming and Montana and other parts of the northwest. There is an army up there headed by someone called the Rattlesnake Kid. He has an army of bikers for his enforcers."

Mac grinned. "But that bunch don't like niggers, Jones. And all you got in your bunch is coons. Have you forgotten that?"

"War makes for strange allies, Mac. I should know. I'm sitting here attempting to converse with an ignorant redneck like you."

"I swear I'm a-gonna kill you someday, Jones!"

Pete laughed at him. "Wait until we've defeated Ben Raines, Mac. We need each other until that time."

"It can't come too soon for me."

"Defeating Raines or killing me?" Pete asked.

"Either one!"

"I've got to get word to this Rattlesnake Kid person." Pete stood up. "And I guess the best way to do that is just to drive up there and see him."

"You best get some hair straightener and some skin lightener 'fore you do," Mac needled him.

"You have no faith in my powers of persuasion, do you, Mac?"

"I have faith in my four-wheel drive and my gun," Mac told him.

"Mac, you are the epitome of redneckism."

"Still makes you a coon."

7

Taking only a few of his men, Pete drove west for a time, until he was clear of Amarillo and Ben Raines, and then headed straight north. He didn't know exactly where this Rattlesnake person and his army of racists were headquartered, but in the end, he figured, that lack of knowledge wouldn't make much difference. Since Pete was black as the ace of spades with a shaved head, and tooling along in a Cadillac limo, he felt reasonably sure *they* would find *him.*

Only problem was he didn't want to get shot right off the bat.

"Ever been to a KKK meeting, Sam?" Pete asked.

"Hell, no!"

"Me neither. But I think we're all going to attend our first one in a few days."

"Whatever you say, Pete," Sam replied glumly.

Pete laughed and patted his main man and bodyguard on the shoulder "Be of good cheer, Sam. One can only die once. I should know. I've killed a hundred or more people and I've never seen one return from the grave yet."

Ben and his Rebels put the rubble and ruin and smoke of Amarillo in their rearview mirrors and headed into New Mexico on Interstate 40. They abruptly ended their journey when Scouts radioed back to the main column that a series of bridges had been blown on the Interstate. The way to Albuquerque was blocked.

"What now, Dad?" Tina asked.

"Well, this 129 looks like it was a lousy road when this map was printed. We won't chance it. We'll backtrack to Tucumcari and take this Highway 104 up to Interstate 25. We'll wait there for the Scouts to return and then take off. New country to see, gang. Hell, that's what this trip is all about."

As the column drove the old secondary roads, the Rebels began spotting signs of life. Smoke came from the chimneys of homes set far back from the highway; homes that were surrounded by high stone fences. The gates to the roads leading to the homes were padlocked. Ben halted the column and walked back to Ramos, CO of A Company of the Rebels.

"What'd you think?" Ben asked him.

The Mexican-American shook his head. "I don't know, General. I get the feeling there are a lot of guns pointed at us right now."

"Hostile guns?"

"Not unless we try to interfere with them. Some of my family, distant relatives, left Texas after the Great War and settled along the Canadian River. Somewhere in this area, I believe. They were separatists;

but not racists. If you know what I mean."

"I do. You want to take a bullhorn and try to communicate with these people—in their language?"

"It wouldn't hurt."

Ramos took the bullhorn and spoke in rapid-fire Spanish for a moment, identifying himself and telling anyone who might be interested who they were and what they were doing. Ben leaned against the fender of a vehicle, rolled a smoke, and waited.

Before he had finished his cigarette, a dozen men, on horseback and all heavily armed, rode out from behind the walls of the ranch compound and up to the fence. Their expressions were not unfriendly, but neither could they be mistaken for Welcome Wagon ladies.

Ramos spoke to them and they returned the greetings. Ben could speak some Spanish, but not enough to follow what was being said.

Ben walked to Ramos's side during a slight lull in the conversation. In English, he said, "I apologize for not being fluent in your language." And being Ben Raines, he concluded by saying, "But I will not apologize for being one of those who believed in English being the official language of the United States."

An older man smiled. "Do you come here to force your beliefs upon us, Ben Raines?"

"No. Not unless you want them."

"Suppose we do not want them but someday might need your help?"

"You won't get it."

Some of the younger men stirred at that flatly given statement. The older man, obviously a leader of some sort, lifted a hand and gave them a dark look. The young men settled down. He swung his eyes to Ben. "Those are hard words, General Raines."

"But necessary, times being what they are."

The older man did not blink nor change expression. "There are several thousand of us along the Canadian, the Mora, and the Conchas. We have been attacked many times over the years. We are still here, General."

"Then you don't need our help."

The man sighed. "That is not necessarily true, General. We are being overwhelmed by our own productivity. We need markets for our cattle and our vegetables and the clothing we produce. And . . ." He hesitated. "Some technical assistance, as well."

Ben had studied the maps of this area before they cut off the Interstate. He took a wild guess. "The Conchas Dam?"

The younger men stirred at his words, not understanding how Ben could have known that. Ben said, "That was a guess, people. I'm not possessed with supernatural powers."

"My name is de Vaca, General," the older man said. "You and your Rebels are welcome here. I think it is time to open our homes to those who are friendly to us. Come, we'll have a celebration."

The Rebels spent three days in the Spanish communities along the Canadian. Ben found some resentment among a few of the younger men, but not enough for any concern. He complimented de Vaca on his organization and the way he had brought order and productivity out of chaos.

"It was not easy," de Vaca said. "After the Great War, many among my people wanted to break away and form a separate state, like you did in the Tri-States. You know that many of those who used to live here went to aid you in your fight?"

Ben nodded. "I know."

The men were relaxing in the spacious and cool den of the hacienda, drinking a slightly sweet, nonalcoholic drink out of tall glasses. Ben had no idea what it was.

"The problem lies in what do we do for money?" de Vaca said. "The barter system is fine for some things, but if this country is ever to be restored, there must be some form of hard currency."

"And something with which to back that currency," Ben added.

"Precisely." The man smiled. "And you have probably seventy-five percent, or more, of all the gold and silver."

Ben returned the smile. "That I do, sir. And I'd be glad to release it for backing."

"We must not fall into the trap that the U.S. government did before the Great War."

"I agree, and have no intention of doing that. We're not going to print more money than we can solidly back with gold or silver. And"—Ben held up a warning finger—"if we agree to do this, gold and silver cannot be allowed in private hands."

"I agree."

De Vaca stuck out his hand and Ben shook it with a smile on his lips. "Congratulations, sir."

"For what?" de Vaca asked.

"You've just been appointed Governor of New Mexico."

It probably was a good thing that Ben did not have much Spanish, for de Vaca proceeded to turn the air blue with oaths.

After much arguing and debating, de Vaca agreed to accept the appointment. Armed with the knowledge that he had the full backing of Ben Raines and the Rebels, the rancher thought he could bring the majority of the state's residents back into the folds of democracy. But, he pointed out, it would not be an easy task.

De Vaca pointed out that there were many outlaw gangs operating in New Mexico, and it would take years to flush them all out. In other words, the rancher said, this was tantamount to a return to the old Wild West.

However, he said with a smile, he had a militia that was ready to go, and they were willing to fight to the death.

Ben left with a good feeling in his guts. Matters were beginning to come together in a solid jell.

Colorado, however, was quite a different matter. That part of the country had been carved up into sections, with various outlaw groups claiming territory. De Vaca had warned Ben that he faced serious problems when he entered Colorado.

"Was there no one trying to bring order?" Ben asked.

"Bob Lucas, up in Trinidad. I have radioed him, telling him that you are on the way."

The Rebel convoy picked up Interstate 25 just north of Las Vegas, and slowly made their way north. The news had spread quickly, and many survivors were now flying American flags in their front yards. Had not de Vaca passed the word, many of these same people would have remained hidden while the Rebel convoy passed.

"We're gonna make it, General," Jersey said. "I feel it."

"There is definitely something positive in the air," Ben agreed. "I felt it back there talking with de Vaca. I don't think we're going to have to worry much about New Mexico. De Vaca will get it done. Now if we can just get this Bob Lucas on our team, we'll have really taken one giant step."

"You've had something worrying your mind for a couple of weeks, General," Jersey said. "What's up?"

Ben smiled. Whenever four or five people worked and lived as closely as his personal team, all became aware of the slightest mental shift in the other. "Across the waters, Jersey."

"Across the waters?"

"I want to know what's going on overseas."

"Oh, shit!" Beth blurted.

Ben laughed outloud. "Relax, Beth. We're not leaving tomorrow."

"But we are going?"

"I don't know; maybe sometime in the future. I haven't discussed this with anyone because it would be such a massive undertaking. And what I know about boats—ships—is nothing. We'd have to find someone who knows the oceans, currents, navigation; all sorts of things that I am totally ignorant of."

"General Ike?"

"Ike would definitely be part of any expedition."

Cooper spoke up. "Thermopolis knows a lot about ships and stuff like that."

Ben glanced at the driver. "He does?"

"That's what one of the guys with him told me. He spent years working in a shipyard somewhere. He sailed all over the place."

"Ummm," Ben replied. "Captain Therm. Not exactly Nemo, but it has a nice ring to it."

"I thought Europe was destroyed by nuclear bombs," Corrie said.

"Yes. Just like we thought New York City and the entire Eastern area was destroyed. One great big hoax. Somebody played a very cruel joke. And the why of it will probably never be known."

"How far is it to Europe?" Beth asked.

"From the upper East Coast to England is about three thousand miles, I think."

"That's an awful lot of water," Beth said dubiously.

"And a whole bunch of sharks," Cooper said with a grin.

"Shut up, Cooper!" Jersey ended it.

"Roadblocks at Raton," Tina's voice came through the loudspeaker.

"Any shots fired?"

"Negative, Eagle."

"Hold what you have, Tina. Lucas may have extended his territory; de Vaca said he was planning that. We're only a few miles behind you. See if you can make radio contact with them."

"Ten-four."

Ben had traveled only a few miles when Tina bumped back. "Go to scramble, Eagle. It's Lucas's people, Dad. They're preparing for an attack by some outlaw bunch. Says it's due to come in about four hours. Their recon people have been tracking the outlaws. They're coming from the southwest, out of the Sangre de Cristo Range; that's where they're headquartered."

"Tell Lucas to open the roadblocks. We're coming in and will lend a hand in this fight."

"Ten-four, Eagle. Says he's looking forward to meeting you."

Ben shook hands with the man and sized him up, liking him almost immediately. Bob Lucas came across as a tough, hard, no-nonsense, law-and-order type of man.

"I was a businessman," Lucas explained as Ben's people rolled past the open roadblocks. "Just getting started when the bombs came. For the first two-three years after that, I was fighting that fool President Hilton Logan. Then the bastard put me in federal prison and kept me there for three years. I busted out and formed this little army you see now. We've been fighting to restore law and order in this part of Colorado ever since."

"How far does your control extend, Bob?"

"From Trinidad up to Pueblo and east to La Junta, then down to Springfield and south to the line. The outlaws and so-called warlords have pretty much left us alone for the past year. We hang them whenever

83

we find them," he added grimly. "But now there's some nut up in Wyoming who is pulling all the gangs together, under one leader . . ."

"The Rattlesnake Kid," Ben said.

"Yeah! How'd you know that, General?"

"That's one of the reasons we're here, Bob. I intend to tear the head off the Rattlesnake Kid."

"Good! That's the best news I've heard in a while. Just who is the Rattlesnake Kid?"

"A man named Matt Callahan. I knew him way back. His daughter is part of our group. Meg. She can tell you all about him—none of it good. But right now, let's deal with what's facing us. How many men are coming at us?"

"Maybe a thousand." He opened a map. "But terrain is to our advantage. They've got to come up this highway." He pointed it out. "Highway 64. At least to this point where the secondary road cuts off and links up with the Interstate. They'll probably come up that way, too. Lots of bikers in this group."

"A two-pronged attack, at least. No way they could be coming from the north or east?"

"Not a chance. We're spread pretty thin in those areas, but we have the roads covered as best we can and we're linked by shortwave. This Barnes fellow— he's the leader of this particular bunch of no-goods— has got a lot of men with him, but he's stupid and arrogant. He thinks he can roll right over us just because he outnumbers us."

Ben nodded and looked at Dan. "Get the tanks under cover, Dan. We'll not use long-range artillery. Have the tank commanders lower the muzzles. I want this Barnes and his men to be looking us in the eyes before we open the dance." Ben pointed across the Interstate and beyond, to a wide field. "Let them get in there before we fire. Let's take a few prisoners for interrogation. It looks like Callahan is widening his base of operations. I want to know how much before we go blundering up into his territory."

"Right, sir. How far out do you want recon teams to go?"

"Couple of miles. No farther than that."

"And as soon as they have this outlaw bunch in sight, report in and get back here."

"Yes. Get the troops down and tell them to stay down. Let's give Mr. Barnes a very unpleasant surprise. His last surprise. Until he meets his Maker, that is."

8

Ben pulled his troops down and low, allowing Lucas to keep his people in the positions they occupied before the Rebels' arrival. He didn't want to spook this Barnes person; wanted the outlaw to commit his people full-force and head-on as he had boasted he'd do.

The Rebel tanks had been pulled back into heavy brush and timber along the Interstate. The 81mm mortar crews had done the same. The Dusters were parked behind bob trucks, ready to wheel about and unleash their twin-mounted 40mm cannon. The Big Thumper crews were ready.

Ben leaned against the fender of a bob truck and waited.

Bob Lucas studied the man, noting that Ben was calm to the point of being about half asleep. Nothing spectacular about the man; except that aura that seemed to linger about him. There was something that seemed to inspire courage, to make a person want to follow him.

Ben pulled out a sack of tobacco and began rolling a cigarette just as Corrie said, "Bogies in sight, General."

"Good." Ben licked the paper closed.

"Forward teams report they have machine guns mounted on flat-bed trucks."

"Any artillery reported?"

"Negative, sir."

"Estimate of strength?"

"Probably a thousand men. They're coming hard and fast. They've split their force, half the advancing forces now heading for the Interstate to come up below us."

"Tell the forward teams to bug out now and tell Dan to shift his command to the south of us."

Bob Lucas watched as the Rebels moved with clockwork precision; no wasted motion. And although they did not appear to react hurriedly, it was all accomplished with split-second timing. He commented on that.

"We're always outnumbered, Bob," Ben told him. "Speed and precision and instant following of orders help keep us alive."

The forward teams drove the twisting roads as fast as conditions would allow and were back at the main body of Rebels a few moments before Barnes's people were due to arrive.

"A woman was in charge of your recon people?" Lucas asked, watching as a very pretty young lady dismounted from a Hummer.

"Yes," Ben said with a smile. "A very capable woman. Her name is Tina. She's my daughter."

Bob decided he'd better keep his eyes open and his

mouth shut until he sorted a lot of things out concerning the Rebel army.

"Approximately two miles and closing," Corrie announced.

"Stand at ready," Ben said quietly.

Corrie passed the orders.

"Western line of bogies slowing, sir."

"They're giving those coming up from the south time to get into position for a simultaneous strike. Have we locked on to their radio frequency, Corrie?"

"That's ten-four, sir. Communications is monitoring all bogie transmissions." She paused. "A lot of profanity and boasts about what they're going to do with the women they capture."

"Pure slime," Ben muttered.

"All bogie columns moving at top speed, sir."

"Hold fire."

Bob was getting just a tad nervous.

"Fifteen hundred meters, sir."

The sounds of roaring trucks and howling exhausts from motorcycles were clearly audible. Men on foot and in various stages of dress were storming across the flats to the west of Ben's position and closing fast, screaming and cursing.

"One thousand meters, sir."

"Fire!"

The ground trembled as the tanks opened fire, the muzzles of the 105s lowered almost to the optimum. They were firing incendiary and Willie Peter, and Bob watched as the flats erupted into a wall of flames and phosphoric arches. The 81mm mortars were lobbing in HE rounds on top of the tank fire, turning the flats into a death trap. Bodies of outlaws were flung into the air, the clothing blazing. Fifty caliber machine guns were yammering, the muzzles spitting out death in two directions. The Dusters and Big Thumpers began singing their war songs. Rebel snipers were having a field day, calmly and coolly picking their targets and dropping them. Bodies were piling up on the Interstate as Dan's people took their toll.

"Tanks and mortars cease firing," Ben ordered.

The heavy crashing abated and the smoke from the battlefield began to drift away.

"Jesus Christ!" Bob muttered, looking out over the flats.

Twisted and mangled bodies littered the smoky battlefield. To the south, bodies were piled on top of bodies on the Interstate and the median and in the overgrown ditches.

"Cease all firing," Ben ordered.

The guns fell silent.

The faint and fading sounds of trucks and motorcycles reached the ears of the defenders. Those of Barnes's command who were not cut down by the almost solid wall of lead were retreating in a rout.

"Corrie, advise Dr. Ling to be ready to receive wounded; Rebel and friendly wounded first. Have interrogation teams ready. Rebels out." He looked at Lucas. "Let's go tour the battlefield, Bob."

On the flats, Ben knelt down beside a man whose legs had been blown off. He was alive, but just barely. His eyes glared hate at Ben.

"Got anything to say to me?" Ben asked.

"Snake'll git you!" the man gasped. "He's waitin' on you, Raines."

"I would give you a message to take back, but you just had your ticket punched for a one-way ride to Hell," Ben told him.

Standing back, listening to the brutally blunt exchange, Bob Lucas knew then why Ben Raines was slowly but surely winning the battle to reclaim America. Ben Raines was a hard-ass from the word go.

The dying outlaw cursed Ben.

"I've heard it all before. Please excuse me. Do have a nice day." Ben stood up and walked to another moaning outlaw. Lucas followed.

This outlaw was no more than a boy, and his shoulder wound was painful, but did not appear to be serious. Ben waved a medic over. "Patch him up. There may be hope for this one."

As the medic went to work, Ben said, "Boy, you want to get straight and try to make something out your life?"

"What you mean?" the teenager gasped.

"Stop outlawing."

"And do what?" The teenager gritted his teeth as the medic cleaned out the wound.

"How about work for a change?"

"And if I don't?"

Ben placed the muzzle of his M14 against the boy's head. "I blow your goddamned brains out—right now!"

The boy's eyes widened and his face paled. Bob Lucas did not think it was due to the wound in his shoulder.

"I reckon I might give that work a try, sir," the boy finally said.

"I sort of reckoned you would, son." Ben lifted the muzzle of the M14 and stood up, walking away. Bob followed.

"Would you have shot that boy, General?"

"No. But he didn't know that. He was born into this mess, Bob; or at best only a baby when the bombs came. Chaos and crime are all he's ever known. He's never known discipline or been exposed to law and order and rules and regulation. When anarchy reigns, I can accept that excuse and give a young person a break."

"And the older men?"

"With few exceptions, we don't take prisoners of the hardcases."

"And what happens to the boy?"

"That's your problem, now. This is your area of control. I'll only interfere if and when you ask me to do so."

"Thanks a lot." Bob said it with a smile. "I get the feeling that like de Vaca, I've just been appointed something or the other."

"Only if you want it."

Bob stuck out his hand and Ben took it, standing in the midst of death and pain on the shattered and still-smoking flats.

"Glad to have you with us, Bob."

"Glad to be with you, Ben."

The badly wounded who, in Dr. Ling's opinion, had absolutely no chance of surviving, were eased out of their pain and out of the ranks of the living with lethal injections. The less-severely wounded were patched up and split up for the interrogation teams to work on. And in many cases, that would prove to be rougher than their battle wounds.

"Sit down!" Ben told one man who looked as if he had just stepped out of central casting for a grade B motorcycle movie.

His head was shaved clean and he was dressed all in animal skins, except for his massive arms, and they were bare and covered with tattoos. Ben thought he was the ugliest son of a bitch he'd ever seen. And since Ben knew something of outlaw biker jargon and what various tattoos meant, this guy was the epitome of slime.

This one had most of the wings tattooed on him. Brown wings, a sign that the wearer had performed oral sex with a woman's anus. Green wings, denoting that he had performed oral sex on a venerally diseased woman. Purple wings, showing proudly that he had performed oral sex with a dead woman.

P.P.D.S.P.E.M.F.O.B.B.T. Which translated to read: Pill Popping Dope Smoking Pussy Eating Mother Fucken Outlaw Brothers Biken Together.

F.T.W. Fuck The World.

The ugly bastard also had two crosses tattooed on his arms. The white cross was earned when a person digs open a grave, removes an article from the deceased with witnesses present, and then wears the article on his clothing. The red cross was earned by committing homosexual fellatio with witnesses present.

There were other tattoos; but Ben had seen and translated enough to know that he was dealing with pure shit.

"What's your name?" Ben asked.

The biker cursed him.

"You're a real tough boy, aren't you?"

"Goddamn right!"

"And nobody is ever going to break you or any of your buddies, right?"

"Bet your ass on that!"

Several of his biker brothers sitting across the room laughed in agreement.

"You ever raped a child?" Ben asked.

"Bunches of times."

"Female or male?"

"Both."

"You proud of that?"

"Goddamn right!"

"You're wearing 666 tattooed on your arm. You worship the devil?"

"Goddamn right."

"You take orders from a biker named Satan?"

"Goddamn right."

"No hope for you at all, is there, tough boy?"

"Goddamn right."

Ben picked up his .45 from the desk top and shot the biker between the eyes. He slammed out of the chair and lay still, his blood leaking out of the back of his head where the hollow-nosed slug had exited.

"Drag that dead obscenity out of here and sit another tough boy in the chair," Ben ordered. "I want to see if he's as tough as his brother on the floor."

He wasn't.

*   *   *

Bob Lucas was a tough man, and all who knew him would agree, but even he had been startled by Ben's shooting the biker in the head. He knew they why the old Tri-States that Ben had formed had been 99.99 percent free of crime.

Ben Raines just wouldn't tolerate it—then or now.

"All right," Ben said. "Here's what we have. Matt Callahan and this biker called Satan have quite an operation going, controlling, to one extent or the other, most outlaw gangs in a half a dozen or more states. Might as well say the entire northwest, and I'll include Utah and Colorado and the north half of California in that.

"Now that doesn't mean that there aren't plenty of communities in those states that are law-abiding and forward-looking. I know there are many of them. We've had radio contact with them. But this outlaw biker business is bigger than I first thought, and I intend to crush it."

"You want me and my bunch to go with you, Ben?" Lucas asked.

"No. I want you people to stay right where you are and continue to stabilize this part of Colorado. You've done a fine job and I congratulate you."

"I have radioed Base Camp One and requested that Dr. Chase have medical teams flown in with plenty of supplies for Mr. Lucas," Dr. Ling said.

"Good!" Bob said. "We have doctors in the area, but damn few supplies."

"We'll get you set up, don't worry about that," Ben assured him.

Gunshots split the night air. Dan Gray was overseeing the disposition of many of the older, hardcore outlaws. Rebel justice came down very, very swiftly, and very, very final.

The warlord, Barnes, had not been among the dead or wounded.

"I have to tell you this, General," Bob said. "There is a group of people who settled up in Walsenburg who ride motorcycles when the weather permits."

"Just because someone is a biker doesn't make them bad," Ben said. "I've never been the type of person who thought that." He smiled. "But I would tell them, if I were you, that this is not a real dandy time to be tooling about on two wheels."

Bob laughed. "Yeah, I agree. I'll give them a bump and so advise."

"Anybody got anything else they'd like to say?" Ben asked.

"Only that when you leave our area of control," Bob said, "you're in real bogie country. You're going to have to fight your way through Colorado. There is not much left of Colorado Springs, and nothing left of Denver. You're going to have to leave the Interstate and skirt those places, using secondary roads. From Pueblo on, General, you're in enemy territory."

"Believe me when I say, Bob, we're used to that."

9

"You either got a lot of nerve, or else you're just plumb crazy, boy!" the guard at the roadblock told Pete Jones.

"I will admit to possessing more than my share of courage," Pete told him. "However, there are some who might question my sanity."

"Talks funny, too," another guard said.

"What'd you want, boy?"

"To see a person named the Rattlesnake Kid. If not him, then Satan will suffice."

A huge biker who looked, if he strained very hard, as if he might be able to count to ten, walked up and looked at Pete. He squinted, then smiled. "Hiya, Pete!"

"Hello, Bruiser. How have you been?"

"I been doin' great, man."

"You know this nigger, Bruiser?"

"Hey!" Bruiser gave the man a sharp look. "Pete ain't no nigger. He's . . . ah . . . just dark, that's all. He's all right."

"Whatever you say, Bruiser. How do you know this n . . . ah, guy?"

"We was in the slam together down in Texas. Me and Pete busted out together. We was tight in the joint."

"He wants to see Snake."

Bruiser looked at Pete and shook his head. "That ain't cool, Pete. Snake don't like nobody that ain't white."

"He doesn't have to like me, Bruiser. Just listen to what I have to say. Ben Raines and his army aren't that many days away. He's coming up to destroy you."

"Snake might like to hear that, awright. OK. You follow me in. Just you." He jerked a thumb at Sam. "Him and the rest of your people stay back here. Come on."

One side of the biker's face had been torn off in an accident years back, leaving that side horribly scarred. He could not completely close his mouth nor completely open one eye. One ear was missing. He stood six feet, six inches tall—without his boots—and weighed about three hundred pounds, very little of it fat. He stared at Pete for a long time, hoping to intimidate the man. But Pete was not the intimidating type. Satan finally gave up.

"Snake don't see no one. You talk to me, then if I decide it's important, I'll get word to Snake."

"Very well. Here is my news and my plan . . ."

*   *   *

"You're passing out of our area of control," Lucas's people at Pueblo radioed Ben. "Bear west up ahead, Highway 50. Take that to 285. It's right at a hundred miles to the junction. Then you're in the mountains and in bogie country. Good luck, General."

At Pueblo, Ben halted the column, off-loaded the bulldozers, and put the tanks on the flatbeds. He had told Lucas they may or may not be back to get the earth-moving equipment. Then he spread a map out on the hood of his Blazer and once more studied it.

"Right through the heart of the Rockies," Ben said. "One hell of a pull."

"What are our options, Dad?" Tina asked.

"Go all the way over to Grand Junction and take secondary roads north. And I don't like that either. Once we leave Grand Junction, we'd have to travel through about two hundred miles of absolutely nothing."

"On our way to HALFASS," Dan said, trying to hide his smile.

"Yes." Ben made no attempt to disguise his grin. "I know they're dangerous and savage, but that name gets to me."

"I think we can make the pull through the mountains with no trouble, General," Ramos said. "All our engines have been recently rebuilt, as have the transmissions."

"It's not mechanical problems that concern me. That's ambush country. And we're probably going to have to clear a dozen or more rockslides." He sighed and folded the map. "Well, let's head north, gang. The Rockies are a sight to see."

They hit their first firefight about twenty-five

miles west of Pueblo. But the outlaws quickly realized they were up against a vastly superior force and withdrew after only a few minutes. The Rebels crashed through the roadblocks and continued westward. They used the loop to bypass Canon City. Lucas had told them the town was a haven for thugs and outlaws. Lucas would deal with them later.

Ben pulled the convoy over early in the afternoon at Salida, a town that had once contained about five thousand souls back before the Great War.

Now it was a looted, ravaged shell of a town.

"We'll set up camp and then inspect the residential area," Ben said. "But I've a hunch any decent citizens were either driven out or killed or captured long ago. It has that feel about it."

They found what the various animals and carrion birds had left of what had once been dozens of human beings. Every scrap of flesh had been picked off the bones. Only a few rotting pieces of clothing remained.

Dr. Ling began his inspection of the bones and it did not take him long. "There is no evidence of any broken bones. Not one sign of bullet-shattered ribs. The skulls are intact. I'd say the Night People stayed here for a while and feasted before moving on. This is not their kind of country."

Ben agreed. He hoped he would not have to come face to face with any creepies on this trip. The memories of New York City still haunted him, and he felt sure, most of the other Rebels. The winter spent in the Big Apple had been an exhausting one, both mentally and physically.

They stood in silence for a few moments, looking

at the piles of bones. Finally one Rebel said, "I'll get some shovels. That's the very least we can do."

No one slept easy that night outside the deserted town. Even though he knew it was an unnecessary move, Ben doubled the guard and shortened the watch hours so no one would get in a mental strain during the seemingly endless hours of the night.

The Rebels pulled out just after dawn, turning north on 285.

"Now it gets hairy," Ben said.

Cooper smiled lecherously and waggled his eyebrows.

"Keep your mouth shut, Cooper!" Jersey warned him.

"I can always dream," he replied with a smile.

Ben looked at the dark forests that lay on both sides of the highway. Battalions, divisions of troops could hide in there.

But Tina and her Scouts, on forward recon, reported seeing nothing. And Ben could take some consolation in the fact that he was not up against highly disciplined troops; he doubted that very many of the bikers and outlaws were even very good or at home in deep timber.

"Jesus!" Jersey breathed, gazing out at the outline of Mt. Antero, its summit pushing over fourteen thousand feet into the air.

"I wonder how the outlaws keep this road open during the winter," Cooper mused aloud.

"I'd wager they don't," Ben said. "I'd say that in the winter, everything grinds to a halt."

"Far-out Scout to Eagle," Tina's voice came through the speaker.

"Go, Scout."

"Roadblocks at what used to be a little town called Nathrop."

"Hold what you have. We're on the way. You catch that, Dan?"

"Ten-four, General. I'm gone."

"Get around those trucks, Cooper."

The few trucks and Jeeps and Hummers that rolled ahead of Ben got over to let him pass.

Jersey looked down at the valley below. "Please stay on the road, Cooper."

"You ain't seen nothing yet, Jersey," Ben told her with a smile. "Believe me when I say the best, or the worst, depending on your point of view, is still ahead of us."

"I can hardly wait."

The roadblock was a chain of human bodies, roped together and rotting all across the road.

Ben got out and walked up to the stinking roadblock. The stench was awful. Tina and her bunch were already wearing gasmasks; the filters knocking out much of the stink, but not all.

Ben slipped his mask on and said, "Any sign of boobytrapping?"

"Not that I can see," Dan told him. "The manner of men we face just seems to get worse and worse as time marches on."

"Dregs of society, Dan. All right, inspect the bodies carefully for explosives and then cut them down and bury them. Tina, take your team in and look over the little town. Head's up, now."

Ben didn't like the position they were in and he could tell Dan wasn't too thrilled about it either. But they had been stopped for several minutes, and if an ambush was coming, it should have already started.

The line of rotting bodies removed, Ben walked on past, waving for Cooper and the Blazer to come on.

"Why the roadblock?" Dan questioned. "And why that type of blockade?"

"I don't know. A warning, to be sure."

"Perhaps to other outlaw gangs?"

"Could be. If that's the case, then all the gangs are not uniting under the leadership of Matt Callahan."

"And that could be both good and bad. For us, I mean."

"Yes."

The Blazer pulled up alongside the walking men. Corrie said, "Tina reports the town is deserted. But it's been recently occupied."

"Go on in," Ben told Cooper. "I'll ride in with Dan."

The Rebels spent only a few minutes in the deserted and ravaged little town. Just enough time to silently tell them that the town was ruined and would probably never again be occupied by humans.

"They're waiting for us at Buena Vista," Buddy called in. "A hundred or so bikers."

Buena Vista was only a few miles up the road.

Ben acknowledged the report and told his son to stay put. "Off-load the Dusters," he ordered. "They'll take the point. Bust through, we'll be right behind you," he told the tank commanders.

The Dusters were unchained from the trailers and roared and rumbled into life.

"Go!" Ben waved them forward, then got into the Blazer, telling Cooper, "Stay with them."

Outfitted with twin 40mm cannon and twin-mounted M60 machine guns, the Dusters roared toward the bikers crouched behind a hastily erected roadblock on the edge of the town. The outlaws must have thought the devil had unleashed his fury at them as the five Dusters came barreling up the road, abreast, all guns snarling and spitting.

The Duster could spit out two hundred forty 40mm rounds per minute with both barrels going. In one minute, twelve hundred 40mm rounds and twice that many 7.62 machine gun rounds tore into the blockade and the immediate area around it.

They turned the blockade into an inferno, the gas tanks of the vehicles and motorcycles exploding, hurling torn and bloody and blazing bodies in all directions.

The Dusters rammed through, with APCs right behind them, and raced toward the center of the small town.

The battle turned into a total rout as the superior troops of Ben Raines locked horns with the bikers. Very little mercy was given to the outlaws. Ben wanted only a few prisoners for interrogation.

The battle was over in less than fifteen minutes and the town was declared secure.

Ben walked to where a small group of sullen-looking bikers were being held under guard by Rebels. He pointed to a store. "Is that building secure?"

"Yes, sir."

"Take these"—Ben looked at the outlaw bikers,

disgust evident in his eyes—"people in there and hold them. I'll question them in a moment."

Before the bikers could be taken inside, Buddy and a team of Rebels walked up, escorting a very frightened and apparently badly used group of women and girls.

"Found them chained in a house, Father. They were taken from a small settlement just east of here."

"Just females?"

"The boys were traded to a group of outlaws whose sexual preferences are a bit twisted."

Ben cussed as he turned to the biker prisoners. "Where is this other group of scum?"

"Fuck you, man!" was the reply.

Ben hit him with the butt of his M14 and his jaw popped as green and rotten teeth flew from his mouth. The outlaw lay on the littered sidewalk and moaned in pain. Ben shifted his hard eyes to another biker. "I'll ask you the same question. And if you wise-ass off to me, I'll shoot you."

"You gonna shoot us anyways, so why the hell should I tell you a goddam thing?"

Ben obliged the biker with one round to the head. The outlaw dropped to the sidewalk.

"Hey, man!" one of the remaining outlaws yelled. "We got rights, man. You can't do this. It's . . . it's unconstitutional!"

Ben's smile was extremely unpleasant as he shifted the still-smoking muzzle of the old Thunder Lizard toward the mouthy biker. He slowly lifted the muzzle and placed it against the man's jaw. "Where are the young boys being held, scumbag?"

"Up the road at Leadville!" the biker screamed.

"Jesus God, man! Who the hell are you?"

"Ben Raines."

The outlaw fainted.

Ben did not shoot the remaining outlaws. He hanged them.

The column rolled out and traveled up to a small town about fifteen miles south of Leadville. The going was very slow through the mountains and Ben wanted some intelligence about Leadville before he struck it. He bivouacked his Rebels in the small town of Granite and sent out recon teams.

"About the time I think we're making some progress, we meet scum like those today," he said to Meg.

"Satan and my father are just as bad." She spoke the words with a bitter tinge. "Or worse."

"I can't imagine what pushed Matt over the edge. He always seemed so steady."

"He had his dark side, I can tell you that for sure," Matt's daughter replied. "Looking back, searching my memory, I can remember some pretty ugly scenes with my father, and some suspicious moments when I'd come home unexpectedly and catch Dad with . . . neighbor boys, or young girls. I guess I just forced them out of my mind."

Ben did not press her on the memories. He felt he had a pretty clear idea of what she had seen and probably personally experienced at the hands of her father.

He watched her walk away, and for the first time in months, enjoyed the view. Jerre would never be totally out of his mind, but he felt he could push her far enough back into the dark reaches where she would not be constantly bugging him.

He turned as Dan approached.

"Recon reporting a fairly heavy force of outlaws are occupying Leadville, General. No way of determining whether they are part of Callahan's bunch or are an independent group."

"Weapons?"

"Nothing to match ours in sight. Handguns and rifles for the most part. No way of knowing where the prisoners are being held. If they're still alive," he added.

"The kids would probably be better off if they were dead," Ben said, disgust on his face. Aberrent sexual behavior between consenting adults was bad enough, but when children became a part of it . . . no punishment was too great for those adults involved.

Ben waved Buddy over to him.

"Yes, Father?"

"You think you can take a team into Leadville, find those kids, and get them out, all without getting yourself killed or captured?"

"Certainly!" Buddy acted as though Ben had insulted him by even asking.

"Well . . . what the hell are you waiting on?" Ben said with a smile.

10

Buddy's team, as Dan was fond of pointing out, was the crème de la crème of his Scouts. They were, to use the words of Jean Larte Guy: young enthusiasts in camouflage uniforms, who would not be put on display, but from whom impossible efforts would be demanded and to whom all sorts of tricks would be taught.

"Stupid thugs," Buddy whispered to a team member. They stood over the bodies of two outlaws who had come blundering out of an alley and almost ran into the Scouts. The Scouts had used their knives, starry pinpoints of light reflecting off the long, sharp blades as they cut and slashed.

Wild drunken laughter came from a building across the street. Buddy and his team darted across the dark street and pressed in close to the side of the building, Buddy peeking inside through a filthy window. No kids were in sight, but the building was filled with outlaws, most of them well on their way to getting drunk on what appeared to be some sort of homebrew. It was an equal mix of bikers and their women, one just as bad as the other.

"The ones who prefer young boys must be in another part of town," Buddy said. "Put a charge on this building."

Grinning, a young Scout slipped out of a heavy pack and began planting enough C4 to guarantee there would not be enough left of the building or its occupants to worry about. The charge would be detonated by radio signal.

"Let's find the kids," Buddy said.

They found them, and they were in a pitiful shape. One of them was being used by an outlaw, gags stuffed in the boy's mouth to stifle his screaming. Buddy lifted a silenced .22 autoloader and shot the biker through the head. The team rushed in, slashed at the ropes binding the children, slung them over their shoulders, and ran from the house of horrors.

At the edge of town, Buddy halted the team and looked at the young Rebel who had planted the charges. "Do it."

Seventy-five pounds of C4 blew, the shock of the explosion rocking the ground for blocks around. The walls of the building collapsed, bringing the roof down on the outlaw bikers and their women. Lanterns and candles caught debris on fire and within minutes the night sky was lit with dancing flames.

Buddy held one scared, trembling, and hurt young boy, no more than five or six, in his strong arms. "You're all right now," he assured the boy. "The horror is over. It will not happen again. Not as long as you stay with the Rebels."

"That was one strange dude, Sam," Pete Jones told his friend, as the Cadillac rolled south toward the preset rendezvous point with Lopez, MacNally, and the others. "I don't think I've ever seen anything like him."

"Tell me about him again, Pete," Sam urged. "I wanna laugh some more."

"Dressed all in black, Sam. Cowboy boots shined to where you could see your face in them—had shiny spurs that jingled. Big black hat with a rattlesnake skin for a hatband. Big belt all studded up with silver dollars. Had twin six-shooters, nickel-plated, pearl handles, tied down low. He used all sorts of cowboy terms, like partner, rattle your hocks, belly up to the bar, fork your cayuse . . . stuff like that."

"What's a cayuse, Pete?"

Pete shook his head. "Damned if I know, Sam. Must be something you eat with a fork, though. Anyway, Snake liked my plan. So we'll be linking up with Lopez and the others and traveling back north."

"Sounds good to me. Pete? I've eat lots of hamhocks in my time. But damned if I ever saw one that would rattle!"

"Take the town," Ben ordered, just as day was pushing night aside. "No prisoners."

He turned to Corrie. "According to this map, there

111

is—or was—some sort of airport in Leadville; or close to it. It's probably not going to be large enough to handle our bigger birds, so Cecil will have to send some of those smaller commuter planes we have. Tell him to stand by, please, Corrie."

Ben had spoken to the kids. They were the only prisoners being held by the outlaws. There had been others, but they had been traded to another gang a few days back.

The 81mm mortar crews began lobbing HE and incendiary rounds into the town as gunners behind .50 caliber machine guns raked their fire areas. Several blocks of the town had burned the night before; as the incendiary rounds began slamming in, it was only a matter of minutes before the entire downtown area was blazing.

"Cease firing," Ben ordered. "Mop it up."

Rebels moved in behind the Dusters, as the 40mm cannon rounds from the Dusters created more flames and confusion and destruction.

Ben looked down at what had once been a thriving little town nestled in the Rocky Mountains. He had read somewhere—long ago—that it had once snowed in Leadville on the Fourth of July.

Now there was very little left of Leadville, and as the fires swirled relentlessly on, soon there would be nothing.

Only sporadic gunshots were coming from the burning town as the Rebels mopped up.

Cooper said, "I told General Jefferys about the condition of the kids and he's starting the smaller birds out immediately. He says to tell you that a hostile force was spotted by our patrols in Minnesota.

They were pretty sure it was Ashley and his bunch."

"I'm beginning to get very weary of Mr. Ashley. That bastard is determined to see me dead."

Dan walked up. "Snake and Satan to the north, Ashley and probably Sister Voleta to the east." He shook his head. "And God only knows what's being plotted by those south of us."

"That same thought just crossed my mind," Ben admitted. He shrugged his shoulders. "Let's go see the airport."

There wasn't much left of it. The buildings had all been looted, and the few planes left in the hangers destroyed.

Dan, who was a pilot himself, viewed the wreckage and cursed. "We'll be able to salvage parts, but that's about all."

"Why do they do it?" Corrie asked.

"Because they're looters," Ben told her. "And looters are greedy, selfish, stupid people. Whatever they don't understand, they destroy. Let's get the runway cleared off. We'll bivouac out here; let the town burn itself out."

"Buddy reporting they have prisoners," Corrie said, after listening to her earphones.

Ben gave Dan a quick look. The Englishman nodded his head and walked toward his Jeep. Ben slung his M14 and began to roll a cigarette as teams of Rebels began the task of clearing the runway. Others began pitching tents and cleaning out a hanger to use as a mess hall.

"It's just all in a day's work, isn't it, General?" Meg asked. "I mean, nobody has to be told what to do . . . it just gets done. It could be said that you have

113

a cult following here."

"It has been said, Meg. Many times. And there may be a modicum of truth to it. But a cult has to have something they worship. For a time that 'thing' was me. But I put a stop to that. For the most part."

"I've seen shrines built in your honor, General."

"I know. The Woods Children and the Underground People have done that. Used to do that. I hope all that is over and done with. A cult? No, we're all fighting and working and sweating toward the same goal, Meg. To rebuild this nation."

"And you're determined to get it done."

"Not in my lifetime. Buddy and Tina will have to carry on after I'm gone."

"Can they do it?"

"Oh, yes." He smiled and his eyes twinkled. "But I don't intend to go for a very long time."

The following morning, Ben outlined the route he wanted to take and a team of scouts pulled out. They would go only as far as Interstate 70, about twenty-five miles from Leadville up Highway 91, reporting back any roadblocks or sightings of hostiles. At the Interstate, they would camp and wait until the Rebels jumped off from Leadville. At that time the Scouts would advance up to the junction of Highway 40 north, repeating the process.

Buddy was leading this team of Scouts.

Late that afternoon, the light planes from Base Camp One began setting down. Ben was not surprised to see Dr. Lamar Chase step out of the first plane down.

The men shook hands. "You old goat," Ben needled his old friend. "Who invited you?"

"I don't need a damned invitation!" Chase popped back. "Besides, you're forgetting this is my country. I used to take leave in this area, hiking and camping. I wanted to see it one more time."

"And, of course, you brought along more of that abysmal goop you concocted that is laughably called field rations."

"Of course. Knowing how you all love it so much. I couldn't bear the thought of you running out."

"You're all heart, Lamar."

"Don't I know it. Where are the children?"

Ben pointed. "Over there. And they're in rough shape."

"The scum who did this to them?"

"They're dead. Dan hanged them yesterday afternoon."

"Good." Chase waved at the medical team who had accompanied him from the base camp and walked toward the building where the abused kids were being kept.

Past seventy, Lamar Chase was still as spry as a man thirty years younger.

The planes began landing ten minutes apart, off-loading supplies to keep Ben and his battalion fully equipped, and gassing up for the return trip the next morning. Ben waved several of the pilots over and outlined the proposed route the Rebels would be taking.

"Fort Collins will probably be our next resupply point. Of course, all that is subject to change, depending on how much we exhaust between here and there."

"Hell, General, we can always come in on some of these little strips all along here," a pilot said, tracing the route with a finger. "We've landed in worse places, believe me. Anytime you want us, just holler. We'll sit them down anywhere you carve out for us."

Ben watched the birds fly out the next morning then mounted up his people and started the pull north to the Interstate. Buddy had reported back that the outlaws in the mountains had pulled out, giving the Rebels a wide berth.

"I would much prefer they stood and fought it out," Ben said to those in the Blazer. "We're just going to have to come back and do it all over again." Then he laughed.

"What's so funny, General?" Beth asked.

"I was just remembering a line from Brother Dave. He said you can't ever do anything again. Once it's done, it's done. You can only do something similar."

And with a smile on his lips, Ben let them all chew on Brother Dave's words for a time.

The convoy made the way to Buddy's location by midmorning. It had been very slow going through the mountains. Highway 91 was deteriorating rapidly, with many washed-out spots, where huge areas of concrete were missing or broken.

Ben couldn't imagine anyone in their right mind wanting to ride a motorcycle through this mess.

They had passed through the small town of Climax, where a few hundred souls had once resided. The town had obviously been used by outlaws—and recently—for the place was a mess. Human feces was evident in every building, usually confined to a corner in one room.

"Filthy buggers!" Dan said. "How could a human being live like this?"

"They're not human beings," Ben had told him. "That's precisely why I am not treating them as such."

When they reached Buddy's position on Interstate 70, Buddy and his team pulled out for Dillon, another tiny town on the route.

"If the outlaws have damaged Eisenhower Tunnel, or just blown it closed, we'll have to backtrack and take this old secondary road up to Kremmling. And then pray that Highway 34, which goes through the Rocky Mountain State Park, is still open. Hell with it," Ben said, lifting his mike. "Eagle One to Rat." Buddy's team had been code-named the Rat Team while inspecting the tunnels in New York City.

"Go, Eagle."

"Check out Eisenhower Tunnel—you should be within a few miles of it—and report back to me. We'll stay put until you do so."

"Ten-four, Eagle. Rolling."

Ben leaned against the Blazer and waited for his son's report. It was not long in coming.

"Rat to Eagle."

"Go, boy."

"The tunnel is blocked, Eagle. Filled with old cars and trucks; a path just wide enough for motorcycles to use is all there is."

"Estimate on time to clear it?"

"Several days at least."

"All right, Rat. Return to our location."

"Ten-four, Eagle."

Ben turned his face north, to gaze at the old highway that would, he hoped, lead them to Kremmling. "It's going to be a rough pull, gang."

That was putting it mildly.

The highway was in such terrible shape the convoy was slowed to no more than a crawl in many areas. It turned out to be thirty-eight of the roughest miles Ben had traveled in a long time.

It was almost dark when they reached the outskirts of Kremmling.

And came very nearly driving smack into an ambush.

Even Ben was later forced to admit that most of the Rebels' attention had been focused on just trasversing the terrible highway. That changed in a hurry when the lead started flying and whining off the vehicles.

Rebels poured out of the vehicles and took up defensive positions wherever they could find them.

"Get those tanks off the trailers!" Ben spoke into his mike as he crouched by the side of the Blazer. "Somebody give me a report."

"Our ass is coming under fire," Buddy radioed from his forward position.

"Very funny, Rat. Can you be just a bit more informative?"

The Rebels had the Colorado River to their backs and hostile fire in front of them.

"Somebody doesn't like us very much, Dad," Tina added.

"Clowns," Ben muttered, very conscious of Corrie pressing close to him. It was not at all an unpleasant sensation.

The Dusters were the first to wheel about and unleash their 40mm cannon fire at the muzzle flashes coming from the edge of the small town.

The main battle tanks were unchained and roaring into life. They lowered their deadly snouts and blew everything in their path to hell with 105 HE rounds.

Fifty caliber and 7.62 machine gun fire began raking the area. Ben let them all rock and roll for several minutes before he called a cease-fire.

He lifted his mike. "If your ass is still intact, Rat, carry it up a few hundred meters and give me a report."

"I don't have to carry it anywhere, Eagle. We were practically looking down the muzzles. They're bugging out on motorcycles."

"Ten-four, Rat. Hold what you've got. Tanks up and check it out. Rebels behind the tanks. Let's go in and do a little night hunting."

11

But the outlaws were gone. As had been the case so often since Ben and his Rebels entered Colorado, the outlaws struck, and then pulled back.

"Do you get the impression that we're being baited?" Dan asked.

"Yes." Ben poured himself a cup of coffee and sat down in a canvas camp chair. "I'm beginning to feel that we are. And if that's the case, and it's Matt doing it, he's got tricks up his sleeve. Or troops would be more like it."

"The outlaws that bugged out of Dallas?"

"Probably. They were the more intelligent ones. Or street-smart might be a better way of putting it."

"There were several hundred who pulled out," Dan said, "And that's being conservative."

"Let's use five hundred for a ball park figure. Five hundred behind us. Say . . . two thousand north of us; with another two thousand that Matt could pull in . . . maybe more than that. Four to five hundred under Ashley's command coming at us from the east.

It's shaping up to be a very interesting scrap, Dan."

"You going to alert Ike and Cecil?"

"I don't think so. Ike can have troops up here in ten or twelve hours. He's got a combat team ready to go that can drop in anywhere we lay out a DZ. I think we'll just play it by ear for the time being. We'll get some rest tonight and inspect the town in the morning."

It was a mess.

"These people have just got to be the trashiest people I have ever encountered," Tina remarked.

Filth was everywhere. It appeared to the Rebels that their enemy did not believe in bathing more than once or twice a year. The lice and fleas left behind in their discarded clothing prompted Dr. Ling to issue a disinfect order once they were free of the small town.

The Rebels got the hell gone from the town.

"For a little bit I'd change the planned route," Ben said. "But I want to resupply at Fort Collins and get back on the Interstate system. As bad as it is, it's a dream compared to the roads we've been traveling."

The Rebels headed east on Highway 40, stopping along the way to bathe in the Colorado River and let the medics spray them with disinfectant. They had all been scratching since the discovery of the lice and fleas.

The town of Granby no longer existed. It had been destroyed by fire. Whether deliberate or by nature was anyone's guess.

They moved on, swinging north on Highway 34. They traveled just eighty miles that day, calling it quits at midafternoon at an old Ranger station in the Rocky Mountain National Park.

"So beautiful and so peaceful," Meg observed, taking in all the splendors of the wilderness. Deer were grazing nearby.

And they could graze without fear of the Rebels. The Rebels did hunt, but only when their food supply was low. The Rebels did not hunt for sport. That was not to say that they all agreed with Ben's philosophy about wildlife, for many certainly did not; the ranks of the Rebels were diverse. It was just that they all knew how Ben felt about so-called sport hunting, when it was not necessary for one's own survival, and they would just rather not bring the wrath of the General down on their heads.

"The way God planned it," Ben replied. "And the way I intend to keep it . . . if possible."

"I remember my father used to disagree with you about hunting," Meg said.

"Then he read me wrong—like a lot of other people. I was never antihunting. Hell, I belonged to the NRA right up the end. I hunted as a kid. And the one thing that people could never rightly accuse me of was being a hypocrite. I was, quite simply, adamantly opposed to animal cruelty. And I despised poachers."

"General," Meg began, shifting the topic, "where does all this end? I mean, surely you *can't* possibly believe that you and a small force of men and women can restore America. "That's an . . . impossible dream."

"We don't think so, Meg. I think that if you stay with us, you'll change your mind. And I have no intention of restoring America to what it was. Far from it."

"Then . . . ?" She looked up at the visionary, questions in her eyes.

"I intend to make it better."

The Rebels reached Interstate 25 in the early afternoon of the next day. They had put the majestic Rocky Mountains behind them—at least for the time being.

They found a small band of survivors in Loveland, once a city of more than thirty thousand. Five hundred determined men and woman had turned the place into a fortress against the roaming bands of outlaws. Many of them, men and women, openly cried when Ben and the Rebels rolled up to their blockades.

It was here that Ben left the last of his settlers.

Ben spoke with Cecil. "Get a team of Rebels up to Loveland, Cec. I'm going to clean out Greely first, then move up to Fort Collins. The spokespeople at Loveland say both towns are infested with outlaws and crud and the like. Bring in the team with the supplies. I'll bump you as to when. Just have them ready and standing by."

"Ten-four, Ben. Recon reports a large force heading straight toward you from the east."

"Ashley and his bunch?"

"That's affirmative. And he's picking up human crud as he goes. And there is a second force moving up behind you. Not quite as large, but big enough to cause you trouble."

"That's the bunch that bugged out of Dallas. We're aware of it, Cec. We're going to sit right here in

Colorado for a few days—maybe longer. Let's see what they do about that."

"Ten-four, Eagle. Hawk out."

"Let's go have a look at Greely, gang."

Ben set up a temporary CP in a small town just east of Interstate 25, on the road leading to Greely. He could not shell the small city because he did not know how many, if any, prisoners were being held in the city.

"It's going to have to be go in eyeball to eyeball," he told his people. "Now this bunch has automatic weapons. M16s, Uzis, AK47s. They have no artillery. Like most outlaw gangs we've faced in the past, this bunch has always relied on brute force to overwhelm people. So we'll play their game. Main battle tanks as spearheaders, followed by Dusters, followed by us. Let's go."

The rumbling of fifty-ton tanks reached the ears of the outlaws and did nothing to calm the already jittery nerves of the men behind the blockades; blockades that they now realized were very flimsy when held up against the main battle tanks rolling and clanking in their direction.

The battle tanks lowered the muzzles of their 105s and turned the roadblocks into smoking piles of bloody rubble. Then the Dusters opened up with 40mm cannon fire and the road was opened.

The Dusters and main battle tanks veered off, splitting up and rumbling up the streets on the edge of town, machine guns snarling and spitting.

"Rebels, out!" Ben told Corrie, and she relayed the message.

This time, before anyone could stop him, Ben

overran his own lines and led the charge, with Beth, Corrie, Jersey, and Cooper right behind him.

"Bogies in there!" Ben shouted, pointing to an old service station as he ran past it.

Cooper tossed a Fire-Frag grenade through the busted window and ran after Ben. When the Fire-Frag blew, and it was perhaps the most powerful and lethal grenade ever manufactured, the explosion and the hundreds of tiny fragments it released splattered the walls with what remained of the outlaws who had taken refuge in the building.

A half-dozen other Rebels, driven toward Ben's position by the roaring of Dan Gray, reached Ben's team. He waved them all down into a ditch. Ben clamped the bipod onto the gas cylinder and cylinder lock of his M14 and slipped a thirty-round clip into the belly of the old Thunder Lizard.

"A group of crud ran into that house right there," Ben said, nodding his head toward a frame home about a hundred meters away. Then he cut loose with half a clip of 7.62 rounds, stitching the wood and bringing screams of pain from those inside. He smiled. "I believe we've found us some bogies, gang."

But not for long. The dozen Rebels cut loose with M16s and M60s, soon turning the frame house into a death house.

"Check it out," Ben told the Rebels who had joined him.

Less than ninety seconds later, the Rebels waved the others on.

Hard-fighting Rebels, offering no quarter and taking no prisoners, cleared a dozen blocks in any direction within the hour, putting the so-called tough outlaw bikers into a rout.

"Chase them down and dispose of them," Ben ordered.

Hummers and Jeeps leaped forward, each one equipped with either a .50 caliber or 7.62 M60 machine gun. Many of the fleeing outlaws were chased and gunned down.

"House to house," Ben ordered, and then with his team, he personally took one side of the block where he was standing. When he had swept his perimeter, he told Corrie, "Tell those back in Loveland to enter this city. Start taking whatever they think they can use, either now or in the future. They have four days, dawn to dusk, to do it. Then we destroy this city."

The Rebels were still mopping up on the east side of the city when the settlers entered the west end and began taking materials they felt they might need.

"Five Rebels wounded, General," Dan reported. "Three will need to be sent back to Base Camp One with the returning birds. No dead on us."

"Corrie, tell base camp to send replacements up with the planes. We want to stay full strength. Dan, an estimate on outlaw dead?"

"Rough guess. I'd say a hundred and fifty, give or take twenty-five. About a hundred got away."

"Prisoners?"

"Fifty or so. Badly used and very frightened. Dr. Ling had them transported back to Loveland. And we have some prisoners . . . reluctantly on our part. They were groveling and snuffling about at our feet. One of them even wanted a lawyer."

"Wonderful. Of course you told him we'd have one

sent in immediately?"

"Oh, but of course!"

"Have them transported back to my CP. I want to talk to them."

They were just as scummy and stinking and sorry a lot as the others of their ilk Ben had encountered on this run.

"You ain't got nary rat to do this, soldier boy," one told Ben.

"What did he say?" Dan leaned forward. "What in heaven's name is a naryrat?"

"Did somebody call me?" Buddy stuck his head in the building, responding to his nickname.

"I think he did." Dan pointed at the outlaw.

"I ain't neber done no sich of a thang!" the biker said.

"What did he say?" Buddy asked.

"Enough!" Ben held up his hand. "Now I'm getting confused." He looked at the outlaw. "I'll be up front with you. You're going to die. That's a one hundred percent guaranteed fact. How you die is up to you. I can hang you or have a medic give you a lethal injection, which, so I'm told, is a much more humane method of execution. Not that you deserve it, for I find you and your kind to be among the least-humane people I have ever encountered."

The outlaw stared at Ben.

"I don't believe the cretin understands English," Dan said.

"I ain't got a fuckin' thang to say to you, soldier boy." The biker spat out the words, filling the immediate area with bad breath.

"Your choice." Ben nodded to Dan, who prodded

128

the biker to his boots with the muzzle of his weapon. "Bring the next one in, Buddy."

"Can I smoke?" the outlaw said after Buddy had pushed him into a chair.

"You might as well. It'll probably be your last one."

The biker's hands were shaking as he finally managed to roll a cigarette. "You're a real hard-ass, ain't you, Ben Raines?"

"Yes. How do you know my name?"

"I seen your pitcher years back, when you was writin' them books. You ain't got no purtier."

Ben had to smile. The biker was just as hard as he was. He knew he was going to die, but he was going to die well. "You're not exactly the last rose of summer yourself. You part of Satan's organization?"

"Yep."

"You kidnap people to trade to the Night People?"

"Naw. We just use 'em as slaves and fuck 'em and so forth. Then swap 'em off to other gangs."

"How about Snake and Satan?"

"What about 'em?"

"They deal with the Night People?"

The biker paused. "I heard they did. But I ain't never seen it personal."

"How many men does Snake have in his organization?"

The biker smiled, then told Ben where to go, how to get there, and where to stick what on the way.

Ben glanced at Buddy. "Put him down by injection."

Buddy looked puzzled. "Why, Father?"

Ben shrugged. "He may be trash, but he's got

129

balls." He cut his eyes to the biker. "Too bad you picked the wrong side."

"Nobody forced me, Raines. So don't go sheddin' no tears for me." He pointed a finger at Ben. A very dirty finger. "I'm gonna tell you something, Raines. I didn't pick the wrong side. I couldn't live under your rules, that's all. I could have cleaned up my act and joined your Rebels. And I probably would have been a good soldier. You believe that?"

"Yes, as a matter of fact, I do," Ben surprised him by saying. "But now are you going to sing me some sad songs about how you were abused as a child, or you are what you are because of society, or some such crap as that?"

The outlaw laughed. "Hello, no! That's garbage and you know it as good as I do. I am what I am because it's what I wanted to be. It's as simple as that. You been right all these years."

"What's your name?"

"Larry. Last names don't matter much no more."

"You want to live, Larry?"

"Everybody wants to live, Raines. But if you're askin' me to suck up to you and be a snitch or whatever, forget it. Just bring the needle out and put me down."

"Why?"

"'Cause eventually, you're goin' to win this fight. It's gonna take you a long time—years—but you'll do it. And just the thought of livin' under your rules makes me wanna puke!"

"Is there not one shred of decency in you, man?"

Larry thought about that for several moments. Then he shook his head and frowned. "Your idea of the word, Raines?"

"If that's the way you want to put it, yes. But decency is decency, Larry. You know that. Stop playing games. We—all of us—have to have a moral foundation to live by. We'll revert back to anarchy without it. Hell, you're living proof of that!"

The biker grinned. "That's true, for a fact. That's a pretty speech, Raines. Why don't you put that on my tombstone?"

"You didn't answer my question, Larry."

"I ain't gonna answer it, Raines. I'm gonna leave you wonderin' about that."

"I won't wonder about it for very long, Larry . . . if that is your name. My back trail is lined with dead men."

"My name is Charles Lawrence Matthews. Put that on my marker, punk." He looked up at Buddy as his right hand dropped out of sight.

Ben put his hand on the .45 lying on the table, cocked and locked.

"Why me?" Buddy asked.

"'Cause Raines is dead!" he shouted, and leaped forward, a boot knife in his hand.

Ben shot him twice in the chest, the slugs driving him back. The biker staggered out the open door and fell to the ground, dead.

Ben leaned back in his chair. "Buddy, find the Rebel who searched this man. And give him a shovel. Tell him to start to work. He's got a lot of graves to dig."

12

With Greely under firm control of the Rebels, and only hours away from being destroyed, Ben and his troops moved up the Interstate to Fort Collins and watched as the planes carrying supplies from the base camp began arriving.

The newly arrived replacements were assigned and the badly wounded Rebels, along with the freed prisoners, were flown back to Base Camp One.

Ben drove back to Greely just as the survivors were leaving, the trucks loaded with lumber, bricks, and other articles that might be useful in the future.

"Bring it down," Ben ordered.

A light rain was falling as the small city went under the Rebel torch. As he stood back and watched the city burn, Ben then ordered every town within a twenty-mile radius of Loveland to be picked clean, the materials inventoried and warehoused, and then to be destroyed.

Ben and his Rebels pulled out for Cheyenne, Wyoming, at dawn, prepared to fight their way through. They did not see one sign of human life during their run of fifty-odd miles. The old Interstate stretched out before them, barren. Buddy and his rat team ranged twenty miles ahead of the main column, reporting back by radio every fifteen minutes. They had nothing to report over the two hours it took the convoy to reach the outskirts of Cheyenne.

It appeared to be a dead city.

But Ben wasn't buying that. A little warning bell kept going off in his head. He waved Buddy to his side.

"Take your team and skirt the city. There was a SAC base here before the war. See what's left of it." He waved Tina to him. "Take this old highway here, Tina, and check out Laramie County Community College. Take some trucks with you. We'll try to salvage all the books we can and fly them back with the other books we've found during our next resupply."

The Rebels saved knowledge much like a squirrel stores away nuts. The book repositories at Base Camp One were very likely the largest in the world. Ben had people who did nothing but oversee the preservation and restoration of books.

Dan walked up to Ben. "I don't like it," the Englishman said bluntly.

"Nor do I, Dan. I'm getting some funky vibes from this city."

"Funky?" Dan said with smile. "That word dates us both, General."

Ben laughed. "Hell, Dan, I still remember *cool* and *hip.*"

The men squatted down on the Interstate and waited.

"Tina reporting the college has been looted and trashed," Corrie informed the men. "But many of the books are salvageable."

"Load them up and bring them back. Any signs of recent habitation?"

"Ten-four, sir. The unmistakable odor of creepies."

Ben and Dan both cursed the Night People. Ben said, "Send an additional platoon of Rebels to both Scout teams, Corrie. Advise Rat and Tina they are on the way."

"Ten-four, sir."

"You think they're in hiding, General?" Dan asked.

"Yes. Hoping that we'll not detect them and just bypass the city."

"However . . . ?"

"They're in for a very rude shock."

"Reinforcements on the way," Corrie said.

Ben nodded, his eyes on the hazy outline of the city. "Contact Rat and Tina on scramble and tell them to start digging in. As soon as the additional troops arrive and their positions are secure, I'll start the push from the south."

He waited until Corrie had relayed that, as he studied a map of Cheyenne, and said, "Main battle tanks prepare to spearhead at my orders, followed by the Dusters. Ramos and Brad will cut off at 80 under the command of Dan, half the tanks with them. I'll take command of Companies C and D and the remainder of the tanks and drive toward the center of the city. I'm going to push straight through to the middle of town and assess the situation."

"Ten-four, sir."

"Get in position, Dan."

"See you at the airport, General."

"Keep an eye out for prisoners, Dan."

"Right."

Ben stood up and waved Corrie into the Blazer, climbing in behind her as soon as she was settled in the specially built rear compartment, so three could still sit comfortably despite all the equipment.

"Let's go, Coop. Swing in behind the tanks."

As soon as Dan veered off onto Interstate 80 toward Holiday Park and Ben's command roared toward the heart of the city, Ben's radio blared the news.

"Under heavy attack," Buddy radioed.

"They're coming out of the woodwork, Dad," Tina radioed.

"If you don't think you can hold, fall back," Ben told them.

"We'll hold," they both assured him.

Ben halted his contingent on Sixteenth Street and spread them out, while the tanks started to work on the lower floors of the ravaged-appearing buildings.

The old Atlas Theatre, long a national historic site, had been gutted by fire, as had several buildings close to it.

Dark, hooded shapes flitted about the charred interior of the old theatre. Ben lifted his M14 and knocked several of them sprawling. A tank commander shifted the muzzle of his 105 and finished whatever else might have been alive in the ruins.

"Lob a couple of grenades into the basement of that building," Ben told Cooper, pointing to the building right behind them. "Let's see what happens."

Cooper tossed two Fire-Frags through a broken window and they all went belly-down on the sidewalk. The exploding Frags brought howls and wild shriekings of pain. Beth crawled over to a smoking basement window and shoved the muzzle of her M16 through the hole, giving the creepies a full clip. The shrieking stopped.

"Colonel Gray says he's found the prisoners, General," Corrie told him. "In a warehouse."

"Tell him to ask the prisoners if any others are being held elsewhere in the city."

"Negative to any further prisoners in the city. That's firm."

Ben took the mike. "Raines to all tank commanders and self-propelled mortar crew chiefs. My command is driving toward the airport. At my signal, start using Willie Peter and incendiary rounds. Dan, you hold what you've got; we're going to box the city as best we can and bring it down."

"Affirmative, General."

"You read me, Rat, Tina?"

"Ten-four, Eagle."

"Let's go, Cooper."

The self-propelled mortar carriers left the original position on the outskirts of town and began circling and getting into position. With the tanks leading the way, Ben's unit began barreling toward the airport, with every gun they could use hammering out lead.

The creeps had automatic weapons, but nothing that could punch through the armor plate on the tanks and trucks and Ben's Blazer. Cooper swerved to avoid a thrown grenade and the concussion as they passed nearly lifted the Blazer off the right-side tires.

"Miserable cannibalistic bastards!" Ben muttered.

"Take 85 right up ahead, tanks," Cooper radioed, after glancing at an old street map of the city. "That'll take us right to the airport. Did you hear that, Cooper?"

"I heard, I heard!"

"Just past the airport, cut right. That'll be Prairie Avenue."

"Yes, Mother," Cooper muttered, just as a hard burst of lead whined off the armor plate of the Blazer, causing everyone inside to wince.

Then a burst of fire knocked out a rear tire. Cooper fought the wheel as he struggled to maintain the same speed. The ride turned very bumpy.

"We're almost there, Coop," Ben told him.

"You all right, General?" Ben's speaker talked to him.

"Ten-four. Getting our innards shook up some, that's all. Cut over, tanks. Start lining up over there next to those mortar crews on the north side of this street."

Ben bailed out of the Blazer as it lurched to a stop, and he grabbed his mike while the others scrambled out. "All units report in if clear of the city."

They were clear. Buddy and Tina were still hard-fighting it, but holding.

Ben turned to Corrie, standing by his side. "Are the units in place around the outskirts?"

She nodded her head.

"Bring the city down," he ordered.

From both the north and south limits of the city, the 81mm mortars and the 105s began blasting, dropping in Willie Peter and incendiary.

"Creepies bugging out." Buddy's report came right on the heels of Tina's radioing in.

Smoke began pouring into the sky as what was once the capital of Wyoming began burning.

As the creepies raced from the burning city, many were chopped down from the units of Rebels scattered around the outskirts. The light rain had long since stopped and a bright sun was warming the land as the city burned and the creepies died.

Ben pounded the city for an hour before calling for a cease-fire. He glanced at his watch. Not yet noon. A lot of history had died in only a few hours, and that wasn't to Ben's liking. But this way was the safest for his people, and the quickest.

"Mount up," he ordered. "Scouts out on Interstate 80, westbound. We're heading for Laramie."

"We wondered what was going on, General," the man said as he shook Ben's hand. "We could sure see the smoke rising."

Buddy had found several hundred survivors living in Laramie.

"There used to be more of us," the spokesperson explained. "But the outlaws and bikers and the warlords are striking us nearly every week. They've taken their toll," he added grimly.

"You're sure this is where you want to settle?" Ben asked.

"We're sure, General."

Ben nodded. "Corrie, get the base on the horn. Tell them to get a team of Rebels up here and to resupply us and prepare to take back those we liberated. And send the books back, too. We're getting top-heavy."

"You've really cleared Colorado?" another settler asked.

"No," Ben quickly corrected that. "We've cleaned out a few towns and cities, and managed to dispose of several hundred outlaws. But cleaning out just one state is going to be a massive undertaking. It's important we get as many outposts set up as possible. Once we're linked in that manner, able to resupply units in the field quickly, the job will become much easier."

The Rebels stayed in Laramie for several days, resting, loafing, working, and seeing to equipment needs. Ben sent out patrols, north and west, and soon became acutely aware of just what he and his Rebels faced.

There were bands of outlaws and bikers and warlords all over the state. Some of them numbered no more than ten or twelve; some numbered several hundred.

And the city of Casper was filled with Night People. Rawlins was a haven for a huge outlaw gang that terrorized the southern part of the state.

"We take Rawlins first," Ben said.

"Destroy it?" Dan said.

"No. I'd rather not. I'd like to set up an outpost there if at all possible. It's about a hundred miles from Laramie, and that's an ideal distance between outposts. We'll take the town building by building."

"There are many families along the way," Ben was told. "Good decent people. But they're forced to live in forts because of the outlaws. We're in radio contact with most of them. I'll advise that you're on the way and for them to get ready to resettle—if they want to. And I think they will."

First reports back from the besieged families along the way indicated they would be more than happy to relocate.

"Fine," Ben said. "We'll put out in the morning."

Ben soon found out that these people were not about to be driven off by outlaws. Their will was strong, but they were going about the task of surviving the wrong way—at least under present conditions. They wanted wide-open spaces between them, and that just wasn't feasible. Not yet. They were too vulnerable to attack.

"We'll clear out everything from Fort Steele to Rawlins," Ben said after carefully studying a map of the area. "Or to make it easier, from the Continental Divide back to Fort Steele. Everything in a twenty-mile radius, north, south, and back east. At least for a start. More as time goes on."

"And from Rawlins?" Corrie asked, to stay on top of things.

"We'll take Highway 287 to Muddy Gap, then 220 up to Casper. We won't destroy that city either. We'll set up an outpost there. Once that's done, the settlers can start cleaning out from the points of the rough triangle inward. We can have hundreds and hundreds of square miles of clean territory."

"And we're going to do this in every state?" Beth asked.

"Yes. Europe will have to wait. We've got to clean up our own act first."

"Folks just outside of Arlington want to talk to you, Dad," Tina informed him.

"That's ten-four." Ben glanced at his watch. "We'll be there within the hour."

"I'll tell you flat out, General," the rancher told Ben. "I don't like some of your rules. But you and your bunch is carryin' the load in this war, so I'll be willing to live under them and not bitch about it . . . much," he added with a smile.

Ben laughed. "I'd be very wary of any type of government that claimed to be perfect, my friend. And we're far from perfect. Good to have you with us." Ben stuck out his hand and the man took it.

They spent an hour discussing Ben's plans, with Ben agreeing to some of the rancher's own plans and ideas. The Rebels pulled out with Ben once more having that good feeling that the light at the end of that long, long tunnel toward restoration of the nation was shining just a little bit brighter.

The Rebels spent the night near Fort Steele. As yet they had seen no sign of outlaws, and neither had any of the settlers they had spoken with.

Buddy's Rat Team had advanced to within a mile of Rawlins, with not a shot being fired from either side.

"They're in there," Buddy radioed back. "We can see cook fires all over the place."

"Estimates?" Ben asked.

"Several hundred, at least. I'd suspect more than that. I think the outlaws have massed in the town; that would probably account for us not having encountered any of them on this run."

"I agree with him," Dan said. "Since we don't

know how many, if any, prisoners are being held, it's going to be a tough fight. Are you planning an end-around?"

"No. We'll go in from the east and take them on nose to nose."

"I'll make it clear to the lads and lassies that they'd better be in body armor."

"Yes. Order a full inspection for the morning. Main battle tanks will spearhead again. Try to keep the destruction down to a minimum; we want to save as much of the town as possible."

"Rat on the horn," Corrie told him.

Ben took the mike. "Go, Rat."

"They have mortars, Father. And plenty of them."

Ben acknowledged that and turned to Dan. "They'll cream us if we wait until dawn to strike. So attack, Dan. Now!"

13

The Rebels jumped into action, rolling within two minutes, the tanks spearheading the column at full speed. The outlaws worked frantically to get the mortars set up and get the range, but the column was moving too fast, and the main battle tanks were too awesome and carried too much firepower. They cut loose with everything they had and crashed through the now-bloody roadblocks, the treads of the fifty-ton tanks crushing the life out of any who were unable to move out of the way.

Dusters were right behind the bigger tanks, their 40mm cannon and twin-mounted machine guns spitting out rapid death as they roared toward the center of town.

The Rebels mauled and mangled the outlaws, knocking them back half a dozen blocks before the crud could recover and try to throw up some sort of defense. At best, it was only a halfhearted attempt now that they had been hammered so severely and so swiftly with massively superior firepower and troops.

Many ran for their motorcycles and cars and trucks and hauled ass out of Rawlins, with most of them heading west. Ben ordered no pursuit; first on his priority list was cleaning out the town.

"Circle the town," Ben ordered. "Fire barrels on every street and keep them burning throughout the night. Company A to the north, B to the south, C to the west, D to the east. No one leaves their perimeter because the passwords will be different in every sector. Rat team and Tina's team will be with Dan and me checking the town. Let's do it, people!"

"General," Beth said, reading an old information packet about the small city. "It says here that there is an old prison located in town, in use from 1903 until 1982. A new prison was build just south of the town then. I bet if there are any prisoners, they're being held in one of those two places."

"Good bet, Corrie. Let's check out the old prison first."

"You ain't takin' none of us, Raines!" came the defiant shout from behind the thick walls of the old prison. "We got the prisoners as hostages."

Ben got a bullhorn from the Blazer and laid it on the line to the outlaws. "I don't negotiate with crud. Ever. Release the prisoners."

"Fuck you, Raines. We'll kill them all!"

"There is nothing I can do about that at the moment. But I tell you this: if those prisoners are harmed anymore than they already are, I'll lock you all down hard in the prison south of town and you will either starve to death or die of thirst—whichever comes first, it doesn't make a damn to me. And don't make the mistake of thinking I'm bluffing."

146

"You ain't that hard, Raines!"

"The hell he ain't," another outlaw said. "You just don't know Ben Raines. That's the hardest-nosed bastard that ever pulled on a pair of boots. I'm givin' it up. I'm comin' out, Raines. The side door. I got a half-dozen prisoners with me."

"You yeller son of a bitch!" he was taunted and cursed by a few of the others. And Ben noticed it was only a few.

"Dan," Ben said. "Get over to the side and see to the prisoners."

Dan and a few Rebels slipped into the darkness.

Beth was looking through night lenses. "I can see the man, General. He's got a gun to a woman's head."

"Keep his face in your mind, Beth. His, and any with him."

A single gunshot cut the night air.

"He killed the woman, General." Beth's words were filled with anger. "Just let her fall and then spat on her."

"I told you, Raines!" the outlaw shouted. "Somebody bring me another cunt up here."

Ben lifted the bullhorn. "Last chance, people," he warned them.

A half-dozen more men, with a dozen or more women and kids, hurriedly left through the side door of the old prison. Dan and his people grabbed them and hustled them to safety.

Another gunshot split the air.

"Another piece of filth killed a little boy," Beth said.

"Take the prison," Ben ordered.

147

It took less than five minutes to secure the old prison. Ben looked at the seven outlaws who had survived the storming.

Then his eyes drifted to the dead woman and dead young boy. He again looked at the outlaws.

"You were warned. Buddy, chain them securely. We'll take them south of town in the morning."

"You ain't a-gonna do that, Raines. That ain't nothin' no law-abidin' puke like you would do."

"If you believe that, then that makes you a fool!"

"Lock them down and weld the doors shut," Ben ordered.

Just past dawn, and one of the outlaws was shaking so badly all present thought his legs might break. He had pissed his filthy jeans as the fright turned him into a glob of jelly.

One by one, the outlaws were shoved into the narrow cells and the doors welded closed. The outlaws were now beginning to realize that Ben Raines had meant every word he had spoken through the bullhorn.

They cursed him and spat on him. Then they begged. Two of them even tried prayer.

The one outlaw who was frightened out of his wits was not locked down.

"Ride," Ben told him. "Get on your goddamn motorcycle or in your pickup truck or on your skateboard or whatever and get the hell gone from here. Spread the word to your scummy-assed friends that I'm on the way. Tell your outlaw buddies and bikers and so-called warlords to either straighten up

148

their act or get ready to die. And be sure and tell them about this!" He pointed to the welded-in prisoners. "Move, you sorry son of a bitch!"

The outlaw didn't need a second invitation. He was gone.

Ben waved all the others out except for Dan, Buddy, and Tina.

"You dirty bastard!" a biker spat the words at Ben. "You know how hard we'll die in here!" he screamed. "This ain't right."

"How many women and girls and boys have you raped and sodomized and enslaved and tortured and murdered, punk? How much grief have you brought to innocent people?"

"But that ain't 'pposed to make no difference!" he shouted. "People like you 'pposed to show mercy to people like me!"

"No," Ben corrected him. "Not people like me. That type of justice was tried for two hundred years, and for two hundred years it didn't work. This works."

"How?" he squalled, slobber leaking out of his mouth.

"Whether or not it proves to be an object lesson to others is debatable. Personally I think it does. Be that as it may, we're rid of you in such a way that allows you, to one degree or the other, to suffer as you have caused others to suffer."

The outlaw sat down on his steel bunk and glared hate at Ben.

Dan opened the outer door at a knock from the other side.

"I just cain't believe this," the outlaw said, over the

crying and cursing of his buddies.

He was looking at one of his former female prisoners. She began relating a story of degradation and evil, of pain and humiliation, of needless death for pleasure . . . at the hands of the outlaws.

Then she turned her back to the welded-in outlaws and left the cellblock.

Ben waved the others out behind her and stepped through the door, closing it behind him.

Rawlins was secure.

With the settlers firmly in place in the liberated town, Ben and his Rebels pulled out for Casper, to once more face the hated Night People.

The news of what he'd done with the outlaws in Rawlins spread quickly throughout the West. For the outlaws and the trash and scum who had terrorized the West, up to this point, Ben and his Rebels were a force to be reckoned with someday.

Someday was now.

Ben Raines and his Rebel army had for several years been off fighting foreign forces who had invaded U.S. soil. And the outlaws operating throughout the ravaged land had ballooned in numbers with no organized force to combat them. Now all that was changing. Ben Raines was on the move, determined to rid the land of human vermin.

The army of the Libyan named Khamsin, the Hot Wind, had been reduced to no more than a demoralized few, at the hands of the Rebels. The Russian, Striganov, and his forces were now on the side of the Rebels, massing along the American-

Canadian border. Sam Hartline was dead. And now Ben Raines was coming after the outlaws.

Many borderline outlaws had a change of heart after the news of what happened in Rawlins spread. They shuddered at just the thought of being welded into cells and left to die.

This just was not the way it was back before the Great War. Criminal justice, back then, had been on the side of the punks and thugs and scum and to hell with the victim's rights and the overwhelming vocal cries of the majority of law-abiding citizens.

Ben Raines had changed all that. It was like a deadly virus: if you had it, you died; if you didn't catch it, you lived. Very simple.

Ben Raines's philosophy was just like that. Obey the laws of the land and everything is smooth. Screw up, and you're in bad trouble.

Those outlaws who did not possess the degree of arrogance and the contempt for others that so many of their counterparts had, left whatever gang they were working with and pulled out. They left their outlaw ways behind them and took up home-steading, raising themselves a garden and becoming a part of whatever community they settled in. It wasn't as much fun as robbing and raping and looting and murdering, but with Ben Raines on the prowl, it was a damn sight healthier.

When Satan brought the news to Matt Callahan, the outlaw leader took it calmly enough. He knocked back a shotglass of rye whiskey—neat—and carefully rolled himself a smoke.

"Well, partner," Snake said, "I reckon there comes a time when everybody throws a saddle on a cayuse he

151

can't ride."

Even Satan sometimes had a hard time deciphering Matt's cowboy lingo. "You mean, like we can't win this fight, Snake?"

"Oh, no, pard. Ol' Slim has done pushed open the batwings and stepped off the boardwalk to face a gunhand that's slicker than he is."

"Ol' Slim?"

"Ben Raines."

"Oh."

"And since our posse didn't come back from Shreveport, and nothin's been heard from Meg, I got to think she's done took her a runnin' iron and changed brands. My own flesh and blood is ridin' for the homesteaders."

Satan understood that. Sort of.

"Send a rider out a-foggin' to the other ranches, Satan. Tell them hardcases to strap on their six-shooters, fork them a hoss, and come on a gallop. We got to get ready to drag iron."

Satan thought about that for a moment. "Ah . . . you want me to get the other bikers in here for a fight with Ben . . . ah, Slim and his boys?"

Matt tilted back his black hat while the smoke from the hand-rolled cigarette that dangled from one corner of his mouth half closed one eye. "That's what I said, partner," Matt drawled.

"He's closing in fast, Snake."

"He's got a week's hard ride ahead of him 'fore he hits our home range. We got time. Tell some of the boys to throw up a line around Buffalo. And to start blowing some bridges on the Interstate all the way over to 59. That'll slow Slim down even more; make him take the country roads so's we can harass him."

"That's good thinking, Snake."

"Naturally. But I don't want all the boys in here. We got to keep us some hired guns in reserve. Ol' Slim is tricky, Satan. Don't never sell him short. He's tricky, he's tough, and he's as mean as a tweaked-tail cottonmouth. He'll punch his way through to here, don't make no bets against that. But what we got to do is keep snipin' at him, keep knockin' out Rebels. Make him use up his ammo and keep him on edge. When he gets up here, we'll have more men than he's got and we can put Slim and his Rebs down. That's my plan."

"It's a good one, Snake."

"Thanks kindly. Toss you a loop on a good hoss, Satan. You got some hard ridin' to do."

Satan left the ranchhouse and stood on the porch for a moment, scratching his head. "The bastard's crazy as a road lizard, but still manages to make sense."

He stepped off the porch and waved for some men to come to him. "Get on the horn and tell Butch to start blowing the bridges on Interstate 87 all the way over to 59. Rest of you come with me. We got to make some plans. Ben Raines is about to knock on the door."

14

The first town the Rebels came to on 287, about thirty-five miles north of Rawlins, was a burned-out shell. There were no survivors so they did not linger there. About ten miles up the road, they left 287 for 220, turning northeast toward Casper. And like so many roads they had traveled, this one was in very bad shape, slowing the column down to no more than a crawl.

They bivouacked along the Sweetwater River and were up and rolling just as dawn split the dark sky with rays of silver and gold.

And they began finding evidence that the creepies were near.

The Rebels found where whole families had been slaughtered. In many cases, only the best cuts of human flesh had been taken—best depending upon the taste buds of the individual creepie.

Thirty miles outside of Casper, Ben made his decision. There was too much evidence that the city was filled to overflowing with creepies to try to save it; it would be too costly in terms of Rebel life.

"We'll destroy it," Ben told his commanders. "Then move on down to Douglas and salvage that to complete the triangle. We want be in position by dawn tomorrow. We want to avoid damaging the air strip. So I want teams to go in and seize that under artillery cover. We'll hold the freed prisoners from Rawlins there, and any we manage to save from Casper. With three-quarters of the Laramie-Rawlins-Douglas triangle secure, I don't believe any outlaws or creepies will chance staying along the east boundaries on Interstate 25. Any questions? All right. We pull out at four in the morning."

There was no way the tanks and trucks of Ben's column could make a silent approach to Casper—so he did not even try. They rolled up to the city and got into position.

Meg, being new with the Rebels, asked the question. "What about survivors that might be in the city?"

"We hope for the best, Meg. That's all we can do. We're facing one hell of a fight just north of us. I can't afford to lose people."

"That's not all of it, is it, General?" She asked it just as Dan walked up.

"No," Ben said softly. "It isn't. If any have been held any length of time, it's been discovered that the majority of those . . . unfortunate people never make it back to any useful"—he sighed—"way of life, for want of a better term. We're being overwhelmed by ex-prisoners of the Night People. We just don't have the personnel or the know-how to treat them. I've got the best shrinks in the world back at Base Camp One. They just can't break through to them. That's the main reason Dr. Chase flew up to Leadville. Even the ones we rescued a year ago, two years ago, just don't respond to any type of treatment we can give." He lifted his hands in a gesture of helplessness.

"So they're better off dead?" Meg asked.

Ben nodded his head. "Considering our limited ability to heal the mind, and the state of the world, that seems to be the general consensus."

"Or the General's consensus," she countered. Then walked away.

"She doesn't understand, Ben," Dan said in a rare use of Ben's first name, even though Dan had tried for years to have the Englishman stop calling him General. "She just doesn't understand so very many things. Namely that we are strained to capacity with various types of . . . unfortunates. And that even though our ranks are gaining in numbers each week, with each outpost we set up, it's much like the child's game of two steps forward and one step back. But that doesn't make the final decision any easier. I just wanted you to know that I understand."

"Thank you, Dan. Tell the gunners to open fire."

Ben ordered the firing to commence at 0430. He kept up the devastating pounding for two hours, then waved his Rebels into the burning city. Strong west winds had begun blowing about an hour earlier, and they fanned the flames, hurrying the scorching of the city.

The Rebels shot the creepies as they found them, and brought out several dozen men and women the Night People had held hostage . . . for later dining. Several of them were completely mindless, driven mad by a fear that most would never know and few could comprehend.

"Get on the horn, Corrie. Birds up to Casper with supplies and medical teams. And tell Ike to send another detail of Rebels this time. We're going to settle Douglas and complete the triangle before we tackle Matt Callahan and his bunch."

He looked up at Dan. "Reports on any Rebel dead or wounded?"

"Two wounded. Not seriously. There would have been a dozen dead if not for the body armor."

Ben nodded. "Tina, take a team and check out Douglas. It's fifty-odd miles over there. Give me a bump when you get close."

"Ten-four, Dad."

"Let's ease over to the airport, gang. We'll bivouac there."

Buddy and his people had stacked up the dead creepies in a field away from the airport and were dousing their stinking carcasses with gasoline for burning.

"What is their fascination with airports?" Dan mused aloud. "That has been gnawing at me for months. I don't understand it."

"Nor do I. But we never fail to find a large number of them located around airports."

"Maybe they use the runways for jogging?" Cooper offered with a straight face.

The groans of Jersey, Beth, and Corrie and the

laughter of Ben and Dan filled the air.

Dan slapped Cooper on the back. "Thanks, Coop. I need a good chuckle."

Cooper grinned and stuck his tongue out at the ladies.

Jersey flipped him the finger.

The Rebels cleared a runway and then rested and waited for the birds to land while Casper burned itself out. The planes began setting down on the afternoon of the second day.

Tina had reported that a nest of outlaws were occupying Douglas and looked as though they were preparing for a fight. Then, abruptly, they had begun pulling out, heading straight north up Highway 59.

"Matt's got something up his sleeve," Ben commented. "Corrie, bump the outpost down at Laramie and bring them up to date. Tell them that those families who wanted to resettle can come on up to Douglas."

He turned to Dan. "We need some people up here to get the oil industry around Casper producing once again. Give it some thought, Dan. See what you come up with."

"That bunch that came in from Texas while we were in New York City. Didn't Cecil say they had oil field experience?"

"Yeah, I think so. All right. That's our crew. Corrie, get them moving up here."

"It's coming together, Father," Buddy said, a big grin on his face.

"Slowly but surely, son. We're getting there."

Ben took a platoon of Rebels with him and traveled the miles over to Douglas. He encountered no unfriendlies along the way.

Douglas was in good shape, considering the type of people that had been inhabitating the place for several years. Settlers from the southern part of the state were beginning to arrive, staking out claims and setting up shops. Ben left the detail of Rebels and their families just arrived from Base Camp One and headed back to the still smoking and destroyed city of Casper.

He found bad news waiting for him.

"Scouts report bridges and overpasses blown all the way up to Kaycee," Dan told him. "And the pilots report that bridges have been blown all along Route 59 north."

"That's why the trash in Douglas pulled out when they did. Damn!"

"I've been consulting a map," Dan said. "It looks rather dismal."

"A lot of the older maps are," Ben said with a straight face.

Dan glanced at him and then chuckled. "The choice of routes, General."

Ben took the map and studied it for a moment. "Yes, I see what you mean. So straight up on the Interstate through Buffalo is out, as is 59. It doesn't leave us much choice, Dan. The only way open is 20/26 west, unless we want to chance these county roads, and I don't."

"Nor do I."

"We pull out in the morning, then. Buddy, take

your Rat Team and head out now. Don't get yourself in a bind."

The convoy was rolling before dawn. Buddy had reported back no sighting of the enemy, but he had seen many signs of survivors, usually smoke from fires, most of whom were living far off any beaten path, back in the hills and mountain ranges.

"They're out there," Ben said, rolling along in the Blazer. "By the thousands, living in small groups, trusting very few outside their immediate little gatherings. Not that anyone could blame them for doing so. The trick will be to pull them into the protective circle of the outposts."

"And how do you propose to do that, General?" Beth asked.

"I don't know," Ben admitted. "By word of mouth, I suppose. We sure as hell can't go into every group in America, take them by the hand, and lead them out."

They passed through Natrona, a dead town. Then Powder River lay in their rearview mirrors; it had been destroyed by fire. They passed by Hell's Half Acre, actually about three hundred twenty acres that back in 1833 were named "The Burning Mountain" by Army Captain B. L. E. Bonneville, because they were, at that time, spewing sulfurous flumes from burning bitumonous deposits. It was an area of white clay, soft and crumbling and dangerous for walking.

Buddy was waiting for them in what was left of the tiny town of Waltman.

"Nothing, Father. And I mean absolutely no firm sightings of human life. With the exception of the smoke I told you about."

"Where's the rest of your team?"

"Up the road about thirty miles. I've laid out a bivouac area just west of Moneta. I don't know what we're going to find in Shoshoni. According to the maps, it had a population of about a thousand before the Great War. A few miles further on is the Wind River Indian Reservation."

"They'll be damn little there," Ben said grimly. "They joined us back in the mid-nineties when we were defending the old Tri-States. President Logan wiped them out, for the most part. There are probably still many living there, but they'd be hard to find."

"Why did Americans hate the Indians so?" the son questioned.

"Complex question, son. Many white Americans hated, or distrusted, or both, anyone who wasn't exactly like them—or how they perceived themselves to be. The term 'Ugly American' fit the majority of us to a T."

"Even you, Father?"

"To a degree, son. Until I embarked upon a quest to improve my mind and open it up to some light. And that was not an easy thing to do in a time of instant so-called entertainment available to nearly everyone simply by pushing a button on a television set, sitting down in front of the goddamn thing, and letting one's brain rot."

Buddy wisely did not pursue that topic any further, knowing all too well his father's venomous views on the subject.

"Lead the way, Rat," Ben said with a smile.

The column rolled on through what appeared to

be a land totally void of human life. But far in the distance, on both sides of the highway, Ben could see faint fingers of smoke lifting up into the sky.

And as he had done so often, he could not help wondering how they were living. Were they teaching their kids to read and write? Teaching them values? Or were they just existing, living day to day in a world gone mad?

The smoke faded from view and Ben occupied his time studying maps of the state.

At Shoshoni, Highway 26 veered southwest, while 20 cut straight north. The next town north on 20 was Thermopolis, and that brought a smile to Ben's lips as he remembered the discussions, debates, and sometimes downright arguments he'd had with the hippie, Thermopolis, during the time they'd spent together clearing out New York City of creepies.

The town of Thermopolis had once held a population of almost four thousand, so it was a pretty good bet that some survivors would be found there. Friendly or hostile was up for grabs.

On Highway 20, at the town of Worland, that once held over six thousand souls, Ben planned to cut over on Highway 16 and drive through to Buffalo. It was there that he felt Matt, or Snake, would have his first real line of defense. He also felt that this close to Matt's home turf, the defenders would be much better fighters than the scum Ben's Rebels had thus far faced.

So far, the fighting had been a cakewalk. All that, Ben reckoned, was about to come to that well-known screeching halt.

The Rebels spent the night just outside the

deserted and ravaged town of Moneta. Ben doubled the guard that night, not knowing what might be coming at them from out of the darkness.

They reached the town of Shoshoni a hour after dawn the following morning. The Rebels could sense death even before the town came into view.

There was nothing left of the small town except for a few skeletons, bones scattered by wild animals. The buildings had been put to the torch, probably after looting.

"This is getting depressing," Ben muttered, climbing back into the Blazer and ordering the convoy straight north following the Big Horn River through Wind River Canyon and toward the town of Thermopolis.

"Hold the column!" Buddy's voice came through the speaker.

"What's up, Rat?" Ben radioed.

"Roadblock, Eagle. And it's a good one. There are people behind it and they appear to be well armed. I can see heavy machine guns and mortar pits along either side of the road."

"Tell them who we are."

A few anxious moments passed for Ben as he waited for his son's reply.

"Rat to Eagle."

"Go, boy."

"I think they're all right, Eagle. Hear the cheering?"

Ben heard it and he smiled faintly. He lifted his mike. "Column advance. Everybody lock and load. Tanks, button down tight. All troops on full alert. Buddy, do not advance until we are on your tail.

Head's up, boy."

"What's the matter, General?" Corrie asked.

"Just being cautious, Corrie. It never hurts."

They rolled past the now-open roadblocks; very well constructed blockades, Ben noted.

"Get behind the lead tank, Cooper, and stay with him."

As they rolled past the cheering crowds, Ben's smile turned grim. Neat, he thought. Now I know what happened to those Rebel patrols who vanished some months back.

"Notice how slick and well fed these people are, gang?" Ben questioned. "You ever seen such a healthy-looking bunch?"

"You're right," Beth said, looking out the window. "They sure haven't missed any meals."

Corrie spoke up. "I still don't see what's wrong. They just look like hundreds of cheering people to me."

"Oh, they're cheering, all right," Ben agreed. "They're looking at the next six months' supply of food. We're smack in the middle of creepies, gang."

15

Those in the Blazer sat stunned for only a few seconds. Then Cooper slowly turned his head to gaze at Ben. "Are you fucking serious, General?"

With a tight grin, Ben picked up his mike. "Eagle to all Rebels. I think we're in the middle of creepies, boys and girls. Those of you in the trucks, as soon as the first shot is fired, hit the decking." He opened the glove box and took out a .45 autoloader and rolled down his window as the crowd pressed closer to the Blazer. "Put it in four-wheel drive, Coop, and get ready."

Ben studied a man who was staring at him. The man's eyes were savage-looking. His lips were slick with anticipatory saliva. "Hey, asshole," Ben said. "You prefer an arm, a leg, or a breast?"

With a savage scream, the man tried to grab Ben's arm. What he got was a .45 slug in the face.

"Go!" Corrie screamed into her mike.

"Tell the tanks to crush as many as possible on the way out of this snake pit," Ben said calmly as the lead began to whine and howl off the armor plate.

The fifty-ton battle tanks and the smaller, lighter Dusters began wheeling and turning and squashing the life out of the creepies as the buttoned down .50s and light machine guns turned the area blood-splattered.

Cooper had gunned the Blazer, driving right through the crowds, knocking screaming and cursing men and women in all directions, including one who crawled up onto the hood of the Blazer. Cooper slammed on the brakes, knocking the creepie off the hood; then he promptly floorboarded the pedal and ran over him.

There were those who tried to climb up into the canvas-covered beds of the deuce and a halves. They were met with a hail of lead pouring through gunslits in the armorplating on the sides.

"Pull over right up here, Coop," Ben told him, pointing.

"Sir?"

"We're the last ones out, Coop." He smiled, adding, "Almost." He lifted his mike. "This is Eagle. Main battle tank 112, stay with me."

"Ten-four, Eagle," the tank commander radioed. "Standing by."

"And I'm on the other side of the street," Dan radioed. "I've traded my Jeep for a seat in a deuce and a half."

"Ten-four, Dan. Eagle to Rat."

"Go, Eagle."

"What's your twenty?"

"Clear of town, on the north end. Getting the mortars in place."

"Ten-four. When everyone is clear, bump me. Shouldn't be long now."

"Ten-four, Eagle."

"Here they come," the tank commander radioed. "Right on the heels of Tina's bunch."

"Lay down covering fire left and right of Tina's vehicles."

The old streets began to echo with the sounds of lead whining off bricks. Tina's Scouts roared past the last remaining Rebels and she told Ben that was it. Everyone was clear.

"Cream them," Ben ordered.

The tank commander unleashed his 105, his 7.62 and .50 caliber machine guns.

"Let's go, Coop," Ben said. "Nice and easy. Dan, you fall in behind me, 112 bring up the rear."

With his turret swiveled, the tank took the drag and continued to lay down a deadly rain.

"Rat, have the artillery commence firing. Bring the town down."

His words were no sooner out of his mouth than the 105 rounds began whistling over his head, followed by the slight fluttering sounds of the mortar rounds as they began dropping in.

Safely back with their own kind, Ben and the others who had made up the last ones out of the town dismounted and watched as the town was turned into an inferno by the incendiary rounds.

Whatever else the Night People might be, they did not lack courage. Dozens came pouring out of the flames, screaming and cursing Ben Raines as they charged the Rebels' position armed only with rifles.

The Rebels cut them down in less than a minute.

"Cease firing," Ben ordered.

The earth ceased its trembling and the warm early summer air fell silent.

Dan walked over to Ben. "That was a chancy thing back there, General."

"No other choice, Dan. They had us. If we'd tried to back out of there, it would have been a confusing disaster for us. The only way was forward."

"That's as close as we've come to being parboiled in some time." Dan removed his beret and wiped his forehead. He glanced up at the sun. "We have many hours of daylight left, sir."

Ben smiled. "Are you trying to tell me you'd like for us to get the hell gone from this area, Dan?"

"In a word, sir, yes!"

The column traveled up to Worland, originally hoping to find some survivors. But with the creepies this close, it was not surprising to any of them when they found a deserted town.

"It was just recently deserted, Father," Buddy said. "I'd guess no more than five or six months ago. I'm just wondering how many of them ended up in the stomachs of creepies."

"I don't even want to think about it. Let's make camp out near the airfield. We've got a lot of scouting and planning to do over the next several days."

The Rebels did not have to be told they were only a few days away from a major confrontation that might last for weeks. But even though they were fully aware of their being vastly outnumbered, the word *defeat* never entered their minds. Many of the older Rebels had been fighting for more than a decade; this was as natural to them as pulling on their boots.

For two days the Rebels rested, checked equipment, and studied what maps were available of the area they were about to enter.

"Any route we take is going to put us smack in the middle of ambush country," Ben told his unit commanders. "If we take the southern route, we'll travel right through Ten Sleep Canyon and then have to go over Powder River Pass to get to Buffalo. If we take the northern route, that's Highway 14, and that takes us north of Buffalo into Sheridan, we'll really be in tough country for about the same number of miles as the southern route. Either way we go, the tanks have to be chained down on trailers. And don't think Matt didn't deliberately plan it this way. He may have gone around the bend, but he's still a smart man.

"Now then, as we move through this Cloud Peak Wilderness Area, we've got to button everything down tight and be constantly on the lookout for snipers. Transfer as many people as possible into APCs and rig cover over the beds of the deuce and a halves. Due to the country we'll be in, for at least a day, and maybe longer, the snipers will be able to fire down at us.

"I'm not going to pull out of here until I am one hundred percent certain we are one hundred percent ready to go." He held up a finger. "Another thing: I've got a hunch that many of Matt's people will be much more mobile than we are. These are outlaw bikers, remember, and they've probably got three-wheelers and four-wheelers that will enable them to attack hard and fast out of terrain that would be impossibly slow for us. We won't follow them when they retreat. That's what they want us to do. They've had time to booby-trap the areas they know well.

"They've got us outnumbered—hell, what else is new?"

That drew a hard laugh from everyone in attendance.

"But we've got them outgunned. And more importantly, we're right and they're wrong. And since Matt, or Snake, wants this played like an Old West gunfight, you just remember the words of that Texas Ranger who said that you just can't stop a man who knows he's right and just keeps on comin'."

"Or woman," Tina reminded him sweetly.

"What's that hombre waitin' on?" Matt questioned, a small bit of impatience in his words.

"I don't know," Satan admitted.

"Ol' Slim just might be sorta cautious about draggin' iron agin the Rattlesnake Kid," Matt mused.

Matt was more and more slipping into his fictional character's manner of speech, forgetting the English usage that he once prided himself on.

"You mind telling me where you come up with this Rattlesnake Kid and Slim business?" Satan asked.

Something clouded Matt's eyes for a moment. They cleared and he smiled. "The Rattlesnake Kid was someone I dreamed up—character in a series of Westerns. Slim Henry was Ben's character in another series of Westerns. He beat me out of the Silver Spur Award with his Western. But mine was better." He said that with just a touch of a pout.

Satan nodded his head. "I see—I think."

"Oh, I accepted defeat gracefully. I shook his hand and smiled and offered a few congratulatory words after the banquet. After all, I am a gentlemen of the West. It's the code, you know?"

Satan didn't know, but he nodded his head as if he did. Codes always confused Satan. A lot of things confused Satan, including Matt Callahan.

Matt slipped back into character. "But that there hombre's books weren't no better than mine. Not as good, as a matter of fact. How could they be? I am a man of the West and he isn't. From some dreary little town in Louisiana."

Matt rose to walk to the window of his ranchhouse, his spurs jingling as he moved across the floor. "I want to face Slim. I want to meet him in the street eyeball to eyeball and drag iron agin him. I want to put hot lead in his belly." He slapped the pearl handles of his Colts. "That damned dirty lobo wolf!"

Ben Raines may be a lobo wolf, Satan thought, but—recalling some of Matt's Western verbiage— you're just plumb loco! However, he kept those thoughts to himself. Loco or not, Matt had put together one hell of a fine organization and ran it well—even during those moments when he drifted off into never-never land, mentally loping across the prairies on his pony, or cayuse, whatever.

". . . we don't even know which route Slim is

gonna use," Matt was saying, bringing Satan out of his mental meanderings.

"I got both of them covered, Snake," Satan assured him. "The only problem is that when Raines pulls out, I ain't gonna have the time to shift men from one point to the other. Not usin' the mountain trails."

Matt shook his head. "That ain't the way I got it figured nohow. As soon as Slim commits hisself, say on the southern route—that's the way I'm guessin' he'll take—you send those hardcases up along Shell Canyon and Granite Pass a-foggin' it down to Worland, usin' the highways, and come in behind Raines and his Rebs. We'll box him."

"That's a good plan, Snake."

"Sure it is. OK, Satan, you get crackin', boy. Saddle up and ride!"

"For sure we're under observation," Ben said. "As soon as we commit to whatever route—and it's going to be the southern route—Matt will know and start shifting people around." He shook his head and frowned.

"What's the matter, Dad?" Tina asked.

"The area Matt chose to live in. He was always, well, obsessed with Custer and his last stand in the Rosebud Mountains. Matt always said that he'd like to go out in such a manner . . . Matt was a nice guy—back when I knew him—but sometimes a little weird."

"But that's not why you looked perplexed a moment ago, is it?" Buddy questioned.

"No, it isn't. Matt is insane, and you can't tell what

a crazy person might decide to do. I just don't want us to go riding into our own last stand." Ben experienced a visionary mental flash that caused him to smile, and then laugh outloud. "No," he chuckled, as the others gave him strange looks. "No, I can't imagine even Matt having that in mind." Still chuckling, he walked away.

"What in the world?" Dan questioned.

Ben stopped and turned around. "All right, people, we pull out in the morning. First light. And we're going to be driving hard. I don't want us caught in the mountains after dark. Rat, take your Scouts out one hour before the main column leaves. That will be about six. Take plenty of explosives to clear any slides or man-made road blocks. We'll trailer the Jeeps; you take APCs and button them down tight. We're not stopping, people. Equipment breaks down, we leave it and double up. Cold rations and a minimum of liquids. We're not going to be stopping for piss calls. Let's get it done, gang."

16

"Raines is on the move!" Satan informed Matt, just moments after first light.

Matt smiled and rose from the breakfast table. "He's headin' for his last showdown, Satan. I'm finally gonna get my revenge. Which route's he takin'?"

"Southern."

"I knowed it!" His expression changed and he viciously slapped a young girl. "Don't just stand there, you stupid girl. Get Satan some bacon and beans and coffee. Move, you lazy bitch!"

Holding the side of her face, the teenager ran from the room.

Satan sighed. They had plenty of chickens and plenty of slaves to look after them and gather the eggs. They had hogs and all kinds of other animals. But Matt insisted upon bacon and beans for breakfast. A real drover's breakfast, he said. Whatever in the hell a drover was.

Satan looked at the ass of the young girl as she

disappeared into the kitchen, doing her best not to cry. Matt sure had him the pick of the slaves. Real cream of the crop and she couldn't have been much over fourteen or fifteen. Satan got himself a boner just looking at her.

"You got the boys shifted to come in behind Slim?" Matt asked.

"Right. And I don't want no breakfast. I done eat."

Matt's eyes narrowed. Anyone else refused to have grub with him, he'd have killed him over the slight. But he did give Satan a few allowances.

The girl served the coffee and left the room quickly, before she did anything else to bring Matt to slap or hit her. Matt liked to slap women around. And abuse them in the most disgusting of sexual ways—when he wasn't fooling around with young boys, that is. And he always kept a couple of them chained in the basement. He never kept the same ones very long, and the reason for that was very simple: they usually died at Matt's hands.

And there was no hope for escape. The ranch was more like a king's castle in terms of guards and stuff. And she'd seen what happened to other girls who tried to run away. She'd been sick for a couple of days after seeing that.

But she did have one hope.

Ben Raines.

"Ten Sleep is clear, Eagle," Buddy radioed.

"Ten-four, Rat. We're about twenty miles behind you. Hold there for a few minutes then pull out."

Buddy acknowledged the transmission.

"What a strange name for a town," Corrie said.

"Lots of different stories about how it got its name," Ben said. "The most popular one being about two Indian bands that were camped ten sleeps apart. The Indians used to measure distance in the number of sleeps."

"And in case you're getting all impressed with the General's memory," Beth said, "he's reading from an old tourist guide about Wyoming."

Ben grinned and held up the guide.

"What else is interesting in that thing?" Cooper asked.

"Six miles east of Ten Sleep, in the Bighorn Mountains, there's a Girl Scout camp. Or used to be."

That perked Cooper up. "You reckon there might still be some there? You know, like survivors, all grown up now?"

The women in the back groaned and Ben laughed. "I really doubt it, Coop."

"I'm picking up something, General," Corrie said. "Everybody stop talking and let me listen." She listened intently for a moment. "I guess it was just a skip. They were talking about somebody called Slim."

"Who?" Ben twisted in the seat.

"Slim."

Ben looked puzzled for a moment, and then shook his head. "Slim. Sure. I never would have guessed that. Slim Henry."

"Who is Slim Henry?" Jersey asked.

"A character of mine in a Western series of books that won me some awards one time. I beat out Matt's character, the Rattlesnake Kid. Obviously he fooled both me and Meg with his taking it so calmly. I never thought it bothered him that much."

"So now you're Slim?" Beth asked.

"I guess so. I sure hope Matt's not counting on me standing up and shooting it out with him in some sort of fast draw thing."

Corrie smiled. "Now that would be a sight to see."

Ben grunted his reply.

Ten Sleeps was remarkably intact for a town that was totally deserted. Ben would have liked to stay and browse around, but he had about seventy miles of hard traveling before the column would be clear of the mountains.

"Go, Buddy. We'll be only a few miles behind you."

Buddy and his Rat Team pulled out in APCs.

Ben rolled a cigarette and smoked it down, then carefully ground it out under the heel of his boot. "Let's go, gang."

The long column began snaking its way toward Ten Sleep Canyon. No sooner had the last vehicle entered the canyon than snipers opened up. But owing to the steepness of the canyon walls, it was almost impossible for them to shoot out the tires. And after fifty or so rounds had been expelled, the snipers found, to their disgust, that all the vehicles had been armor-plated.

They radioed that information back to their base.

"Then cool it with the sniper fire," Satan told them. "Roll some rocks down on the bastards."

"All main battle tanks and Dusters swivel your turrets and give those up in the hills something to remember us by," Ben ordered.

The big tanks could not use their 105s for fear of breaking the chains that lashed them onto the flatbed trailers. But they could use all their heavy machine guns and the Dusters could use their 40mm cannon.

All along the snaky column, Rebels began poking gun barrels out of the slits and opening fire. No one among the Rebels knew for sure whether they hit anything or not, but the awesome display of firepower sure put a crimp into any further plans those outlaws in the hills might have had.

They radioed the news of this new development to Satan.

"Well . . . piss on it!" Satan yelled. "Git out of there and come up behind them Rebels as soon as they pass. Them boys comin' up from Worland will pick you up. Shit!" he yelled. There wasn't nothin' workin' out.

Then Satan had him an idea. He grabbed up the mike. "All you boys in the hills. Don't do nothin' to keep Raines and his Rebs from leaving the mountains. We want them out. We'll put them in a box in Buffalo and cream the hell out of them!"

Back at his ranch, Matt Callahan listened to the transmissions and shook his head. But he did nothing to countermand Satan's orders. "It ain't gonna work, partner. Ol' Slim's too slick for you. He's got too much firepower for your boys to box him in. But I might as well let you learn a hard lesson about hard men."

Matt propped his boots up on a hassock and rolled him a smoke and waited.

It really didn't make any difference to him who

won this war. Just as long as he got him a chance to put lead into Slim's belly and see Ol' Slim Henry die in the dirt at his boots.

Nope, it just didn't make a damn to the Rattlesnake Kid.

It'd serve him right. How in the hell could anyone who lived in Louisiana write Westerns, for Christ's sake!

"That always bothered Matt," Ben said. "He was one of those die-hard Western writers." The firing had ceased from the ridges above the column and Ben felt he knew why. "Matt figured a writer of Westerns ought to have been born on a ranch or have a stable of horses . . . or at least live in one of the Western states."

"And you two were friends?" Beth asked.

"I sure thought we were."

"All firing has ceased," Buddy radioed back.

Ben took the mike. "Yeah. They want us to clear the mountains so they can box us in at Buffalo, I'm thinking. I'm betting Matt had both routes covered, and just as soon as we took the southern route, he shifted men down from the northern route. They're lying behind us a couple of miles."

"You want me to set up an ambush, General?" Dan asked.

"Negative." All Rebel radios had been set on scramble to avoid being intercepted. "We'll do that just before reaching the edge of the Wilderness Area. We'll teach them that it isn't polite to tailgate people."

"Ten-four, sir!" Dan said with a laugh.

"You hear that, Cooper?" Jersey stuck the needle to him. "So don't tailgate."

"Mind your own business, Short Stuff," Cooper told her, cutting his eyes to Ben. "Can you just imagine being married to three or four women at once? No wonder they made it illegal back in the old days."

"You mean back before the Great War, Coop?"

"Right, sir. The old days."

"Keep talking, Cooper," Jersey said with a smile. "You're just about to stick your boot in your mouth."

Cooper got it then. He flushed and said, "No disrespect meant, sir."

"None taken!" Ben laughed. "To people of your age, Coop, I guess they are the old days."

The miles passed slowly as the convoy wound its way over and through the Bighorn Mountains.

"What's your mileage, Eagle?" Buddy radioed the question.

Ben glanced at the odometer and called it out.

"You're eight miles from the end of the wilderness area, Eagle. It's about five or six miles from there to Buffalo."

"Ten-four, Rat. Hold what you've got. Dan, check your odometer. Two miles inside the exit point, set up an ambush."

"Ten-four, Eagle."

Ben knew that any ambush the ex-British SAS officer set up would be extremely deadly and one hundred percent effective. He would use his team of Scouts, all of them multitrained and especially skilled in guerrilla tactics and the use of explosives.

Ben listened to Dan's radio traffic. "Fall back and join me, Tina."

"Ten-four, Colonel."

"That's gonna be interesting," Jersey commented.

"At least that," Ben agreed.

Dan hid his team's vehicles in the deep timber and heavy brush some five hundred meters east of where he was setting up the ambush site. His Scouts began placing electronically detonated Claymores along both sides of the road, being very careful that THIS SIDE TOWARD ENEMY was properly positioned. The Claymores were set up along a two-hundred-meter stretch, on both sides of the highway.

The Rebels melted back into the brush, above the Claymored stretch, and got into position. Any who survived the murderous wrath of the Claymores would not survive the equally murderous gunfire from the Scouts.

Ben joined Buddy at the end of the wilderness area and halted the column. The town of Buffalo lay only a few miles to the east of them.

"A fair-sized little town," Buddy observed, glancing at a map. "But no mention is made about whether or not it has, or had, some sort of airport."

"I'm sure it had a strip large enough for our birds to land on. If it didn't, we'll carve one out, after we take the town."

"Are we going to save the town?"

"I would like to. I'd like to use both the towns as outposts. But if Buffalo has to be destroyed, then we'll just do it. With the bridges blown on Interstate

87, those outposts in the south will have to rely on those set up in Colorado. Sheridan will connect with those we carve out in southern Montana." He took the map from Buddy and studied it. "If all works out, those will probably be Hardin and Miles City. We'll just have to see."

"There they are," Dan said into his walkie-talkie. "Coming along like strutting cocks of the walk. We'll be able to take out about half of the vehicles. We'll use rocket launchers on the rear half. Get ready."

Those outlaws in the first fifteen cars and pickups had only a few seconds of very painful knowledge that they had driven into a death trap. The Claymores blew and their hundreds of ball bearings literally shredded the vehicles and the occupants. Machine guns and rockets took out the rear half of the column. Those outlaws who jumped from the burning tangle of twisted hot metal, or who were thrown out from the initial blast, were shot down by automatic weapons' fire from the Scouts above the road.

One man did manage to get off one frantic and short-lived message via his radio.

Satan sat stunned in his headquarters in Sheridan. Raines had taken out about a hundred men in less than a minute. The outlaw biker sat with his mouth hanging open, too shocked to utter a sound.

Matt sat with his boots propped up, sipping strong cowboy coffee. "I told you, Satan," he muttered, a grim note to the statement. "You just don't jerk around with Ben Raines."

Matt unzipped his fly and motioned to the young

185

girl he had summoned to his side. "You know what I want. So get to it."

Dan and his Scouts picked their way among the burning vehicles. There was little left to salvage and no prisoners to take.

Using his .45, Dan made certain of that. And it was not done with any type of wonderful humanitarian motives in mind.

The Rebels put out any small fires that were burning along the roadway and cleared out fire breaks that would, hopefully, stop any blazes from spreading once they were gone.

"Ambush concluded," Dan radioed to Ben. "Do you want us to clear the roadway?"

"Negative, Dan. Any type of retreat is not in my plans. Toss the dead into the ditches for the carrion birds and scavenger animals and link up with me."

"Ten-four, General."

The Scouts began dragging and dumping the bodies of the outlaws into the ditches.

Ben had deliberately gone off scramble with his last remarks, wanting them intercepted by the outlaws.

"Goddamn!" Satan said. "That there ain't nothin' no decent man would do."

Matt just smiled as he approached climax, the girl on her knees between his wide-spread legs. The callousness of Ol' Slim did not surprise him. He'd accurately pegged Ben as a hardcase when he'd first met him, years back. The man had the mark of the warrior all over him . . . if you knew what to look for.

Some of the outlaws in Buffalo shifted nervously and looked at one another as Ben's calmly given orders on how to dispose of the bodies came over the speakers and earphones. And the thought came to them all that if any of them had second thoughts about this operation, now was the time to act on them.

A few did. They walked to their cars or trucks or motorcycles and cranked up, heading out and away from Ben Raines and his Rebels. They fully understood that they were all hard men in a hard time, but those with any sense at all knew they didn't want to become hard men in a hard bind facing a much harder man.

Ben Raines.

Ben leaned against a fender of his Blazer and alternately sipped a cup of coffee Jersey had brought him and studied a map of Buffalo that the Chamber of Commerce had issued years back, the map taken off one of the dead outlaws miles back.

He really wanted to save the town. He would have liked to have both Sheridan and Buffalo as outposts. He just didn't know, at this time, whether that was feasible. Ben glanced up at the sky. The trek through the mountains had taken far less time than he had imagined. They still had hours of good light left them.

Dan walked up to his side.

Ben met the man's eyes. "We'll attack the town, Dan." Ben's smile was hard. "But not in any manner they might be expecting."

17

Dan Gray's Scouts slipped close to the town and its now very nervous defenders. The outlaws all knew that somewhere south of their position, Pete Jones and his gang were coming north hard; but no one knew exactly where they were or when they were due to arrive.

What they did know was that Ben Raines was close enough to practically stick the muzzle of a rifle up their collective asses and pull the trigger while the hard bastard laughed at their discomfort.

One outlaw made the mistake of showing an elbow. A slug from a .50 caliber sniper rifle took off his lower arm. Another caught a bullet right between his eyes when he peeked around the side of an old warehouse on the edge of town. A third outlaw tried to run from one house to the other and was spun around and around like a lurching top as half a dozen slugs from Rebel rifles struck him.

"Man, we need some help down here!" a biker yelled into his mike. "We got three or four guys down dead or dyin' and we ain't even seen no Rebs."

"They's five hundred of you guys down there!" Satan screamed into his mike. "You got machine guns, mortars, and enough ammo to last a fuckin' year! Start droppin' some rounds in on them Rebs!"

"How the hell can we drop rounds in on people that we cain't even see, you asshole!"

And while they were arguing, Buddy and his Rat Team were silently infiltrating the town. On this trip, Buddy was armed with his crossbow for more silent killing. Colonel Dan Gray was personally leading the rest of his Scouts into the town.

Had the outlaws been a bit more industrious about keeping the brush and grass cut around the outskirts of town, it would have made the infiltration much more difficult.

One team of Scouts had swung wide, coming up on the south end of town and planting explosives all along a thousand-meter stretch. At Dan's orders, the explosives blew.

"They're attackin' from the south end!" the leader of the bikers in Buffalo yelled. "Gary, swing your people around and beef up Leadfoot."

But Leadfoot was cursing and kicking and trying to get his butt up off the floor where he had been knocked when the building next to him was demolished by C4. The force of that explosion had caved in one wall of the building he had occupied.

One of his brother bikers had been running to Leadfoot's assistance when he rounded the wrong corner. His eyes widened and his mouth opened for just a second as his unbelieving eyes watched as the heavy machete blade impacted against the softness of his throat. The blade very neatly took his head off.

Leadfoot got to his feet just in time to feel something squishy hit him the center of his back. "Goddamnit!" he yelled, turning around.

He stood seemingly rooted to the floor, his eyes mirroring his horror as they stared down at Shorty's head, the wide-open and forever unblinking eyes staring back at him.

It took only a few seconds for Leadfoot to react. He hit the floor and began crawling around looking for his M16. He found his weapon and his walkie-talkie. He punched the side button and whispered into the cup, "Leadfoot to Beerbelly."

"I's 'fraid you was dead, Leadfoot."

"Shorty is. Somebody cut off his head and chunked into the house. Hit me in the back with it. Most Godawfuliest damn thing I ever seen in my life. Where's the rest of the boys?"

"Keepin' they asses down. Injun Sam and his boys has done swung around to your sector. You readin' this, Injun?"

"Yeah. But I ain't swung nowheres. I got Rebs all around me, man. The sneaky bastards has done slipped into town and is all over the place. I just seen Texas Jim; as a matter of fact, I can still see him. He's on the end of a rope danglin' from a tree. The bastards hung him! Turrible thing to see."

A hard burst of gunfire caused Injun Sam to get a little closer to the floor. The only thing that prevented him from getting any closer were the buttons on his shirt.

Injun Sam crawled under a table as a grenade exploded right outside his position. He said a lot of very hard and uncomplimentary things about Ben Raines.

But he said them under his breath, not wanting to give away his location. Damn Reb might be listening right outside the window. Sneaky bastards!

Wanda, the leader of a bunch of dyke bikers, had taken cover, along with her Sisters of Lesbos, behind the walls of an elementary school.

"I hate that goddamn Ben Raines," she hissed at no one in particular.

"I bet he was a Republican," Sweet Meat whispered.

"He's a goddamn man," Sugar summed it up. "That's enough."

"I hate Ben Raines," Wanda repeated.

"About two hours of daylight left," Ben said to Corrie. "Advise Dan to hunt a hole until dark. Then really start headhunting."

Corrie relayed the orders and Dan's operator acknowledged them.

"Received, General. They're going deep."

"I'm hoping that if nothing happens during the next several hours, the bikers will think we've pulled out and they'll try to do something cute."

"We're going to try to save the town?"

"If at all possible."

After two hours of silence, the outlaws began to relax just a bit. Some even began to believe those Rebels who had infiltrated the town had pulled back with the approaching darkness.

Many of those who believed that would not live out the night.

As full night pushed dusk out of the way, and finished spreading her dark wings of concealment over the town, Dan Gray and his Scouts slipped from their hiding places and went about their very silent and very deadly work.

The first to be very brutally tossed into that long sleep was a careless biker who thought he'd slip over to where the female slaves were held and knock himself off a quick piece.

He got knocked off and the piece of himself that got the most attention was not the member he originally had in mind.

The outlaw died with his eyes wide open, the blood staining the front of his dirty shirt, and his head nearly severed from his body just as he was unlocking the door to the slave quarters.

Buddy cautiously pushed open the door and looked inside the darkness. He smiled and waved several members of his Rat Team inside. Working very swiftly, and whispering to the slaves to be very quiet, the Scouts freed the men and women and children.

"Are there any more prisoners being held in this town?" Buddy whispered the question.

"The north end of town," the woman told him in a soft voice. "About twenty or so girls and a half a dozen boys. They were hand-picked to serve Snake."

"Tell me exactly where."

"Get the others out of here," the woman said. "I'll lead you there."

"It'll be very dangerous," Buddy warned her.

The woman's smile, which Buddy observed in the moonlight coming through a very dirty window, was only slightly less than savage. "I've been using a Mini-14 for years and I can probably outshoot you with a pistol. It took these scum three years to finally corner and catch me, and before it was over, I left a dozen of them on the ground that last day."

Buddy smiled. "Welcome to the Army of Ben Raines. I'm his son, Buddy."

"You're a handsome devil, for a fact. But you're a little young for me." She cut her eyes as Dan Gray slipped like a shadow into the slave house. "Now that one!" She let that remark speak for itself.

"We don't have the time for socializing," Dan softly chided his people. "Let's go! Get these people back to our lines."

Buddy waved him over and pointed to the woman. "This is, ah . . ."

"Sarah," she said, sticking out her head. "Sarah Bradford. And you'd be . . ."

"Colonel Dan Gray." He took the offered hand and looked into her eyes.

"She'll be leading us to the other prisoner house," Buddy told him.

But Dan and Sarah were busy gazing into each other's eyes.

Buddy squatted on the dirty floor and smiled at the man and woman. After a few seconds, he asked, "Are you two going to make a career of this?"

Dan shifted his eyes. "Don't be impertinent, young man. Get the lady armed and let's go." He moved to the door and slipped out into the darkness.

"I like a tough man," Sarah said, belting a dead outlaw's pistol around her waist and taking the M16 handed her.

"Well, you have certainly met one. You ready?"

"Let's go. You follow me. I was raised on a ranch over on Crazy Woman Creek. I know this town better than you know the back of your hand."

"After you, ma'am."

Outside, Dan looked on with admiration as Sarah came upon the body of another outlaw with his throat cut and reached down with no qualms and took his sheath knife from the cooling body, slipping it onto her belt, then testing the edge.

"I wouldn't want to dress out a steer with it," Sarah said. "But it'll do to cut a throat until I can find a stone."

They slipped away into the darkness, heading for the second prisoner house.

"What a magnificent woman!" Dan was heard to whisper.

The Scouts escorting the freed prisoners swung wide around the town, using the same trails they came in on, and reached Ben's position.

Dr. Ling then took command of the survivors while the Scouts briefed Ben.

"I think he's in love."

"Who?" Ben asked, startled.

"Colonel Gray."

"Who the hell did he fall in love with?"

"One of the prisoners."

Tina smiled. "Isn't this all rather sudden?"

Ben held up a hand. "Wait a minute, wait a minute! Let's back up. Where is Dan now?"

"Going to free the other prisoners, with his lady love leading the way."

Ben walked away, mumbling to himself, heading toward the truck that was temporarily serving as a coffee and ration wagon. "Love!" he muttered. "Love! I'm trying to fight a war, not run a lonely hearts club!" He passed by Dan's Jeep, where Chester was sitting on the front seat, waiting for Dan to return.

The little dog wagged its tail at Ben's approach. "You're about to have some competition, Chester." Ben stopped and petted the animal. "But I don't think you'll mind at all. Just one more person to spoil you."

Chester jumped up into Ben's arms and Ben carried it toward the mess truck, enduring Chester's licking his ear as they walked.

"There's the house," Sarah said.

Dan glanced at his watch. "The diversion team should be in place. Give them two clicks," he told his radio operator. The signal to open the ball.

Seconds later, a huge explosion rocked and destroyed half a dozen buildings at the south end of town. Outlaws began shifting about, beefing up that end of town, believing a major attack had once more begun from the south.

Leadfoot and Beerbelly and Injun Sam and the others braced for attack. Wanda and her followers began once more to curse Ben Raines.

Carefully placed Scouts began directing heavy machine gun fire into the buildings at the south end of Buffalo. More outlaws were shifted to the south to repel the attack.

Buddy lifted his crossbow and put a bolt through a guard's back, the force of the heavy bolt knocking the man down, dead as he hit the ground.

"What the hell was that?" an outlaw's voice carried to the Scouts. "Luddy—Luddy? What was that sound?"

But Luddy was on the ground, a crossbow bolt through his heart.

The outlaw biker who called for Luddy slipped around the house. He experienced a few seconds of hideous pain as a knife blade slammed into his stomach and the blade, cutting edge up, tore through vital organs, finally ripping the heart.

Rebels stormed the house, expecting more guards, and were pleasantly surprised to find none.

That frightened prisoners were quickly freed from the ropes that bound them. "Come on, people," Sarah said in a hoarse whisper. "Let's go. Ben Raines and his Rebels are here."

And while the outlaws were busy fighting the "Big-ass bunch of Rebels that attacked them from the south side," as Leadfoot would later report, Dan Gray and his Scouts exited the town from the north end, with all the prisoners.

"Ol' Slim conned you," Matt announced to the defenders of Buffalo by radio the next morning. "I warned you about that sneaky no-good. You got to stay on your toes all the time when he's around. He'll stick a knife in your back and twist it. Just like he done to me years back."

"I didn't know Ben Raines ever stabbed Snake," Beerbelly said.

Injum Sam blinked. "Me, neither."

"He didn't," Leadfoot enlightened them. "'At there's a figger of speech."

"Leadfoot's pretty smart," Wanda said, adding, "For a man."

"You shuck them drawers, Wanda," Leadfoot replied, "and I'll show you just how much of a man I really am."

Wanda flipped him the finger.

Matt Callahan, aka the Rattlesnake Kid, then gave a speech that just about bored the boots off those listening, calling on his boys to defend the ranch against invaders.

Since the outlaws had been up all night, too spooked to go to sleep, many of them dozed off during Matt's long-winded harangue.

Three miles away, Ben was climbing into the Blazer. Settled in the seat, he picked up his mike. "We don't have any prisoners to worry about now, gang. Let's take the town."

18

"Holy shit!" Beerbelly said, looking through binoculars at the fifty-ton battle tanks slowly advancing up Highway 16, all buttoned up and ready for action. Behind the main battle tanks came the smaller Dusters.

Beerbelly had been a Grunt in 'Nam—one of the few bikers who'd ever had any actual combat experience—and he knew firsthand what those twin-mounted 40mm cannon on the Dusters could do.

He also knew that the old World War Two Army surplus mortars Snake had supplied them with wouldn't dent those big-assed battle tanks.

The tanks stopped about two thousand meters out and elevated the muzzles of the 105s for range.

Beerbelly cussed. Since most of his mortars were the old M19 models, without mount, the maximum range was about five hundred yards. Add to that the bubbles were all screwed up on them and none of the crews assigned to handle them knew what a klick was . . . so the sum total of all that was a disaster waiting to happen.

Beerbelly lowered the binoculars. "Let's get the hell out of here! We'll set up about fifteen miles north of the town on the Interstate. Move, goddamnit, move!"

"Snake ain't gonna like this," Blackie told him.

"Snake can kiss ass, too. We ain't no good to him dead. Move, man."

"Bugging out," Ben said, standing on top of the Blazer and watching the exodus through binoculars. "As soon as they're clear, Dan, take your Scouts in and inspect for booby traps."

"Right, sir."

"Buddy, take your Rat Team in and find the airstrip. Get it cleaned up for our birds. We're in no hurry. I intend to make Buffalo an outpost. We'll probably need to widen and lengthen the strip for PUFFs."

"Yes, Father. You'll need a CP. I'll find one suitable for you."

Ben and the main force of Rebels stayed clear of the town for more than an hour, until Buddy and his people announced the all-clear. Then the Rebel Army of Ben Raines rolled into Buffalo, Wyoming, and began the job of cleaning it up for use as an outpost.

Ben and Dan inspected the small airport and Dan said he felt the birds from Base Camp One could use it as is, as soon as it was cleaned up.

Meg and Sarah walked up with a group of Rebels.

"How do you feel about staying here, Sarah?" Ben asked. "Becoming part of the settlers?"

She shook her head. "No, thanks, General. Satan

and that bunch of trash with him burned her old ranch out on the Crazy Woman. They chased me all over the north half of Wyoming for a couple of years. I think I'll dedicate the rest of my life to helping clear the nation of crud like that . . . if that's all right with you."

"Fine with me, Sarah. You're certainly welcome. You hid out in this part of the country for a long time. How many people are out there?" He waved his hand.

"Hundreds, General. I roamed from the South Dakota line to the Middle Fork of the Powder. I'd guess about half of the people were too scared to help me. You can forget about them; they're losers any way you cut it. I'd guess many of them have already pulled out for what they think are safer areas—if there is such a thing—or have been killed by outlaws. The rest of the people, the tough breed, well, they're making it. But they're not doing it by being real gentle. They will shoot you." She wrinkled her nose. "What is that smell?"

"An outlaw by the name of Texas Jim," Buddy told her. "Some of my team hanged him the other afternoon. I'll cut him down and get him in the ground."

"Thank you," Ben said drily. He cut his eyes to Sarah. "You said you hadn't been a prisoner long?"

"About three weeks, I think. You tend to lose track of time after the first week."

"What are we facing, Sarah?"

"A pretty tough bunch of people, General. I'll give them that much. They've had a long time to get their act together. These outlaw bikers were pulled in from

201

all over the west by Matt Callahan. Snake. It'd be safe to say that Snake controls most of the Northwest. This part of the country is the easternmost section of his territory. His headquarters is just north of Sheridan. A ranchhouse that's built like a fort. I'd say he keeps about fifty or seventy-five men on the grounds all the time. And those guys are really tough. Snake handpicked them. They're tough, but they're filth. The worst of the lot. And that's really scraping the bottom of the barrel.''

"How easy is the access to the house?"

"Almost impossible. For a year, I tried to figure out a way to get in there and kill Callahan. I never could get close enough to get a shot at him. When he does leave the house to go riding, he's got dozens of men with him. And they can sit a saddle, make no mistake about that. They cover him like a blanket. With you this close, though, I don't imagine he'll chance leaving the house. And if you're thinking about cutting the head off the snake, namely Matt Callahan forget it. You couldn't get your tanks with the big guns within ten miles of that place without being spotted. There's one road in and one road out. Callahan destroyed the rest of the roads. He's crazy, but smart.''

"You say there is a group of women bikers riding for Matt?"

"I'd call them anything but women," Sarah said with a grimace. "Bunch of damn dykes. And they are pure crud. Cruel. Don't cut them any slack because they're of the female gender. They're just as bad, or worse, as the men. And they'll fight just as hard.''

"Can you give me some numbers, Sarah?"

"If Callahan pulls all his people in—something I don't think he'll do; he'll keep some in reserve—we'll be looking at several thousand people. And I heard talk about more coming up from the south and some sort of army moving this way from the east."

"That's the story of our life, Sarah," Dan told her. "We're almost always outnumbered. But seldom outgunned. What we have that Callahan doesn't is organization. We can resupply in ten hours by air."

"That's good, because you're going to need to do that, probably more than once." She looked at Ben. "Matt Callahan hates you, General. You're an obsession with him."

"I am fully aware of that, Sarah. Do you have any idea how he plans to conduct his . . . campaign against us?"

She shook her head. "No. Satan might. But he would be the only one . . . that's providing Callahan even knows himself."

"He's that far gone mentally?"

"I met him when he first came into this area, several years ago. He's fascinated by the area around the Little Bighorn River—Custer's Last Stand. He used to go there quite often. I'd say he knows as much about that part of the country as any man living." She studied Ben's face. "Does that have some significance, General?"

"God, I hope not," Ben said, the remark puzzling them all.

"What's he doin' down yonder?" Matt asked Satan.

"Looks like to me he's settlin in to stay."

It was the fourth day after Ben and the Rebels had occupied Buffalo. Those rescued had been flown back to Base Camp One and Rebels in Wyoming had been resupplied to the point of overflowing.

And still Ben waited.

"Ol' Slim's shore got something up his sleeve," Matt opined. "I just can't figure out what."

"Nothing good for us," Satan said glumly. "You can bet on that."

"We'll whup him, Satan," Matt assured the biker. "What's the latest on them hardcases comin' up from the south?"

"They're in Wyoming. But they're having to work their way up slow to avoid being spotted by them people Raines put in Rawlins. They're comin' up 191 and then will cut over on 28. Wind their toward us that way."

Matt moved to his desk and studied a state map. He shook his head. "I don't like it but I reckon it can't be helped. We might have been a tad hasty in havin' them bridges blown on the Interstate."

We, hell! Satan thought. That was your idea.

"But . . . we done 'er, so there ain't no use a-whinin' about it now. What'd you hear from this Ashley person and that crazy woman he's with? What's that crazy bitch's handle?"

"Sister Voleta. They're getting close. Last transmission was sent from around Bismark, North Dakota. I told them to start heading in a more southwesterly direction. That Ashley feller got all uppity with me. Said he was perfectly capable of reading a map without any help from a cretin." Satan wasn't really sure what a cretin was, but he figured it was an insult.

"We'll deal with him after Ben Raines is defeated."

Satan just had to say it. "There ain't no one ever beat him yet, Snake."

Matt's eyes turned killing cold as they slowly lifted to stare at Satan. Physically, Satan could have easily ripped Matt apart without working up a sweat. But deep down inside the man, Satan both strangely feared and respected the smaller and older man.

"I'm gonna kill him, Satan. You can just go head on and carve his name on a marker. 'Cause I'm gonna kill the sidewinder."

And for the first time in a week, Satan felt that Snake really just might pull it off.

Ben had spent the four days studying maps of Sheridan and being briefed as to the locations of Pete Jones and his outlaws, and the advancing army of Ashley and Sister Voleta. Rebel communications had them both locked in and descrambled.

Ashley and Sister Voleta were still days away. But Pete Jones and his bunch were just about close enough to start breathing down the Rebels' necks.

And Ben was worried about Buddy having to face his mother—admitted nut and perverted killer that she was—in combat. He called Buddy to his CP.

"You wanted to see me, Father?" The son stuck his handsome head into his dad's office.

Ben waved him to a chair. "I want you and your Rat Team to get with Captain Tony of D Company. Draw supplies for a long field run. Take two of the self-propelled 81mm mortar carriers with you. One fifty-caliber machine gun per platoon. Your team take one also. I've already sent a crew out to clear the ambush site in the mountains so you can get through." He stood up and walked to a state map thumbtacked to the wall and covered with clear plastic. "I want you here, son." He pointed to the town of Worland. "This Pete Jones person and his army of crud was last reported, about two hours ago, just south of Lander. You should reach Worland by dawn. That'll give you plenty of time to pick your ambush sites and get some rest.

"Now, boy, I don't expect you and Captain Tony to stop Pete Jones cold. From what we've been able to piece together, this Jones person has put together between five hundred and six hundred outlaws. But I want you to slow him down. None of this nonsense about standing or dying. You know how I feel about that. If you get in a bind, haul your butt out of there. You'll take your orders from Tony. Is that clear?"

"Yes, sir."

"Start drawing equipment and supplies. I want you on the road as soon as possible."

Dan had stood just outside the door, with Ben knowing he was there, listening. As soon as Buddy left, he entered Ben's office.

"You approve, Dan?"

"Definitely. For more than one reason."

Ben arched an eyebrow.

"We can handle Matt Callahan and those coming at us from the east. Oh, before I forget, the PUFFs are on the way."

"Good. The other reasons, Dan?"

"Buddy knows his mother is a kook, a killer, a psychopath. That doesn't mean he has to be present

206

should she be killed."

"Thank you, Dan. My sentiments exactly." Ben sighed. "I sometimes wonder if the bitch can be killed."

"She certainly has been a thorn in our sides for longer than I care to think about."

"Tennessee, wasn't it?"

"Ummm? Yes, I believe it was."

"What have you been able to piece together about their strength?"

"We're going to be badly outnumbered."

"That large a force?"

"Yes, sir. They're picking up outlaws the way a magnet draws metal."

"I want Sheridan intact. So we're going to have to go in and take it house to house, meeting the bikers nose to nose."

"As much as I admire Sarah, I have to question her opinion as to the outlaws standing firm and fighting us. I do believe they will make a show of force—at first. Oh, they'll fight us house to house, but all the while they'll be falling back. That's my opinion."

"And mine, Dan. When are the birds due in from the base?"

"This afternoon. They'll be landing with the PUFFs to throw off any observers Callahan might have watching us."

"Cecil confirm he's sending in those spares that I requested?"

"Yes, sir. Like you, I think we're going to suffer some casualties taking Sheridan. With the extra birds standing by, we can fly out any hard-hit immediately."

Ben turned to stare out a window in the office.

"Any word as to whether, ah, HALFASS . . ." He couldn't keep the broad smile off his face at just the thought of that stupid name. ". . . has made any moves against Emil or Thermopolis?"

"No moves so far." Dan, too, was smiling. "I think Callahan is concentrating solely on us. The man just may be realizing what a big bite he's taken."

"Can we get any number at all concerning the prisoners being held in Sheridan?"

"Sarah thinks several hundred, at least."

Ben nodded and continued to gaze out the window. "Make certain Buddy and Captain Tony have everything they need, Dan. Then report back to me. We're going to be on the outskirts of Sheridan at dawn tomorrow."

19

Ben stepped out of his CP several hours before dawn. He was in full battle harness. His personal team knew his habits well, and they were waiting for him. The entire encampment was up, but moving very quietly and using very little light so those observers watching them from a distance wouldn't be alerted.

Ben looked up at the sky. "Going to be a beautiful day," he remarked.

Jersey handed him a mug of coffee without comment.

"Teams in place above the roadblocks on the Interstate," Corrie informed him.

"Who led them?"

"Colonel Gray, sir."

"He made good time." Ben took a sip of coffee. "He probably pushed them pretty hard."

"Buddy and Captain Tony?"

"They made it to Worland about an hour ago. Setting up now."

"The mortar carriers have their rubber pads on?"

"Yes, sir. Done last evening."

"Tell the crew chiefs to move them out, Corrie."

She radioed the orders and the self-propelled 81mm mortar carriers began their trek up the Interstate to within range of the roadblocks set up by Beerbelly and the other bikers.

"Breakfast?"

"Cold rations, sir. All personnel have eaten and are standing by to mount up."

"Let's take a walk, gang."

Ben walked the long lines of Rebels, stopping to speak a few words to as many of his troops as time would permit. He stopped when he reached Tina and her contingent of Scouts.

"Move them out, girl. When the 81s have done their bit, you link up with Dan and spearhead."

She nodded and slipped back into the darkness, gathering her team around her.

Ben walked on, making sure that all his Rebels had their body armor on.

Corrie listened to her earphones for a moment and then turned to Ben. "General Striganov and his people have crossed the border, sir. They're meeting heavy resistance from an unknown force."

"Bikers?"

"Negative, sir. The general believes it's one of those racist hate groups that have flourished since the war."

"They flourished before the war, too. And a few of them of them had legitimate beefs against the government. Now they've just turned outlaw and they're really coming out of the woodwork," Ben muttered. "If it's Malone's group, they're well armed and well trained."

"Malone?" Beth asked.

"We go way back, Beth. Sort of a mutual hate relationship. I knew he was up in the Northwest, but I didn't know exactly where."

Company commanders, platoon leaders, and other Rebels had gathered around Ben, listening. Tina had paused in her pulling out to hear what her father had to say.

"Malone started out in Ohio, back in the mid-seventies, I believe. He always had a large following of fanatics. He had a few good ideas and a boxful of very bad ideas. People like Malone gave the word *survivalist* a bad name. Let's make sure it is Malone then I'll give you all a rundown on him. Move, Tina. We're fifteen minutes behind you. Mount up, people."

The Rebels were in position to strike an hour before daylight.

Beerbelly stared out at the darkness from behind the roadblocks. The Interstate stretched like a long silent snake before his eyes.

But it wasn't empty, and he knew that for a ironclad fact. Rubber pads on the tracks, or not, he'd heard those damned 81mm mortar carriers come up. Beerbelly was many things: rapist, murderer, dope-head, slaveowner, but he was not a fool. Of all the bikers and outlaws, Beerbelly held a fair education in his head and was combat-experienced. He'd had listening equipment set up along the Interstate and knew what various sounds meant.

"Shit!" he whispered as he crouched behind the blockades that he knew Ben Raines could, and would, roll over and squash like an egg . . . any damn time Raines felt like doing it.

"What's the matter with you?" Wanda asked, crouched down beside him.

"We're playin' a fool's game, Wanda. We ain't got a snowball's chance in Hell against Ben Raines."

"But Snake said—"

"I don't give a damn what Snake says. Hell, Wanda, you know the guy's elevator don't go all the way to the top. I been doin' some powerful thinkin' the last couple of days. I don't think Snake gives a damn whether we all die or not. Whether we win or lose. Just as long as he can get a good shot at Ben Raines. His hate has him all fucked up in the head." Beerbelly pointed a thick finger at the darkness looming before them. "You know what's out there, Wanda?"

She shook her head. Others had gathered around, listening.

"Eighty-eight-millimeter mortars. They can toss a round something like thirty-eight hundred meters. Right behind them are the main battle tanks, armed with 105s. And here we squat behind this pissy-assed blockade that wouldn't stop nothin' that Ben Raines has got."

"Well, what the hell are we doin' here, then?" Wanda's voice held a shrillness that clearly gave away her fear.

Beerbelly was blunt. "Gettin' ready to die, far as I can tell."

"For what?" She almost shouted the question.

"That's the big question, baby."

"That's your big ass! Why in the hell didn't you tell us all this before now?"

"'Cause I had to put it all together in my head first, that's why."

"I'm gettin' my girls and pullin' out, Beerbelly. Like right now!"

"We're right behind you, baby!" Beerbelly said, standing up.

"I think they're quitting," Dan radioed back to Ben. "They're leaving the blockade and heading straight for my position."

"Take them out, Dan."

"Ten-four."

The bikers and outlaws rode and drove straight into an ambush. The guns of Dan Gray's Scouts sparked the still-dark early morning hour and turned the Interstate slick with blood. Beerbelly and Wanda and several other biker leaders and their followers were in the middle of the column and veered off and into the brush. That quick move saved them. But half a dozen of them died when they hit rocks and ravines and were tossed from their bikes.

They would be left there for the carrion birds and the ground scavengers.

Bullets from the Rebel guns ignited gas tanks on the downed and still spinning motorcycles, some of the tanks burning, some of them exploding.

Tina held her Scouts on the south side of the blockade, not wanting to go barging up into a free-fire zone and be mistaken for an outlaw. They began tearing down the blockade.

As dawn began brightening the western skies, Tina and her team had torn down or pushed aside the last of the blockade and were waving the mortar carriers and Dusters and battle tanks through. When the last of the heavy-tracked vehicles were through, Tina and her Scouts followed them.

"We'll secure the airport first," Ben radioed to his commanders. "That's vital. Tina, you know the cutoff to the airport; it's right up ahead off 87. Secure the airport."

"Ten-four, Eagle."

Beerbelly and Leadfoot and Wanda's group had cleared the wrath of Raines' Rebels and had pulled up in a group, shutting down their engines. They knew some of the others had made it, but just who and how many was, at this point, unknown.

To a person, they were badly shaken.

"Beerbelly," Wanda asked, her voice betraying her fear, "what are we gonna do?"

"I been thinkin' 'bout that, too." Beerbelly would have loved to roll a joint and toke it right down to where it blistered his fingers. But his hands were shaking so badly he had to hold on tightly to the handgrips to keep them still. He did not want any of the others to see how scared he was. "We'll give Raines and his people plenty of time to clear the Interstate. Then we'll jump across and take 90 east for Gillette. We'll head north out of there and then cut northwest, try to get up to where this Malone person has his operation."

"Malone and his kind ain't got no love for people like me and my girls," Wanda said glumly.

"It's either that or Ben Raines," Beerbelly reminded her.

"In that case I reckon I could put up with a stiff dick in order to stay alive."

"Wanna try mine just to get back in practice?" Beerbelly said with a grin.

Wanda told him where he could put his dick. And it wasn't where Beerbelly had in mind.

Some tiny, tingling warning bell sounded in Pete's head as he approached the blasted and shot-up town of Thermopolis. And it wasn't the bloated and stinking bodies of Night People that did it. Even though that in itself was enough to make a buzzard puke.

"We're taking 120," he told Sam. "I got a bad feeling, man."

Sam got on the CB and advised the others of what was going down.

"What the hell's the problem, Jones?" MacNally demanded. "Other than this goddamn stinkin' town. Jesus, them bodies would gag a maggot."

"Just a hunch, Mac. Stay with me. It would be like Raines to set up an ambush at some point along the most likely route through the mountains. You want to stay alive, don't you?"

"Yeah, yeah!"

"All right, boys, here's the way it's going to be. No talking on the military radioes. We use CBs only and only then if somebody's got something important to say. In other words, for you rednecks and other assorted honkies, keep your damn mouths shut."

215

"You an uppity nigger, Jones," Mac shot back over the airwaves. "You know that."

"You keep telling me, Mac. You keep telling me."

Tina's Scouts were brought to a halt at the airport. The facility was heavily manned and the defenders were determined to hold it at all costs. Matt Callahan had told them that the airport was critical to Ben Raines being resupplied and the outlaws took Matt at his word.

Nine o'clock in the morning, and after two hours of close-up fighting, the Rebels had advanced only a couple of blocks into Sheridan. Ben stood on the outskirts of the town and pondered the situation as the radios from his Rebels kept him informed.

"Still meeting heavy resistance on all fronts, General," Corrie relayed the messages. "Tina is bogged down at the airport. She's badly outnumbered but holding her own."

Ben turned to Dan. "Take over here, Dan. I'll take my team and help out at the airport. Corrie, what's the word from Buddy."

"They're in position but so far it's a no-show from the outlaws."

Ben nodded. "Let's go, gang."

Ben and his teams skirted wide around getting to the airport and it still took them nearly a half hour to reach it. Matt had dug his people in deep and it was as Sarah had predicted: they were a tough bunch and they knew they were fighting to preserve a way of life.

But as tough as they were, they were not as trained or as disciplined as Raines's Rebels, and they did not possess the firepower of the Raines's Rebels. Like nearly all thugs and punks and bullies from the dawning of civilization, and before, the outlaws had always relied on brute strength and savagery and fear to get their way. That didn't work with the Rebels. They could be just as savage as those they faced and fought—more so if need be.

"They're dug in deep, Dad," Tina radioed to Ben. "And the little terminal is filled with crud."

"Lob some tear gas in and shoot them as they try to escape," Ben ordered.

Rifle grenades were readied and the tear gas cannisters were fired into the terminal. The outlaws came coughing and tear-blinded out. They were coldly and unemotionally shot down in the parking lot.

"Occupy the terminal," Ben radioed to his daughter. "I'm swinging my people around to clean out the hangers. Snipers, get in place with those fifties."

Rebel snipers, using the Browning model 5100 sniper rifle, which is capable of extreme accuracy in excess of two thousand yards, bipodded their weapons and dug in for long-range killing. The .50 caliber projectile, even at the full one-mile range, still had over one thousand foot-pounds of punch upon impacting. And the men and women behind the 36-pound weapons possessed all the qualifications of a sniper: sharp-eyed, vulture-patient, and deadly accurate. They began taking a fearful toll on the outlaws.

"Inside the terminal," Tina radioed. "Stinks like a boar's nest in here."

"Considering the caliber of people who recently

exited the building," Ben told her, "that's being very unkind to a hog. You forward people, give the mortar crews some coordinates to work with, please."

The range coordinates were quickly calibrated and called in. Mortar rounds began dropping in on the outlaw bunkers and one by one they were taken out. Even with the superior firepower of the Rebels, it took them nearly an hour before the airport was declared secure.

Leaving a small force at the airport, Ben and Tina took their people and moved back to the town.

"Slow going," Dan told him. "But we're making some headway. We've got a toehold. We've taken some prisoners. You want to talk to them?"

"Might as well. For all the good it will do me."

"I've set you up a temporary CP. The prisoners are being held there. They're a sullen, uncooperative lot."

"They can be sullen," Ben said, checking his .45 and returning it to leather, "but they'll talk to me or get seriously and quickly dead."

20

The outlaws might have thought Ben was bluffing. But after the second body was dragged from the building, with a .45 caliber slug between the eyes, the remaining thugs and outlaw bikers became very much aware that Ben Raines did not give a tinker's damn about such amenities as constitutional rights, the Geneva Convention, the right to remain silent, or much of anything else except ridding the land of human crud.

They all became very talkative, all at once, each one trying to outdo the other.

Ben listened to them babble on for a few minutes and then turned them over to interrogation teams.

Picking up his M14, Ben walked outside and rejoined his personal team.

"What's the word from Buddy, Corrie?"

"Still nothing, General. And he reports absolutely no chatter on the radio."

"The bastards smelled a rat. They're probably using low-range CBs to communicate." He pulled a map from the pocket of his BDUs and studied it for a moment. "They either cut east at Shoshoni and plan to work their way north using county roads, until they get past the blown bridges on the Interstate, or they took 120 out of Thermopolis and plan to come into Sheridan on 14. I doubt they'd try old 30." He shrugged. "But who knows? Corrie, tell Buddy to come on back. We need him here."

"What'd you get out of the prisoners?" Tina asked.

"Nothing we didn't already know." He looked around for Meg. She was nowhere in sight. "Corrie, tell the PUFFs to get airborne. They have the coordinates. Destroy the ranchhouse of the Snake."

But Matt Callahan aka the Rattlesnake Kid, had seen the handwriting on the wall. He read it with bitterness on his tongue, but he read it nevertheless.

The Rattlesnake Kid was making ready to rattle his hocks.

He and his personal crew of range-wise and gun-ready hands were heading north. There would be another day to deal with Ben Raines, and he could always put together another army.

Matt swung into the saddle. "Let's ride, boys."

At his command post in downtown Sheridan, Satan's radio operator looked at him and shook his head. "No use, Satan. I can't get Snake on the horn."

Satan spent the next few minutes giving the Rattlesnake Kid a cussing.

"What's all that mean?" he was asked.

"It means that the Snake just wiggled away and left us behind to face Raines alone. That's what it means." He turned around as Rowdy busted into the room.

"The guys is fallin' back, Satan. They just can't hold the Rebels no more. But we still got the north end of the town open."

It took the outlaw biker only a few heartbeats to make up his mind. "Let's ride! Tell the guys to start falling back. We'll hold the north end open until they all get clear."

Satan began frantically tossing a few items into a dufflebag. He looked up as his buddy, Bruiser, entered the room.

"I guess you heard the Snake turned yellow and run, huh, Satan?"

"I figured you'd run with him, Bruiser. Seein' as how you and him is so tight."

"Naw. We got my buddy, Pete Jones, and his bunch comin' in, remember."

"So?"

A frown passed the ape's face. "You just gonna leave them to be chewed up by the Rebs?"

Satan stood up and faced the man. Satan was bigger then Bruiser, but not by much. Just uglier. "What do you want me to do, Bruiser?"

"I don't know, man. But it ain't right to just go off and leave our buddies."

"Your buddies, Bruiser. Not mine. I don't like niggers."

"Well . . . I don't neither. But I like Pete Jones."

"That don't make no sense, Bruiser. But very little you ever say makes much sense to me."

That bounced off Bruiser like a rubber ball. "You reckon Pete took the northern route over the mountains?"

"He may have, Bruiser. Come to think of it. The way he was movin', he should have been here by now. All right, Bruiser, we'll ride up to the junction and wait for an hour or so."

"Yeah! Awright, man!" They did a little hand-slappin' and jivin' and then kissed each other on the mouth.

"What you gonna do with the prisoners, Satan?"

Satan's eyes turned cruel hard. "Go kill as many as you can, Bruiser. I know how you like that."

"Awright!"

Just as he said that, the sounds of two prop-driven planes were heard flying high over the town.

Matt Callahan pulled his men into a huge stand of timber only a few miles south of the Montana line and watched as the PUFFs began their slow circle. It took less than a minute for his fine ranchhouse to be reduced to smoking rubble.

"Too bad you kilt them boys and girls 'fore we left," a hand said to Snake. "Even though it was fun watchin' 'em kick and choke. Raines could have done it for us with all that farpower."

Snake nodded absently. "I overestimated my boys and grossly underestimated Ben Raines. I won't make that mistake the next time we meet."

They watched as the PUFFs made their way back south, toward Sheridan.

Snake and his now considerably smaller army

222

turned their horses' heads toward the north. Toward the Rosebud Mountains and the Little Bighorn River.

"Do we pursue, General?" Dan radioed the question as the outlaws rode and drove frantically out of Sheridan.

"Negative. Let them go. We've got to sweep this town and see about any prisoners."

It did not take the Rebels long to find one home that had been turned into a slaughterhouse by Bruiser and his submachine gun.

Ben viewed the unnecessary carnage through eyes that were flint hard. "People who would do this . . ." He let that statement slide, then said, "More and more I find myself agreeing with George Orwell's pigs."

BOOK TWO

All animals are equal, but some animals are more equal than others.

George Orwell

1

"That was a good guess on your part, Bruiser," Satan said, his bulk on the saddle of his Harley. "Yonder they come."

"Yeah. I know some of them ol' boys. There's Pipes—I ain't seen him in years. And Bass is ridin' right behind him. Yeah, this is good."

"How is that?"

"Them boys can fight. Like you, Satan, they's a bunch of them saw combat in 'Nam."

"How come you didn't, Bruiser?"

"I was in reform school. I raped a woman and broke her neck. Didn't mean to kill her, though. I just wanted some pussy. Since I was a minor I only served three years. War was over when I got out."

"You didn't miss nothin', believe me. We got to have us a sit-down, Bruiser. We'll ride on up into Montana and then all of us can talk this thing out. We got to get some organization if we're goin' to fight Ben Raines and win."

"You the boss, Satan. Whatever you say is fine

with me."

The long line of bikers and cars and pickup trucks began to stretch out as they moved north. More than a thousand thugs, punks, and trash.

Beerbelly and his bunch had safely jumped the Interstate and had barreled eastward for about an hour, turning north at Gillette. Once they crossed the line into Montana, they would continue north for a few miles, and then cut westward, hoping to link up with Satan and Pete Jones. Then they would decide what to do about Ben Raines.

"The town's in pretty good shape," Ben said after an hour-long ride through Sheridan. "Remarkably so." He turned to Sarah. "You think you could convince some of those hiding out in the hills to come in and resettle this place?"

She grinned. "I'm sure of it, General. It'll take about ten days for me to touch base with those the others will listen to."

"Draw what you need and get ready. I'll get a team together and have them standing by to accompany you. I won't know how much to request from Base Camp One until I see how many people you bring in."

"I'll be on my way in an hour, General. You'll be surprised how many people are out there." She waved her hand at the vastness that lay beyond the town. "General, you're the last hope the people have to put this country back together."

As he watched her walk away, Ben muttered, "It certainly wasn't a job I asked for or wanted."

Ben chose as his CP a building in the downtown part of Sheridan. He and his team cleaned up the place and set up quarters in the rooms above the first floor.

Rebels had scoured the town, searching house to house, locating several more buildings where prisoners were being held. Many of them were in pitiful shape. Those who had been held the longest sat in stunned silence, hollow-eyed and staring vacantly at nothing, unable to comprehend the fact that they were finally free from their captors.

"Will the doctors back at the base be able to bring them out of their . . . I don't know what to call it," Meg said to Ben. "Condition?"

"Some of them, yes. Healing the mind is a long, slow process. Many of them will always be as you see them now. After suffering so long their minds simply shut down. The human defense mechanism, I suppose. All the doctors can do is try, Meg."

"And you believe that the fault of their being captured lies, to some degree on their own heads, don't you, General?" There was an odd glint to her eyes that Ben didn't understand.

"Yes, I do, Meg. As you say, to some degree. Lone wolfing it is fine, if one has the mental conditioning to survive. A lot of people don't. Especially the older ones who grew up in society where they were constantly being bombarded by TV commentators and so-called intellectuals who told them the use of force was wrong in defending home, loved ones, or self." Ben shut his mouth and smiled. "Don't get me wound up, Meg. I'll bore you to tears with a speech about liberals and their ilk."

"You're forgetting that I grew up in California, General. We had a neighbor who killed a rattlesnake in his back yard—with one of those so-called terrible handguns. The police arrested him and took him to jail for discharging a weapon within the city limits."

"Exactly what I'm talking about, Meg."

"You're missing the point. It didn't take me long to learn to shoot first and ask questions later. Why me and not these people?" She pointed to the hospital where the freed prisoners had been taken.

"Probably, Meg, your father—back in his more lucid days—raised you to stand alone. I would imagine that every time one of those anti-gun/anti-use-of-force messages came on the TV, Matt would tell you it was all a bunch of crap. Which it was. That had a lot to do with it."

She nodded her agreement. "What about that large gathering of men on horseback that the pilots of the PUFFs reported seeing?"

Buddy said the ranchhouse Matt was using as his headquarters was deserted except for those poor unfortunates they found strangled to death in the basement. Matt took his hardcases and headed for the wilderness."

"You know where he went, don't you, General."

Ben sighed. "I have a pretty good idea, Meg. From all indications he was heading for the Rosebud Mountains. Where Custer made his last stand."

"He wants you to come after him, you realize that, don't you?"

"Oh, yes. The Rattlesnake Kid wants to face Slim in a stand-up, shoot-'em-out gunfight. I'm going to disappoint him, Meg."

"You're going to let him go?" Her eyes narrowed and her lips tightened into a thin line.

"For the time being, yes. His army is scattered and Matt poses no immediate threat to us now. I'll eventually have to deal with him, but not now. Not unless he forces the issue."

"He will if he gets a chance."

Ben shrugged. "That's his problem, Meg. But if he thinks I'm going to strap on a pair of hoglegs and face him in some sort of a quick-draw affair, he's not only crazy, he's stupid."

Meg studied Ben's face. "You'd better track him down and kill him now, General. I know the man far better than you. He'll never give up."

"I'm aware of that. But I'm not about to commit troops and send them searching all over the Rosebud Mountains. It'd be like looking for that needle in the haystack. Matt will have to wait."

The Rebels went to work in Sheridan, cleaning up the town and tearing down those buildings they felt could not be used.

Communications reported that Ashley and his group had veered north, apparently heading for Malone and his people, rather than try to launch an offensive against Ben—at this time.

Striganov and his Russian-French Canadian forces were holding their own against Malone, but making no progress in their attempts to move south. Ben knew he was going to have to head north to aid Striganov, but he didn't want to leave Sheridan until Sarah had rounded up enough people to defend the place. And Cecil had radioed from Base Camp One that Kahmsin had made his way back to South Carolina and regrouped what was left of his shattered army.

Ike was champing at the bit to head for South Carolina and once and for all wipe Khamsin from the face of the earth.

"Negative, Ike," Ben had told him. "The Hot Wind is nothing more than a slight breeze now. I might need you and your battalion up here with me before this mess is over. Just stay put and be ready to go."

Sarah and the team of Rebels Ben had sent with her had rounded up more than five hundred people by the end of ten days. And from all indications, they were a tough and resourceful lot, just the types Ben was looking for to resettle the outposts. Among them were a dozen doctors and dentists and nurses.

Ben radioed Cecil and told him to get the requested equipment on the way to Sheridan. The town was once more on the map.

Ben was studying maps when Dan entered his office.

"You wanted to see me, General?"

"Get the people ready to pull out, Dan. We've done what we can here in Sheridan. It's up to the settlers now. We've got to head north and give Georgi and his people a hand."

"I can have them ready to go in the morning."

"Then that's when we'll pull out."

Ben walked to a wall map. "The lines have shifted. Last reports state the main concentration of fighting is centered along this line, between Cut Bank and

Harve. And that's a hell of a lot of territory."

"Malone must have quite an army," Dan said, studying the more than one-hundred-mile-long battlefront.

"Obviously. And when Ashley and Voleta and the various bikers and outlaws link up with him . . ." Ben let that trail off.

"Yes," the Englishman picked it up. "And if we get careless and let them put us in a box, we could be in serious trouble."

Ben nodded. "This time we're really outgunned. We're going to have to go into this fight with a root-hog or die mentality. Saving towns and cities for future use as outposts will have to be put on the back burner during this push north. Since we're going to be so badly outnumbered during this campaign, we'll have to make up for it by using every ounce of firepower we have. And Striganov says Malone has mortars and heavy machine guns. But no tanks or long-range artillery."

"I shouldn't wonder," Dan said drily. "We've spent the past three years scouring the country, hauling in every tank we could find."

Ben grinned. "And we've stripped for parts the ones we didn't haul in. We've got ten tanks for every qualified driver."

"When will the reinforcements arrive?"

"I started them moving exactly one week ago. They should be arriving any day. With the addition of the vehicle-drawn 105s and the tanks, we'll give Malone some new headaches. I plan to have the added tanks lay back, protecting our rear. Get the people geared up, Dan. We move out in the morning.

We'll advance to Hardin and secure that town. By the time we're through there, the new equipment should have reached us and we'll start our push north to take some pressure off of Georgi and his people."

Dan was studying the map. "Miles City?"

"Will have to wait until we're finished up north."

"We'll be passing right by the old Custer Battlefield site. Do you anticipate an attack by Matt and what is left of his army?"

"I'm not going to give him a chance, Dan. We're going to be moving as fast as the roads will allow us. Your Scouts report the Interstate is in good shape, and they have seen nothing of Matt or his people. There hasn't been a shot fired at them. We'll deal with Matt when we've finished with Malone."

"Spearheading?"

"Tina. Have her take command of those Scouts already north of us, and move out today. She'll stop on the outskirts of Hardin. And assign a Duster to her just in case. I can't believe Malone is going to just let us come up behind him unopposed."

"He may be having his hands full with General Striganov."

"Georgi will damn sure give him all he can handle; bet on that. I'd like to think if we hit Malone fast and hard, we can settle this quickly. But something tells me this is going to be a long campaign."

"I'm afraid you're right." Dan seemed reluctant to leave. As if he had something on his mind and didn't quite know how to say it.

Ben helped him along. "Spit it out, Dan. What's eating at you?"

"Very well, General. Do you trust Meg Callahan?"

Ben hesitated. "I don't know, Dan. It just doesn't seem reasonable that a very attractive woman, kidnapped by outlaw bikers, was not raped by them. And Dr. Ling was emphatic on that point. I've toyed with the idea that my so-called assassination attempt back in Shreveport was all rigged."

"With Meg to be planted within the Rebels." Dan did not present his remark as a question.

"Yes. But to do what? Kill me? Hell, Dan, she's had ample opportunities to do that. What has she done to arouse your suspicions?"

"She's just too smooth, General. Everything that comes out of her mouth is too pat. It's almost as if she's been rehearsed."

"By whom? Her father? She's managed to convince nearly everybody that she genuinely despises Matt."

"But not you?"

"I don't know," Ben said softly. "But I do sense that something is out of kilter with Meg. Go on, Dan."

"General, you've seen the caliber of people we've been facing. Do you believe that type of scum would allow a lovely young lady to live undisturbed within arm's reach of them for a couple of years, as Meg claims?"

"It doesn't seem reasonable. And if her father sexually abused her as a child, as she claimed, why would he not do the same as an adult?"

"That thought entered my mind as well."

"And she's been gently pushing at me to attack Matt in the Rosebuds. Our interrogation teams back at Base Camp One have not been able to corroborate our suspicions by questioning of the biker women, however."

"They might not have had prior knowledge. Although that seems a bit unlikely. I think it's just because they're very tough women and hard to break."

Ben nodded and stepped into the radio room, telling Corrie to get Base Camp One on the horn and tell them to start using drugs on the biker women; find out what they can about Meg Callahan.

"No!" Ben suddenly said. "Ten-twenty-two those orders, Corrie."

"Yes, sir."

Ben slowly turned to face Dan. "I don't think she's in cahoots with Matt. I think she really wants to see her father dead."

Dan spread his hands, while confusion filled his face. "She certainly says she does. But if she isn't working for her father? Then?"

"Dan, you were there in Shreveport when I spoke with Meg for the first time. She mentioned that survivalist group that her father shared power with. And she mentioned that they did not get along. That somebody had to have been Malone."

"Yes, I remember, and I agree." Dan was thoughtful for a moment and then he smiled. "Ahh, yes. Now I am beginning to see."

"She wants to see both Matt and me killed. If money was worth a damn, I'd bet you that she takes her orders from Malone."

2

"So we do what, Father?" Buddy asked.

Ben had called a gathering of Buddy and Tina, Dan, Dr. Ling, and his company commanders.

"We watch her. We have nothing but suspicions. We have absolutely no solid proof. I'm just going to play this by ear and be careful."

"Oh, quite," Dan said, giving Cooper, Jersey, Beth, and Corrie a glance. They got the message.

The eye contact did not escape Ben, but he said nothing about it.

"Do you want me to switch her ammo?" Buddy asked. "Substitute blanks for real?"

"No. As I said, we have zero proof that she has done anything wrong. It may just be that I'm getting paranoid."

"That *we* are becoming paranoid," Dan corrected.

"That's it, people. Tina, you all set to go?"

"Sittin' on ready."

"Take off. Follow the Duster and we'll see you in Hardin maybe late tomorrow. For sure in a couple of days."

Tina waved and left the room.

"Let's start packing it up, people," Ben said.

The Rebels rolled out of Sheridan just as dawn was spreading light over the valley. The extra tanks and artillery that Ben had requested from Base Camp One were a day behind them and coming hard.

Ben pushed his people hard and they made Hardin by dusk of the first day out, driving right through the area where Ben thought Matt was hiding. But if Matt Callahan thought Ben was going to waste his time hunting him, the Rattlesnake Kid was sorely disappointed.

Tina had radioed back that Hardin was a ghost town.

During the noon break, Sarah had said, "The people are all along the Yellowstone. When the outlaws came, many of them left the towns for the country."

"We don't have time to contact them now," Ben said. "After we deal with Mr. Malone, then we can backtrack."

"Meg appears to be a bit edgy this evening," Dan said, walking up to Ben, two packages of cold rations in his hands. He handed one to Ben.

"Does she now? It wouldn't break my heart if she were to desert."

"Nor mine."

The men sat down on a curb and opened their field ration packs, the contents all carefully mixed under the eagle eye of Dr. Chase, ensuring the troops the correct amounts of vitamins and fiber and nutrients and with all the taste of a tennis shoe.

All the Rebels carried small bottles of hot sauce around with them to slop generously on their field rations. Ben requisitioned homemade hot sauce by the hundred-case lot.

"Are you sure Chase retired from the Navy, or they forced him out before those in his command mutinied?" Dan asked, looking with distain at the goop he had dumped into his mess kit.

Dan gave the paper to Chester to lick and the dog took one smell and carried it off and buried it, returning to sit by Dan's side.

"That has to tell us something," Dan remarked as he scratched the small animal behind the ears.

The next morning, Ben held up the column while Tina and her Scouts checked out Billings. He took that time to radio back to Louisiana and tell Cecil to start sending up tins of meat and dried beans and sacks of rice and potatoes. And if Chase had the nerve to send along any of his nutritious field ration goop, have the pilots dump it into the first swamp they flew over.

"What's the matter, old hoss?" Cecil said with a laugh, knowing perfectly well what the matter was.

"Very funny. And send along a case of vitamins for us to take. I'd rather take a pill than eat any more of Lamar's concoctions."

Cecil was still laughing when Ben broke the connection.

Ben stopped smiling when Dan stepped into the tent and said, "Tina reports Billings is filled with creepies, General."

"Here we go again, Dan. All right. We'll hold up here and wait for the extra tanks and artillery."

"And if they're holding prisoners, sir?"

Ben sighed, remembering the sign that President Harry Truman had on his desk. THE BUCK STOPS HERE. Ben knew only too well what that sign meant.

Ben hand-rolled a cigarette, taking that time to weigh his options—and they were few. "We'll hope they will survive the shelling," he said, knowing he was sealing the fates of many, but having no other choice.

"If it helps," Dan said, "I would have made the same decision."

The main battle tanks and the vehicle-drawn 105s joined the column the next afternoon and Ben gave everybody an extra day to rest before beginning the attack on Billings. The vehicle-drawn 105s had a range of about ten miles, or slightly farther, depending upon the type of shells used.

Ben laid out the plans, and they involved the splitting of his command.

"Ramos, take your A Company along with your assigned 105s and approach Billings from the southeast, on this old secondary road. Brad, you and B Company will cross the Yellowstone here"—he pointed to a map—"and assault the city from the north. Anderson, you and Charlie Company will lay back on the Interstate and drop in your rounds from the east side. I'll take Captain Tony and Dog Company and swing wide, coming up on the Interstate west of the city. Buddy, you and your Rat Team will secure the airport." Ben sighed and minutely shook his head. "We'll start the bombardment at oh-six-hundred tomorrow, using Willie Peter and incendiary. That's it, people."

The smell emanating from the city was strong even to those Rebels several miles away as they waited and glanced at their watches. It was the unmistakable smell of rotting flesh and death.

The hands on their watches straight-lined and Ben's voice came over the speakers. "Fire!"

Billings, the city on the Yellowstone River, founded back in 1882 by the Northern Pacific Railroad, began to reel under the bombardment from Rebel gunners.

Buddy and his Rat Team hit the airport coming off Black Otter Trail, and they struck hard, with a cold, fighting fury. Rebels did not take prisoners of Night People. Attempts to do so had invariably and consistently failed miserably, almost always resulting in the death of those Rebels who tried to extend the olive branch of peace to the creepies.

The cannabalistic Night People were shot down upon sighting, with the wounded receiving a bullet to the head. Orders of Ben Raines.

The earth-shattering pounding continued until eight o'clock. By that time, the city was burning, black smoke twisting like mortally wounded snakes into the big skies of Montana.

"Shut it down," Ben said to Corrie.

Corrie relayed the orders and the guns fell silent.

"Snipers in position," Ben instructed.

Rebel snipers, armed with .5- caliber rifles, slipped into position and waited.

"Airport secured, sir," Corrie told him. "Buddy is clearing a runway now."

"Approximate time for clearing?"

"Two hours."

"Advise the communcations truck to notify Base Camp One of that."

"Advance teams into the city, sir?"

"Negative. All units hold their positions. We won't enter the city until tomorrow at the earliest. Move Tina and her team to the airport for security."

"Colonel Gray has a few freed prisoners that came out of the north end of the city."

"Take them to the airport. Advise Dr. Ling to move a medical team over there. Tell Buddy to prepare to receive freed prisoners. Put them in a hanger."

Sniper rifles began cracking as robed Night People began staggering out of the burning city in a futile attempt to escape the inferno. They left the flames behind them in exchange for a bullet.

The Rebels maintained their positions all that day as the city slowly began to burn itself out. The flames leaped into the night skies, dancing macabre ballets before sparking and vanishing into the darkness.

The breeze picked up, bringing with it a moist touch. Ben awakened once during the night, as a soft rain began falling. The rain picked up in intensity as thunderstorms began rolling through, dousing the land and gradually putting out the most savage of the fires that had devoured Billings.

When Ben stepped out of his tent that morning, the fires were still burning, but the most intense had burned themselves out. The thunderstorms had lashed out their fury and drifted on; the early predawn skies were pocked with stars as Ben walked to the coffee truck.

Coffee mug in hand, he leaned against the dew-covered fender of a deuce and a half and sipped and watched as his team drew coffee and walked to him.

"The spare planes will be leaving Sheridan at dawn," Corrie informed him. "The resupply birds from Base Camp One left at midnight. ETA here is approximately ten hundred hours."

"We will not enter what is left of Billings," Ben said. He had already studied a map and knew where they were going and how they would get there. "Make sure all units understand those orders. When the birds have come and gone, we'll pull out. Advise all units to begin concentrating along Highway 3, just off the airport. Tell Tina to get her team ready to roll and check out Highway 3. She is to wait for us at Lavina. That is approximately fifty miles north of our present location, at the junction of Highway 3 and 12."

Ben turned his back to the dead and smoking city and walked back to his tent to pack. If he had to adpot a scorched-earth policy in order to rid the land of outlaws and scum and Night People, so be it. Regrets, if any, he could deal with later.

"You killed about a hundred prisoners!" the woman screamed at Ben. "Murderer!"

Ben stood at the edge of the tarmac of the airport and listened to her tirade, his face expressionless. She cursed him until she was breathless.

"What would you have had me do, madam?" he asked.

"Free us!"

"Madam, you are free."

"But many of my friends are dead! Thanks to your callousness."

Ben stared down at the woman, her clothing no more than rags, and with her face baering the marks of recent beatings. He knew he should just turn his back and walk away; knew it was pointless to stand and argue with her. But with Ben Raines being what he was, he wasn't about to do anything like that.

Ben pointed toward the smoking ruins of the city. "Madam, how far away do you think you were from being served up as dinner to some of those loathesome creatures who were holding you captive?"

"I don't know! That isn't the point. You could have attacked the city with your army and saved us all."

"To tell you the truth, I'm beginning to wonder if you were even worth saving."

"You can't talk to her in that manner!" a man said, stepping away from the hanger and walking to the woman's side.

Ben blinked. "Now, just who in the hell are you?"

"I am her friend."

"Well, friend, you best carry your ass back inside that hanger before you get on the wrong side of me. And I might point out that your mouth is awfully close to getting you there."

The woman opened her mouth and the man said, "Sybil, let me handle this. General Raines, we are not ungrateful for being plucked from the hands of those dreadful creatures. But it is distressing that more than half of our group was killed by the bombings and the fires that followed."

"Your . . . group. All of you were from the same group?"

"Oh, quite. We are—were—all from the same scientific organization."

"And that would be . . . ?"

"Peace without violence."

Ben sighed. "And how long has this organization been around?"

"Only recently. I would say about six months. We all felt we could reason with those poor unfortunates who have turned to a life of crime and violence."

"Poor . . . unfortunates?"

"Quite."

"Ah—yeah! Right. And some of those 'poor unfortunates' came along, grabbed you up, and swapped you to the Night People, right?"

"Well . . . yes. But that doesn't mean that our plan won't work with some other group, at some other place and time."

"Ah . . . you mean you want to try again?"

"Oh, my, yes."

"Do you want us to arm you?"

"Oh, no, General. Indeed not. We do not require arms to exist. We are vegetarians, so we don't have to kill for food."

"I wasn't talking about hunting, mister . . . whatever your name is."

"Morris Deason. Oh, I see what you mean. Oh, no. We don't want arms. If we do come upon some ruffians, I feel we can convince them that we are

245

peaceful and mean them no harm."

"You do, huh?"

"Yes."

In a pig's ass, Ben thought. "Well, I wish you lots of luck, Mr. Deason." 'Cause you're sure going to need it, he silently added. "Can we, ah, drop you and your group off somewhere?"

"That's very kind of you, General, but no. We must first bury our dead and then take a vote as to where we will relocate."

"I would suggest that you don't go north."

"Oh?"

"That's where we're going."

"To kill more innocent people?" Sybil asked, enough venom in her voice to kill an ox.

Ben glanced at her and then deliberately turned his back. "Dan, see to their needs. You can be much more diplomatic than I." He walked away.

"Murderer!" Sybil screamed after him.

3

The Rebels saw no signs of human life on the way to Lavina, and when they reached the small town, there was nothing left of Lavina.

The tiny town and its few buildings were no more than piles of charred rubble.

Ben ordered Tina and her Scouts out toward Harlowton. As they drove Highway 12, which was in surprisingly good shape, they followed the Musselshell River, flowing on the south side of the highway. The lack of any sighting of human life was beginning to be depressing to all of them. Beth said as much.

"They're out there," Ben told her. "Some of them probably watching us right now. They know what we are, they just don't know who we are."

"Maybe I ought to get a brush and a can of paint," Cooper said with a grin. "Start painting your name on all the vehicles. General Ben Raines and the Rebels. Enlistees please fall in at the rear of the column."

Tina's voice coming out of the speaker cut the laughter short. "Far Out Scout to Eagle."

"Go ahead, Tina."

"Got a few people outside of Harlowton you might like to speak with."

"Ten-four. We're about half an hour away."

"We been down around Lake Lebo," the man told Ben, after shaking his hand. "We had us a pretty good little beginning here in Harlowton until that goddamned Malone and his people showed up. They hit us hard one afternoon. Killed about a hundred. All we could do was grab what we could and run like hell."

Ben had studied a map and liked what he saw about this area of Montana. "Is there an airstrip in this town?"

"If you want to call it that. I reckon we could clean it up. But it can't handle nothing big."

"Twin-engine prop cargo planes?"

"Oh, yes, sir."

The man's name was Jim Tower and he was the sterotype Western man. Tanned faced, lean-hipped, and looked tough enough to handle double just about anything that came his way.

"You've heard about the outposts I'm setting up, Jim?"

"We still got pretty good radio equipment, yes, sir."

"You game for running an outpost here?"

Jim smiled. "You just try me, Ben Raines."

Ben halted the column at Harlowton and sent word

to Cecil to start rounding up more settlers and equipment. On the morning of the second day, he spread a map out on the hood of a Jeep.

"Here's what I have in mind, Jim. Down south, Sheridan, Hardin, Miles City. Up here, Roundup, Harlowton, Lewiston. Eventually, if I live long enough, I plan to have anywhere from six to twelve outposts in every state in this battered country. It isn't going to be like the old days, Jim. It's going to be run just like the Tri-States. No handouts, no free rides, justice comes down hard and swift and, in many cases, final. It's going to smack of autocracy, but until we get a grip on this nation, that's the way—in my opinion—it's going to have to be."

"You don't hear me complaining, do you, Ben?"

"What do you know about the present inhabitants of Lewistown—if any?"

"Trash. Outlaws. Scum. But there used to be a pretty fair little airport there."

"All right. Jim, you begin getting your people settled in back here. Lewiston is close enough to the battlelines to serve as our depot and as a jumping-off place for us. We'll bring the birds in there." He glanced at Corrie. "Let's go clean it out."

Ben left Jim and his people well armed and well supplied. He also left behind as squad of Rebels, with mortars and heavy machine guns, just in case those outlaws Ben knew were still tagging along somewhere behind him decided to hit the town.

"We want Lewistown taken intact," he told his people. "It's small enough for us to do that. The airport is on the south side of the town; that's another reason we want to use it for a depot. When things start looking in our favor, we can always shift the operation elsewhere. But not Great Falls. Jim says it's full of creepies. And Corrie, tell the PUFFs down at Sheridan to stand by. I want Lewistown cleaned out by this time tomorrow. Let's go!"

Ben and the Rebels were knocking on the outskirts of Lewistown at dawn the next morning.

Standing between two rumbling main battle tanks, Ben lifted powerful binoculars and looked over the scene. What he saw was a bunch of unshaven and dirty crud armed mostly with hunting rifles and pistols, staring back at him from behind crude roadblocks.

"Dan, use loudspeakers and tell those men to lay down their arms and stand aside if they want to live to see tomorrow."

Dan relayed the message, the cold, hard words hurled electronically over the short distance.

The outlaws' reply was expected. A volley of gunfire erupted from the edge of town, the bullets wanging and howling off the armor of the tanks.

Ben lifted his walkie-talkie. "Let's show them that we have just a tad more firepower than they, people. About a minute's worth should be convincing enough."

Ten tanks opened up with .50 caliber and 7.62 machine gun fire. Big Thumpers began roaring. And the Dusters opened up with 40mm cannon fire just as mortar crews began laying down patterns.

The roadblock had been rusted-out old cars and trucks and concrete blocks and sandbags spread along a five-hundred-foot line.

When Ben ordered the firing stopped, there were great gaps blown into the blockades. Vehicles and nearby buildings were burning, and bodies lay sprawled in bloody heaps all along the line.

Ben looked at Dan. "Dan, tell them we are a very understanding group of people . . . but not very patient. So if they want to live, they had best lay down their weapons and stand aside."

Bedsheets and pillowcases and handkerchiefs and T-shirts began waving in surrender from that part of the town that was visible to the Rebels.

"That's better," Ben said. "I do so enjoy dealing with reasonable people."

Tina and Buddy looked at their father and rolled their eyes.

"Take your Scouts in, Dan."

Lewistown was in Rebel hands.

They numbered just over two hundred and they were a scabby-looking lot. Ben walked up and down the line, looking at the men and women, disgust evident on his face. He could see fleas jumping about on all of them.

Chester sat on the front seat in Dan's Jeep, not wanting to get too close to the prisoners.

"You ain't got no right to come a-bustin' up in here and jist take over!" one mouthy man popped off to Ben.

Ben surprised the entire group by saying, "You're quite correct. I have no right to do that. But we did it. Now the immediate problem facing us is this: what are we going to do with you?"

"I be your woman, General!" a not-unattractive female called from the lines.

Ben looked at her. "Madam, I wouldn't touch you with a sterilized crowbar."

She glared hate at him.

"I can do all sorts of happy things for a sweetie like you," a man simpered, batting his eyes at Ben.

Ben shuddered and tried to ignore the laughter from Tina and Buddy.

Not accustomed to taking prisoners, Dan walked up to Ben and whispered, "What in the world *are* we going to with them?"

"I haven't the foggiest notion, Dan. Lock them all down and get Jim Tower up here. We'll dispose of the murderers and rapists and so forth; try to talk to the others."

"Paul Simpson"—Jim Tower pointed him out— "he's the so-called leader of this pack of filth. He's a cold-blooded killer." His eyes turned flint hard. "He killed my mother and father just after the bombs came . . . just for the fun of it."

"I shore liked the way they hollered and begged 'fore I kilt 'em, you pussy!" Simpson shouted at him. He spat at Jim. "You ain't got the guts to do nothin' to me, you puke."

Jim did not reply. He reached into the back of his pickup and took out a coil of rope and began building a noose.

Ben backed away. "You're in charge here, Jim. Salvage the ones you think have any decency left in them . . . do what you want to with the rest of them."

Paul Simpson and twenty-one others of Paul's gang were hanged that morning. No one among Jim's group could positively state that any of the others had ever killed or raped or terrorized—although all knew they had.

"What the hell do we do with the rest of them?" Jim asked.

"That's a problem we face all over the country," Ben replied. "But I am certainly glad I have someone else to help make those hard decisions."

"Who?"

"You," Ben said with a smile.

In the end, Jim turned the others loose, unarmed, and with a warning that if they ever showed their faces in any area of the country that he and the Rebels controlled, they would be shot on sight.

"That ain't fair!" a woman said. "We din't have no choice in the matter."

"That's crap!" Jim spat the words. "No one forced you to follow Paul Simpson. You could have done what the rest of us did: live as decently as possible, plant gardens, open schools, try to pull this country back together."

She sneered and spat at him, verbally hanging several uncomplimentary titles on him.

"If you're in my sight one minute from now," Jim warned, slowly pulling a pistol from leather, "I'll kill you."

The freed outlaws and their followers scattered, most leaving at a run.

Ben looked at Jim Tower. There was not a doubt in his mind but that Jim would have killed the woman had she pressed her luck. Ben had made another good choice in picking people to help lead the nation out of the ashes of devastation and near hopelessness. It was a hard time—much harder than the opening and winning of the West a century and a half back—for those earlier pioneers, many of them, at least, once the mountain men had blazed the way, had the support of friends and family back East, and in many cases, the Army was there to help out.

Not so now. Now there was no one to turn to for help. Now the help had to come from within, and it would take hard men and women to reclaim the land and enforce the few laws that Ben would hold over from the old system.

Yes, Jim Tower and men like him would make it work. Ben had met Jim's wife, and had been impressed by her. She had worked right by her husband's side, both of them sharing equally in the seeing to it that the kids in their group had at least some schooling every day, the planting and harvesting of small gardens . . . and in the day-to-day struggle to survive in a land gone hostile.

The light in that long, long tunnel shone just a bit brighter. The end was still years away, and Ben doubted that he would ever live to see it. But it was comforting to know that now they could at least see the light.

Ben drove around to the airport. It could handle the Rebels' twin-engine cargo planes with no problem.

Ben walked to the communications truck to talk

directly with Cecil and Ike.

"I'm going to make Lewistown my jumping-off pint, Cec. From here, the supplies can be trucked up to Fort Benton. That's going to be about fifty miles south of the present battle lines. Great Falls is out; it's full of creepies, or so I've been told. I don't have the time to check it out now."

"You want me to get some trucks rolling up there, Ben?"

"That's ten-fifty, Cec. Jim Tower, the man who will be in charge of this section once we're gone, tells me there are plenty of vehicles in this area to more than adequately do the job. If I can pull it off, by that I mean keeping the towns intact, I'd like to have the other triangle of outposts be Fort Benton, Shelby, and Harve."

"You going to need some help up there."

Ben hesitated. "I . . . don't know yet, Cec. I just don't know what I'm up against. If I need help, it'll be West and his men, I'm thinking. We're beginning to spread ourselves pretty damned thin leaving troops behind at every outpost."

"Ike is not going to like that."

"Ike is needed where he is and Ike knows it. He's got to stay there and see to the training of new personnel. And speaking of that, how's it look?"

"Fantastic, Ben. We'll be able to field another battalion in a few months. Ben, I believe, by God, we're really going to pull this thing off!"

Ben paused before keying the mike and replying. So the feeling or sensation of victory was that infectious. "Years of hard fighting ahead of us, Cec."

"I'm champing at the bit to get back into the

field, Ben."

"How's Patrice, Cec?" Ben brought his friend back down to earth.

Cec sighed. "Right, Ben. And Ike has a family to look after. So you're telling me that you're in the field and we're back here."

"That's it. I'm doing what I do best, Cec. And I have nothing to bring me back there."

"And no one, you think," Cec added.

Ben said nothing. Damned if he was going to discuss Jerre. Only he and Jerre knew the cold hopeless depths of their strange relationship.

"You still there, Eagle?"

"Right here, Cec."

"What do you need, Ben?"

"Sharpen your pencil, Cec. It's going to be a long list."

4

The supplies began coming in around the clock. Using portable generators, the Rebels lighted the runway and kept the small airport going twenty-four hours a day.

Ben had spoken to General Georgi Striganov several times since arriving in Lewistown, and the Russian's situation was getting grimmer with each radio transmission. Malone seemed to have what appeared to be an inexhaustable supply of men—kill one and two took his place.

"All right, Georgi," Ben radioed his onetime enemy and now close friend. "I've got my CP set up in Fort Benton and we're ready to strike. Start shifting your troops. I'll take everything east of Highway 223 to Harve. You take everything west of 223 to Cut Bank."

"That's ten-four, Ben. And be alert. We captured several who stated a large group of outlaws are moving up Highway 89 to attack you from the rear."

"That would be Pete Jones and his bunch."

"That is correct. He has perhaps a thousand men with him. The numbers vary with each man we interrogate."

"Any intel on Ashley and his bunch?"

"We've lost them. I personally believe they plan to attack from the north and try to box us in."

"How are your supplies?"

"More than adequate. We have factories in Alberta and Saskatchewan working around the clock. It's the sheer numbers of Malone's army that are threatening to overwhelm us."

"We're on the way, friend."

"Looking forward to seeing you again, Ben."

Ben ended the transmission and glanced up at Dan. "Take Tina and her section, and Companies C and D. You'll head up 87 to Harve. I'll take Companies A and B and head up 223 to Chester."

"Meg Callahan?" he questioned.

"I'll take her with me. It will be interesting to see her reaction when we get to the front."

"You watch your back, Ben."

"Don't worry," Ben assured him. "I think Meg began to suspect she was under observation some miles back."

Dan stuck out his hand and Ben took it. "Nut cuttin' time, Dan," he said with a grin.

The Englishman faked a grimace. "What marvelous expressions you Americans have."

Fort Benton had been turned into a staging area. It was from here that supplies would be trucked to the battlelines. And just moments before Ben and Dan were to jump off, forward recon teams radioed back the grim news.

Corrie broke it to Ben. "We're looking at four or five thousand men, General. Well armed and well trained and seeming to be highly dedicated and motivated."

Ben took it stoically. "It doesn't surprise me. These are second-generation race-haters. Their mothers and fathers belonged to every hate group known to mankind back in the seventies and eighties. They've had twenty-five years to fine-tune their hate. Motivated? Oh, yes. I can believe that. The sad thing is, the government—back when there was a government—helped them fuel their hate." Ben was very conscious of Meg's hot eyes on him. It was not a very comfortable sensation.

"Whenever the government singles out so-called minority groups and helps them over the majority," Meg said, "there is certain to be resentment. The government should have stayed out of the private lives of white people."

Ben sighed heavily. There it was. "Your first statement has a ring of truth to it, Meg. Your last statement smacks of racism. But we put your personal puzzle together some days ago."

"I felt that the game was just about over," she admitted.

Beth took the weapons from the daughter of Matt Callahan while the muzzle of Jersey's M16 was pressed against the woman's belly.

"You going to kill me, General Raines?" Meg asked.

"No. You may be salvageable, Meg. We'll just have

259

to wait and see about that."

"You're living in a dream world, Ben Raines. Are you even aware of why you and your Rebels can mix the races and get along?"

"You tell me, Meg."

"Because you've got the cream of the crop, that's why. A cottonpatch nigger or welfare-raised slope or greaser wouldn't last a day in this organization. Hell, they don't have the mental capabilities to pass your goddamned tests, so consequently they don't try."

"People of any race who do not meet our requirements are not accepted," Ben admitted. "But that doesn't mean we wash them out and forget them. You're only half right in your thinking, Meg."

She cocked her head to one side and narrowed her green eyes. "What do you mean, General?"

"Those who don't make it on the first try are not tossed to one side and forgotten, Meg. We have the finest schools in all the world. There is no limit to the number of times a person may try to join us. Sometimes a man or women is just sized up by a Rebel and admitted into our ranks and accepted without question. If there are any doubts, they're sent to school and evaluated. We don't distrust or dislike people because of race, Meg. It's concepts and ideas that contradict ours that we're wary of."

She opened her mouth to argue and Ben waved her silent. He turned to several Rebels. "Lock her down in the old jail and keep her under guard."

He watched as Meg was led away. She offered no resistance, knowing the Rebels would not hesitate to shoot her. "Corrie, give base a bump. Tell Cecil to get West and his people up here by bird. Land at Lewistown."

"Do we push on, General?" Dan asked.

"Yes. Get your troops moving. Let's go, people."

They met their first resistance twenty miles outside of Fort Benton and it was a stiff attack by disciplined and well-armed troops of the survivalist Malone's army.

The two sides slugged it out for over an hour until Ben's superior firepower finally drove the racist survivalists back. But they retreated grudgingly, fighting all the way, not giving up one inch of ground easily.

In his command post in the town of Conrad, Malone listened to the field reports coming in.

"Root hog or die time," Malone said to the men gathered around him. "Raines doesn't give up. And don't sell his Rebels short. They may be a mixture of niggers and other inferiors, but they can fight, and fight damn well." Malone stood up and walked to a wall map. He was stocky, and in excellent physical shape, as were all the men who were members of his organization. Malone's hair was peppered with gray. He was the same age as Ben, and had hated the man for years. No particular reason was outstanding in his hatred; Malone just didn't like anybody who had anything to do with those he considered inferior . . . and that included anybody who was not white, Anglo-Saxon, and Protestant.

Malone considered himself to be a very religious and God-fearing man. He could point to passages in the Bible which he interpreted to read that all nonwhites were inferior. So were Jews and Catholics and so on and so forth. Malone did not smoke, did not drink, did not consort with loose women—he'd been married for years—and only rarely cursed.

When he did curse it was almost always directed at either some inferior . . . or Ben Raines.

Back when civilization was the rule rather than the exception, Malone was always organizing some book-burning or book-censoring event. And anyone who did not agree with his whacked-out views was a "damn hairy hippie commie pinko Godless queer!"

Either that or they worked for some national network news team and everybody knew those types couldn't be trusted. Bunch of damned left-leaning liberal punks.

"Where is that pack of hoodlums that is supposed to be joining up with us in this fight?" Malone asked.

"Between Helena and Great Falls the last report," he was informed. "But I believe they were changing routes."

"War certainly makes for strange bedfellows," Malone muttered.

"That's profound, sir," one of his lieutenants complimented him.

"Thank you."

Ben paused at the battle site long enough to make a thorough inspection of the dead and wounded and their equipment. Their weapons were well maintained, their clothing well kept, and their boots in good shape. Ben knew then he was up against a paramilitary group that was well trained and motivated.

He squatted down beside the body of a young

man—maybe eighteen or nineteen years old. Unlike so many of those the Rebels fought, this was a nice-looking and clean-cut young man, from all appearances the kind any father would be glad to see his daughter date.

Until the boy opened his mouth and started spouting his political leanings.

Ben stood up with a sigh that had nothing to do with the fact that he was middle-aged. For Ben was in better physical shape than most men half his age. He had heard his son walk up and stand just behind him and to his left.

"If you're thinking that there but for the grace of God go I, Father," Buddy said, "you are wrong."

Ben turned to look at his son. "Oh?"

"I learned how to think very early in life, Father. And I have very little patience with those who are content to stagnate in the murk of their minds."

Ben smiled as he looked at his son. The boy was built like a weightlifter and was as handsome as he was strong. More importantly, Buddy could think. Just a few more campaigns, Ben thought, and he'll be ready to take over his own battalion. After that . . . ? Buddy knew he was being groomed, along with this sister, Tina, to take over if something happened to Ben.

Ben shook those thoughts away. "Get your team up the road, boy. Let's see what's happening north of us."

Buddy's team was stopped cold and thrown back at the junction of 223 and Highway 366, about fifteen miles south of Chester. He pulled his people back a mile or so and radioed the news to his father, calling in the coordinates.

Soon the air over his head was filled with 105 rounds from the vehicle-drawn howitzers. Buddy corrected the range until the rounds were dropping in right on target, clearing out a line five hundred yards east and west of the highway. Buddy called for the barrage to cease and waited for Ben to come up.

It wasn't a very long wait.

At Ben's orders, Corrie got General Striganov on the scramble frequency.

"Georgi, I just heard from Colonel Gray. He and his people are stalled between Big Sandy and Box Elder, on Highway 87. I'm pulled up short about fifteen or so miles south of Chester. I'm going to start spreading out and digging in. Colonel West and his mercenaries should be here sometime tomorrow. We will then attack on three fronts south of your lines. You copy that?"

"Ten-four, Ben. You will need my coordinates and I shall need yours so our artillery will not overshoot."

They exchanged coordinates and agreed not to shift present battlelines without notifying the other.

"Dig in," Ben ordered. "And bunker deep. I expect mortars in very shortly. I want forward observers on the high ground to spot enemy mortar sites. The instant you get something, bump it to me so we can lay in artillery. Captain Ramos, have the 105s deployed well back, out of mortar range. Get them stabilized for action."

"Yes, sir."

"The rest of you people get busy digging. I want to see that earth fly. Get to filling bags for use around the pits. Move, people!"

Malone did have mortar capability, but they were light mortars and did not have nearly the range of Ben's heavier pieces. But a suicide or sneak attack was not out of the question . . . not when one was dealing with any type of fanatic. And Malone was a fanatic of the worst type.

He actually believed his was a Holy War, sanctioned by God.

"About the same mentality as that nut over in Iran," Ben muttered.

"Beg pardon, sir?" Jersey asked.

"Nothing, Jersey. You were just a gleam in your daddy's eye when that disgrace went down."

"How come we never heard of this Malone character before now, General?"

"He was busy building his empire and army and keeping his head down. I knew about him. But I never guessed he'd ever get this strong. That's what I get for guessing, I suppose."

"We'll deal with him," she said confidently, her head just about even with Ben's chest. But the M16 she held and could use with expertise made her as tall as anybody in Ben's command.

"You damn right, Jersey!" Ben said with a laugh. "Especially if they mess with you."

"Fuckin' A," she told him.

Laughing, Ben began a quick inspection of the digging-in of his people.

The Rebels had just completed their bunkering in—some of them with holes dug just deep enough to cover their butts—when Malone's mortars began chugging.

"Order everyone to stick their berets in their

pockets and get into helmets," Ben told Corrie as the first volley of mortar rounds came crashing in, jarring the ground.

"FOs calling out enemy positions," Corrie said, after relaying the helmet orders.

"Advise the artillery to adjust and commence firing."

The long range 105s soon silenced Malone's mortars.

"Get some night glasses up to the FOs," Ben ordered. "As soon as it's dark, Malone's people will be moving back up. Double the guards. Tell them to be alert for any sneak attacks. Malone might have knee mortars; if he does, he'll sure use them if he can work his people in close enough. Corrie, get Dan on the horn."

"Coming under heavy attack, General," Dan reported. "I don't know if we can hold. I don't know if we should."

"Explain that reasoning, Dan."

"We'll plant Claymores and fall back. Make it look like we're running for our lives and suck Malone's people in. The Claymores will shorten the odds against us."

"Sounds good, Dan. Go ahead. Report back to me when the operation is concluded. Corrie, have we locked in on Malone's frequency?"

"That's ten-four, sir. Fort Benton is monitoring now. He's being very cautious on the air."

"He would be. Malone is a fanatic but he's not a stupid man."

"Troops from Base Camp One are on the way, General. They'll be landing in Lewistown around midnight. Colonel West had an accident. Broke his ankle. He will not be leading."

"His XO taking over?"

"Ten-fifty, sir. Third battalion of Rebels coming up."

"Under whose command?"

Corrie smiled. "Ike."

5

Ben opened his eyes as soon as the person drew close to his sleeping bag. He closed one hand around the butt of a cocked and locked .45, then relaxed as he made out Corrie's shape.

"What's up, Corrie?"

"General Ike, sir. He pushed his people hard as soon as they deplaned. He's at Fort Benton now. Be here in about an hour."

Ben looked at his watch. Three-thirty. He unzipped and rolled out of his sleeping bag, pulling on his boots and speed-lacing them. "Let's get some coffee."

"You'll really be glad to see Ike, won't you, General?" Corrie asked as they walked to the coffee truck.

"Oh, sure. I bitched about his coming up, but I'm never going to keep Ike out of the field. He loves it as much as I do and hates paperwork as much as I do. Cecil, on the other hand, enjoys administrative work, and is the best I've ever seen at it. Ike and I go back a long way, Corrie. I gather Malone didn't try anything last night?"

"No, sir. Nothing spectacular, at least. Some of his people tried infiltration. They didn't make it."

Dan had successfully pulled off his fake rout and the carefully planted Claymores had done the rest. Dan's people had returned, deactivated those Claymores that were not triggered, and counted the dead. Malone had lost more than a hundred of his men, and that was sure to be very demoralizing to the man who believed he was engaged in a Holy War.

Over hot coffee and cold field rations, Ben waited for Ike and his battalion to arrive. He knew Ike would exit his vehicle whooping and hollering like a painted-up buck on the warpath, and he was not disappinted. If any Rebels were still in their sleeping bags when Ike arrived, they weren't in there long. Ike jumped out of his Hummer and hit the ground yelling.

Ben and Ike shook hands and stood for a moment grinning at each other. Then Ike's eyes narrowed as he began making out the hastily dug bunkers.

"Outnumbered again, huh, Ben?"

"You got it, Ike. You know it's a tough crew when Georgi and his people can't punch through. You and your people want to catch some sleep?"

The ex-Navy SEAL shook his head. Like Ben's, Ike's close-cropped hair was peppered with gray. "We slept on the planes and dozed some on the way up here. Let's get something to eat and go over this operation. Then we can kick some ass."

Walking over to draw rations, Ben said, "How's West?"

Ike laughed. "Mad as hell! It was one of those freak accidents. He was stepping out of a shower stall, stepped on a silver of soap, and went elbows over butt on the floor. Busted his ankle. He was still cussin' when we pulled out."

"He probably wanted to see Tina as much as getting into combat."

"There is that to consider, for a fact." As they approached the truck, Ike put out his hand. "This is not some of Dr. Chase's goop we're having for breakfast, is it?"

"I buried that crap."

"Good. I hope it doesn't poison the earth."

Buddy and Captains Ramos and Brad joined them, and after drawing their breakfast packages and mugs of coffee, they walked over to a vehicle and sat down on the ground. Ben pulled a map out of a pocket of his BDUs and Buddy shone a light on it.

"Dan and two companies are here," Ben said, placing a finger about halfway between Box Elder and Big Sandy. Georgi has swung his troops around and is covering from Chester over to Cut Bank."

Ben explained what Dan had done the previous afternoon and Ike smiled with satisfaction. Ike was Mississippi born and reared, but he despised bigotry and all those who practiced it.

"Where is Malone's CP—anybody know?"

"Somewhere around Conrad. Right here." Ben punched the map.

"Pretty good move on his part," Ike said "Things get too hot, he could easily duck into this wilderness area just west of his location and it'd take ten times the people we have to flush him."

"I'm thinking that's where he and his people live. I'm recalling that back in the mid-eighties the government had to go in there and arrest him a time or two."

"That's right," Ike replied, looking up from the map. "I remember this bunch now. So where do you want me and mine, Ben?"

"There is no way in hell you could effectively spread your people out, north and south along Highway 89, to put Malone in a box. We just don't have the troops. Ike, we've got a bunch of outlaws and bikers and crud coming up behind us. Up Interstate 15 or using county roads, we really don't know what route they're taking. And we don't know how many. It might be five hundred, it might be fifteen hundred. Both Georgi and I feel that Ashley and Sister Voleta have swung north to try to box Georgi. But I think we've pretty much nixed that by shifting Georgi over to this other sector. I've left one frequency open so Ashley can listen to us . . ."

"And hope that he's arrogant enough to stop his westward advance and cut south to butt heads with you," Ike correctly guessed.

"That's it. We're a lot fresher than Georgi and his people. They've been getting a pounding for long enough. They don't need Ashley and Voleta breathing down their necks."

Ike glanced at Buddy. The young man caught the glance and said, "I'm tired of being shifted around, Ike. If I have to meet my mother in combat, so be it. Though I am *of* her, that does not mean I am *for* her."

"My, my," Ike drawled in his Mississippi best.

"The boy shore do talk fancy, don't he?"

"Put it in your ear, Ike," Buddy told him.

After the laughter, Ben said, "I've already notified Georgi of this move. Now then, we're going to punch a hole through Malone's lines and cut his people in two. When that is done, one battalion will turn east to push those troops back and eventually link up with Dan, the other battalion will push west, to link up with Georgi."

"Sounds good to me, Ben."

"Sounds good . . . but will it work?"

"There is one way to find out, Father," Buddy said, standing up.

"Oh?" Ben looked up at his son.

"Do it."

The Rebels struck Malone's lines at dawn. There was nothing fancy about the attack; it was straight out of a textbook. Tanks and mortars and vehicle-drawn 105s laid down a smoke pattern and the tanks led the advance, ground troops coming in behind them.

And when Ike and Ben said they were going in with the troops . . . who among them was going to argue and tell them they could not?

Jersey and Beth.

"Stupid!" Jersey said, a disgusted look on her face.

"Foolish and childish!" Beth said, a reproachful look in her eyes. "It smacks of typical male bravado."

Ike beat it back to his own battalion and left Ben to handle it.

"Coward!" Ben called after him.

Jersey and Beth bitched and pouted, with both

knowing it was not going to change Ben's mind. Ben leaned up against a fender in the predawn darkness and let them wind down.

"You all through?" he finally asked.

Jersey and Beth glared at him.

"Get into body armor and helmets if you're coming along with me. Corrie, Cooper, the same goes for you. Gear up, we're moving out."

The Rebels busted through Malone's lines at the junction of 223 and 366. For almost a half hour it was eyeball to eyeball and hand to hand along a two-mile stretch of Montana countryside. Cooks, medics, supply personnel, clerks, and radio operators fought with pistols and camp axes against the troops of Malone.

Ben came face to face with a man who looked as if he ate trees for breakfast, lunch, and dinner. Out of ammo, the ape reversed his AK47 and swung it like a club at Ben. Ben ducked and pumped the man's belly full of .308 rounds from his old Thunder Lizard and kept on advancing.

Jersey was tackled and brought down by a young man, screaming out his hate. She gave him a knee in the balls and a knife blade across his throat, grabbed up her M16, and kept pace with Ben.

Corrie's backpack radio took the brunt of automatic weapons' fire, knocking her off her boots. Cooper tossed a grenade into the nest of hate mongers and hauled Corrie to her feet.

Ben, Beth, Jersey, Corrie, and Cooper found themselves a full two hundred yards ahead of the main body of Rebels, looked around, not liking their openness, and jumped into a bunker. Ben and Jersey

274

and Corrie began heaving bloody dead bodies out of the bunker—brought to their present state of final unpleasantness by two Rebel-fired mortar rounds—while Cooper righted the .50 caliber machine gun and yelled for Beth to feed it.

Then he turned the weapon on Malone's men and let the big .50 rock and roll.

A breech in the line had been opened and secured.

"Cease fire!" Ben finally yelled. "Pass it up and down the line. Cease fire!"

The landscape was littered with the ghostly silence of the dead and the moaning and crying of the badly wounded and the dying.

Ben used a walkie-talkie for communications while Corrie waited for another radio to replace the ruined backpack. "Approach the wounded cautiously," he ordered his people. "Work in two-person teams. One medic with an armed guard to watch for suicide tries. Bear in mind that these people are fanatics."

"I got a wounded man over here won't let Jimmy work on him," Ramos radioed. "He says no goddamn nigger is gonna play doctor on him."

Ben did not hesitate with his reply. "Then let the son of a bitch die."

"Our lines have been split," Malone was informed. "Raines pulled in more troops from down south and busted through. He's now controlling about a five-mile stretch along Highway 2."

Malone took the news stoically. There was no point in ranting and raving about it. That would not accomplish anything. Casualties?"

"Unknown at this time, sir. But from first reports, it's going to be at least several hundred. And the Rebels have seized mortars and hundreds of rounds."

"Crabtree's men?"

"Cut off."

"Communications?"

"Spotty. He's trying to keep it to a minimum to avoid being electronically pinpointed by the Rebels."

"Damn Ben Raines and his black heart to the pits of Hell!" Malone let a little of his temper slip through as he walked to the wall map.

Malone studied the map for a moment. "Tell Crabtree to make a run for it. Head north and try to link up with this Ashley person. He should be between Willow Creek and Wild Horse. Tell him to pull out now."

"Yes, sir."

"Get in touch with this Pete Jones person. . . . Is he a white man?"

"No, sir. I mean, I don't think so. But you can't tell by talking to him."

"Probably one of those educated niggers. They're the worst kind. Uppity. Don't know their place." He looked again at the map. "Tell him to attack Fort Benton. But don't do it head on. Make a series of sneak attacks. That might force Raines to shift some of his men back down south."

"Yes, sir." The aide hesitated. "Sir? We have word that Meg is in jail in Fort Benton. We picked it up by monitoring radio transmissions."

"She's too good a soldier to waste. Tell this Jones

nigger to get her out of there and bring her to me. If he can pull that off, that will be points in his favor. I might give him a watermelon."

Laughing, the aide left the room.

"Dan and his people have taken the airport at Harve," Corrie informed Ben. "Tina says Malone's men have bugged out."

"Which direction?"

"North."

"They're going to link up with Ashley and Voleta. Advise Ike of this development and tell Dan to stay put. Also advise Fort Benton to go to middle alert. Jones and his outlaws just may try to attack there."

Ben stepped out of the building he was using for a CP and looked up and down the street. There was not much left of the small town, certainly nothing salvageable. It had been carefully picked over, probably by Malone and and his people. He mulled matters over in his mind, rubbing his chin as he thought.

Stepping back into the building, he picked up the mike and got Ike on the horn. "Ike, swing your people around and head for Harve. Get with Dan and finish Ashley and his bunch once and for all. I'm going to hold what I have here until you're finished. I've got a feeling Fort Benton is going to come under attack and they might need our help. We can be down there in about ninety minutes."

"Ten-four, Ben. Rollin' now."

"Corrie, locate Buddy for me and get him over here."

His son was in the CP within moments. "Buddy, take your Rat Team and an additional platoon and get down to Fort Benton. Take heavy mortars and heavy machine guns. If an attack comes from this Jones person, it will more than likely come from the south." He walked to the wall map. "Move into position here," he said, pointing out the area.

Buddy studied the spot. "Your thinking is that the outlaws left Highway 89 and are moving north on these old county roads?"

"Yes. They had to avoid Great Falls and the creepies. They know we're using 90 as a supply route. That doesn't give them many options. Get your people together and move out."

Buddy hesitated, meeting Ben's eyes. "And you intend to do what, Father?"

Ben's smile was slight. "You're quick, boy. What do you think I'm going to do?"

"You're sending Ike east to link up with Dan, and you used an open frequency doing it. Now you're sending me south to Fort Benton. I think you're giving this Malone person an opportunity that will be too good fr him to pass up."

"That's right, Buddy. I'm the bait that's sitting on a nice sharp hook just waiting for the big fish to swim by and grab it."

6

"What do you make of it?" Malone asked his staff.

"I think Raines is taking a big gamble. I think he's too confident and this may be our chance to move in and cream him once and for all."

But Malone wasn't sure. He had carefully studied Ben Raines over the years. Had read, with some distain, most of the man's action/adventure books, and knew the man was, among other things, totally unpredictable when it came to unconventional warfare. The man was as sneaky as a snake and totally void of morals . . . why, he didn't even attend church!

"I don't know," Malone finally said. "He's certainly leaving himself vulnerable. Whether by accident or design is something I can't be certain of. I do know this: before we commit to an assault against his position, we'd better review the options very carefully."

"He only has two companies of Rebels with him. We've got him outnumbered ten or twelve to one."

"Ben Raines went into New York City out-numbered *fifty* to one and came out victorious," Malone reminded them. "I warned you all from the outset: do not underestimate this man. Leave me, I've got to think about this for a time."

"You think Malone will take the bait?" Ramos asked Ben.

"I'm hoping. As badly as he hates me, I can't see him letting an opportunity this good pass by. Are the people getting into position?"

"Quietly and quickly."

"Now we wait."

"How are we gonna do this?" Sweet Meat asked Beerbelly.

Everybody had linked up with the instincts of a homing pigeon. Beerbelly, Satan, and Pete Jones and his crew.

"This is all Pete's show," Satan said. "And I'm damn glad of it."

"Why is that?" Bruiser asked.

"Just to prove once and for all that a nigger can't do nothin' right."

Pete looked at the man. "If you feel that way about it, you ugly ape, why did you link up with us?"

"So I can watch you make a fool out of yourself, that's why. And when this is all over, I'm gonna kill you!"

"You ain't neither," Mac said. "I am."

"Why don't you draw straws?" Pete suggested. "Or

have some sort of raffle?"

"Why don't we all settle down and plan out the job ahead of us?" Lopez suggested.

Mac muttered something about coons and spics and then shut his mouth.

"Because I'm waiting for the scouts to return and give me a report on the town," Pete said patiently. "Just as soon as they return, we can map out strategy."

"You sure you can spell that word?" Satan smiled after the question.

"Can you?" Pete popped back.

"I got a suggestion," Wanda said. "Why don't we all put the hard feelings behind us until this job is over and Ben Raines is dead. We're never gonna get anything done if we don't work together."

The majority of those biker leaders and warlords gathered around agreed with that.

"All right, all right!" Mac said, after receiving a nod from Satan. "I don't like your black ass, Pete, but you give the orders and we'll carry them out."

"Agreed," Satan said.

"Fine." Smiling, Pete rubbed his hands together. "Here come the scouts. Now we can put our heads together and plan this operation."

Crabtree met Ashley's column about twenty-five miles north of Havre, just about the time Ike's battalion was dismounting in Havre and Ike and Dan were preparing to map out the campaign.

"Beautiful!" Ashley said with a laugh. "We've been monitoring Raines's radio transmissions and know that he's vulnerable. We've got him, Crabtree. I'm finally going to put an end to Ben Raines." He looked at the man. "You are Southern, aren't you?"

"Michigan," Crabtree corrected.

"Oh. Well . . . no matter. You had no say over your birthplace. Here's what we're going to do . . ."

The Rebels had the finest and most sophisticated radio equipment in the world, and given the least little break of luck they could track the movements of any enemy. Just as they were now doing with Crabtree.

"Crabtree has linked up with Ashley and Voleta," Corrie told Ben seconds after the communications truck relayed the news to her.

"I was hoping he would do that," Ben said with a smile. "Now let me put myself in that arrogant bastard's boots for a moment. We've deliberately been transmitting on an open frequency, so Ashley knows I've split my command and I'm sitting here with about two hundred and fifty people. If I were he, I would drive straight south and hook up with Highway 2, then as fast as I could, I'd head for my enemy's position. The enemy being me. I would smash into my enemy's position with a frontal attack, depending on sheer numbers to completely overrun the position." He winked at Jersey. "How's that sound to you, Jersey?"

"Frankly, not worth a shit, General! Are you tryin' to get us killed?"

Ben laughed and patted her on the shoulder. "Relax, Jersey. This place is going to be filled with people, but those people ain't gonna be us."

"Sir?"

"Malone has just given the orders to move out," Corrie told Ben.

Ben glanced at his watch. "All right, people. It's going to take Malone and Ashley about an hour and a half to get here. That'll put them here at sixteen hundred hours; with about two and half hours of good daylight left. We've got an hour to set things up and a half hour to get into position. Let's get to work."

"You in position, Ike?" Ben radioed on scramble.

"Ten-four, Ben. Me and Dan are about ten minutes behind. Bogies should be passing through Rudyard right about now."

"That's ten-four, Ike. Malone's main force is just below us. They used 336 to travel east, and they'll be cutting north at any moment. How's it looking on your end, Georgi?"

"Fantastic, Ben!" the Russian radioed. "I can't believe our luck. They're taking the bait like a hungry shark."

"What is your position, Georgi?"

"Just approaching Galata. That will put us eleven miles from your position in about five minutes."

"That's ten-four. Say a prayer for luck, boys and girls. We just might break the back of the snake this afternoon."

From a few hundred feet out, the town of Chester looked as though it had an armed Rebel in each window. What the buildings and houses contained were the bodies of Malone's men who had been killed earlier that day, stiffly and permanently grinning and grimacing in puffy death, the staring eyes seeing nothing—so far as mortals have been able to ascertain.

Ben lifted his walkie-talkie. "Mortar crews, when they get within range, start dropping a few rounds in on them. But keep it wide as if we're unable to get on target. We want them close enough to smell their hate before we open up with everything we've got."

And that was plenty. Some of the rear walls of buildings had been knocked out in order that tanks could hide, the muzzles of their cannon lowered to the max—they would be firing at almost point blank range.

The Duster and Big Thumper crews and many machine gun crews were hiding in the ditches and behind the ridges and in the underbrush at both ends of the town. Claymores had been planted alongside the roads, and every Rebel had his or her pockets bulging with grenades, for this was going to be very close up work.

Not to mention one hell of a gamble on the part of Ben Raines.

From the top of the tallest structure in town, a Rebel lifted his walkie-talkie. "I have them in sight, and there is a bunch of them, General."

"The more the merrier," Ben said brightly.

"Everybody got what they're supposed to do?" Pete asked the group.

"We make a bunch of noise upriver from the

town," Bass said.

"Create a diversion, yes," Pete acknowledged patiently. "Fire off lots of rounds, toss a couple of grenades . . . and keep it up for several minutes. Give us time to get into position. That way, the Rebels in town will have to split their forces to see what is going on."

"This better work," Mac warned.

"You'll never know if it doesn't," Pete said with a smile.

"Huh? What you mean?"

"If it doesn't work, Mac, you'll be dead!"

"Fire!" Ben gave the signal to attack as the trucks entered the perimeters of the Rebels.

The first thirty seconds of the ambush turned the road into a hideous deathtrap for the advancing armies of Malone and Ashley. The first ten trucks entering the town from both east and south, with each truck carrying twenty men, were torn apart by the deadly shards from Claymores, heavy machine gun fire, and the hot balls of fire from Big Thumpers.

When the men of Malone and Ashley realized—much too late—that they had been neatly suckered into an ambush, they attempted to turn around and run for their lives. When they did so, they found escape routes blocked by Striganov's people who had cut across country in all-terrain vehicles, and Ike and Dan from the east, the Russian and the Rebels advancing ruthlessly.

The tiny, nearly ruined town became the Waterloo for Malone and Ashley. But as Ben suspected and would later prove to be correct, neither Ashley nor Malone would be counted among the dead. Unlike Ben, those two did not lead men into battle, they only directed from a distance.

There was no place for the badly shaken survivors to run, and death was waiting impatiently to take them into cold bony arms.

Rebels began popping up out of hiding places to hurl grenades into the confused mob. Crossfires were the order of the day. Booby traps were the order of the bloody afternoon; every door seemed to be wired to explode.

And then the ultimate plan of Ben came true: Malone's men and Ashley's men began shooting at each other, each one believing the other was the enemy.

Those who did escape the town were cut down by an almost solid line of fire from Ike, Dan, and Georgi Striganov and his army of Russians and Canadians. Perhaps forty percent of the attackers managed to escape, most by running into the countryside, some by taking Highway 223 to the south and a gravel road to the north.

The fight was over in twenty minutes.

"Cease fire," Ben ordered, and gradually the area fell silent except for the moaning and screaming and crying and begging of the wounded. And they lay several deep in places, piled on top of one another. The streets of the town were littered with the dead and wounded. Burning trucks added fire and smoke to the confusion and the screaming.

The Rebels did not have to be told what to do. This scene had been played out many times over the long and bloody years. They began gathering up weapons and ammo, stripping the boots from the dead. The Rebels wasted nothing; everything that could be later used was taken, cleaned up, inventoried, and warehoused in any one of a dozen locations around the battered nation.

The wounded were cared for, the Rebels and Rebel supporters first, regardless of the severity of the wounds. Ben Raines put the well-being of his people first, the well-being of his enemies last.

Ben had once told a wounded outlaw, who was loudly protesting that he was being denied treatment while Rebels, not wounded nearly as badly, were getting aid, "I am not the Red Cross, punk."

7

"It's all gone to shit!" Pete was notified by a badly shaken biker who was manning the radio. "Malone and them others comin' from the east was damn near wiped out by Raines up near the border."

It did not take Pete more than a few seconds to recover from his shock and begin to issue orders. "Call the people back. Let's get out of here. Abort the mission."

"Do what to it?"

"Call it off."

No one needed to be told that twice. As the news of the ambush north of them spread, the bikers and warlords and outlaws went into a near panic getting the hell gone from the vicinity of Fort Benton.

But as they headed back south, to eventually cut west and then . . . who the hell knew where, Pete's mind was working frantically. This might not be as bad as he'd first thought. Perhaps something good could be salvaged from the ruins of what remained. Yeah, it just might work. Hell, he could make it work!

With Pete Jones in charge, he thought, a smile

cutting his lips.

Ben stuck out his hand and the Russian shook it. "Good to see you again, Georgi."

"The pleasure is mine, Ben. But I have to say I was holding my breath there for a moment. If this had not worked, we would have all been in a hard bind."

"Tell me about it. I wasn't breathing two times a minute for a while there."

Ike and Dan walked up and shook hands with the Russian. Dan said, "Neither Ashley nor Voleta are among the dead. At least not so far."

"Nor is Malone," Georgi added.

"That doesn't surprise me. Ashley and Voleta seem to lead charmed lives." Ben looked around him. "Where is Buddy and his Rat Team?"

"I told him to stay in Fort Benton." Dan said. "The main reason is to keep him away from the scene should we find his mother's body," he added.

"I'm sure you didn't fool him."

"Oh, I'm certain of that. But he didn't question the orders."

"We're going to be here working the better part of the night," Ben said, looking around him. "Ike, take your battalion and go after Malone. Before dark, shut it down. Resume the chase at first light and bump me as soon as you make contact."

With a smile and a sloppy salute, Ike trotted off, hollering for his people to mount up.

"We've broken the back of the monster," Ben said. "But the head and teeth are still venomous. They'll never fall again into what happened today, so tomorrow morning begins the slow and dangerous job of hunting them down and killing them. Let's mop it up here and get some rest. We shove off in the morning."

In his command post in Conrad, Malone was still not functioning at one hundred percent. The shattering news of losing more than half of his men had numbed him.

He had worked for years to build a pure Aryan nation, weeding out the inferiors, with an army of men who would spread his message across the land.

Now it was devastated, destroyed, what was left of his army scattered and demoralized, stumbling around in the darkness like lost children.

All because of Ben Raines and that bunch of inferiors he had gathered around him, clinging like bloodsucking parasites to his every utterance.

Then the thought came to him that while Ben Raines's Rebels might be made up of inferiors, they had sure kicked his ass and had done it soundly.

"More men coming in, sir," an aide told him, jarring Malone out of his bitter reverie.

With a sigh, Malone heaved himself out of the chair, forcing himself into action. "Have the women and children been evacuated?"

"Yes, sir. Most of them have been moved toward the wilderness area and the rest will be clear of the town by dawn."

"How do the men look?"

The aide hesitated, unsure of how to put his answer. He plunged ahead. "Scared, sir. And badly disoriented. More than a few are in some sort of shock. Babbling incoherently."

Malone suddenly snapped out of his depressed mood, if not completely, at least enough to once more take command and make the necessary decisions. "We can't spend any time here. Ben Raines will be after us very soon. Treat the more severely wounded and then get everybody onto what trucks we have left. Move them into the wilderness. Go, Carl. We'll rebuild; that's a promise."

When Carl had gone, Malone turned toward the east and muttered, "And I'll kill you someday, Raines. And that, too, is a promise. For I have God Almighty on my side, you heathenistic nigger lover!"

"How come you look so worried, Pete?" Mac asked. The outlaws had made camp deep in the timber, fixed their meager dinner, and doused the fire. "Ben Raines likes coons. He'd probably pat you on your bald head and make you a colonel or something in his army."

Pete sighed. "Once again, you have your information all twisted, you redneck. Ben Raines doesn't give a damn about a person's skin color."

"That's what I just said!"

"No, what I meant is this: Ben Raines will shoot me just as fast as he would you."

"Well, that don't make no sense, Pete, not when you takes into consideration that all you people look alike."

Muttering under his breath, Pete picked up his blankets and moved far away from MacNally. Ignorance could be catching.

*   *   *

Meg Callahan had asked to see a doctor; said she was feeling really rotten. The Rebel hesitated, then reached for the keys. He figured that since she hadn't caused any trouble up to now, maybe she really was sick. For a fact, she didn't look so hot. He opened the cell door and Meg jammed stiffened fingers into his throat, smashed his nose with an expert blow, and then using the heel of her hand, drove the cartilage up into his brain. The Rebel was dying as he hit the floor.

She belted his sidearm around her waist and picked up his M16. She slipped out into the hallway and worked her way to the front office. Another Rebel sat at a desk, reading an old magazine.

Damn!

She turned and slipped toward the back. If the luck was with her . . . It was, and the back door was unlocked. Meg Callahan slipped out into the night. Even if someone did spot her, she probably wouldn't be recognized, since she was still wearing her Rebel tiger-stripe BDUs. She felt pretty good. She had a fully loaded sidearm with two extra clips for it, and a fully loaded M16, with a half-dozen clips for it on the web belt. Now to find out where Ben Raines was and get to him.

So she could kill him. All in the name of and for Malone.

Ashley and Sister Voleta and their remaining troops had beat it when the frantically broadcast news of the ambush reached them. Ashley and Voleta had halted their personal troops at the junction of a gravel road leading south, about ten miles outside of Chester.

When they heard the news, they split. At the next intersection, they turned west and both almost had collective heart failure when the next road they came to was 223 and they realized they were only a few miles south of Ben Raines. They sped on across, cut south at the next intersection, and then once more west when they came to a sign telling them that Conrad was sixty miles.

Meg had killed another Rebel with a club and stolen her Jeep. She knew this country and didn't need road signs or maps to tell her where she was. She wound around a series of county roads until coming to 218 and followed that into Conrad. She arrived just moments after Ashley and Voleta and was stunned to see the place nearly deserted.

"I don't understand!" she shouted at Malone.

"My dear, listen to me. I'm overjoyed that you're still alive and free of that jail. But we've been badly mauled by the Rebels. We've lost, conservatively speaking, sixty percent of our troops. And it took about fifteen minutes for Raines to do it," he added with the bitter copper taste of defeat on his tongue.

"We're going back to the wilderness?"

"We have no choice. Raines won't come in there after us. Even that arrogant, Godless dictator knows that would be a foolish thing to do. We'll rebuild, Megan. We have time and God on our side."

Ashley and Sister Voleta exchanged glances at that. Even though the both of them were a couple of bricks shy of a load, they knew they didn't want to get tied up with some religious fanatic . . . he might pull something like what happened years back down in Jonestown. And Ashley had never acquired a taste for poison.

"You're welcome to join us, friend," Malone told Ashley. "Since your ranks are free of Inferiors, you obviously are a man who believes in maintaining the purity of the races."

"Oh, quite, sir. But I fear we must push on at first light. We're going to gather more troops and strike again at Ben Raines."

Malone was pleased to hear that. This Ashley fellow seemed to be a man with some breeding behind him and was quite the gentlemen, but that woman with him looked like a witch.

Which she was—a practicing witch of the Dark Arts, known as the Ninth Order.

"I wish you luck," Malone said.

"Thank you."

"They've bugged out, Ben," Ike radioed from the deserted town of Conrad. "They left a trail that a fool could follow. Leads straight toward the wilderness area."

"That's ten-four, Ike. Do not pursue. Repeat: do not pursue. We'll deal with them on a later date. Hold what you've got. We'll make Conrad our westernmost outpost. I'll start tanks and troops out within the hour. Let's clean out Great Falls."

Leaving a contingent of Rebels at Haver, busy cleaning up the airport, Ben and his people pulled out about an hour behind the tanks, taking Highway 2 over to Shelby—which turned out to be only a burned-out shell of a town—and then cut south on the Interstate down to Ike's position at Conrad. There, at Fort Benton, he sent Buddy to take his Rat Team, with one extra platoon of Rebels and a couple of Dusters, on ahead to check out Great Falls.

"Used to be a city of sixty thousand," Ben said, checking the maps. "It might hold anywhere from five hundred to five thousand creepies."

"Considering the sparseness of this country—speaking in terms of human population, that is," Dan said, "I would opt for less than a thousand of the buggers."

"Yeah, I'm with Dan," Ike said. "This is some of the most beautiful country in the world, but it always was kinda short on people."

Ben glanced at his watch. "Buddy should be there in about half an hour. Corrie, tell him to take the airport first, if possible, and stay put. We can fly supplies in from Lewistown if the runways are operable."

"You reckon this Callahan woman linked up with Malone?" Ike asked.

"Yeah . . . probably."

"I think we all know where our next campaign is going to be," General Striganov said. "and it damn well better be during the summer or early fall."

"Yes," Ben agreed softly. "And Beth has done some figuring on that place."

"Approximately one hundred and seventy-five miles long, from the Canadian border down to Mullen Pass, near Helena. Approximately one hundred and thirty-five miles deep; that's over to the Idaho line. That's roughly twenty-four thousand square miles."

"Holy shit!" Ike said.

That pretty well summed up everybody's feelings.

8

"The airport at Great Falls is secure," Buddy radioed back to his father. "We met some resistance, but it was put down."

"Runways?"

"Oddly, they are clean and in good shape. And we have taken possession of half a dozen cargo planes, which are also in good shape."

The people who had gathered around the radio in Malone's old CP in Conrad all exchanged quick glances, none fully understanding what this latest development meant; but all of them with the same thought, and it was an unsettling one.

"Any estimates on the strength of the creepies in the city?" Ben asked.

"Only a guess, Father," Buddy radioed. "I would put them at about seven hundred and fifty."

"Based on what information?"

"Six planes with a capacity of thirty-five human beings. That comes to two hundred and ten people being transported in each month, with each person weighing an average of one hundred and sixty pounds. Say fifty pounds of eatable flesh per person comes to just over ten thousand pounds to consume. We know that the creepies eat only about three times per week. That would give each of the seven hundred fifty Night People in the city approximately fifteen pounds of food a month."

"Holy Jesus Christ!" Ike blurted, then grimaced and belched.

"His arithmetic is correct," Beth said.

"Thank you both," Ben said, his breakfast lying like a lump in his belly.

Dan opened a window for a breath of fresh air.

"Hold what you've got, Buddy," Ben radioed. "We're moving out within the hour."

"That's ten-four, sir," the son acknowledged.

Ben did not ask if his son had taken any prisoners, or if he had, what to do with them. The Rebels did not take adult Night People prisoners. That was standing operational procedure.

"The slimy, hideous bastards are setting up outposts around the nation!" Dan said, turning from the window, his tanned face mirroring the inner shock and disgust of the man.

"Yes," Ben said. "That is my feeling."

"How many fronts are we going to have to fight, Dad?" Tina asked.

Ben cut his hard eyes. "Every one that rears up before us. Everything that stands between us and rebuilding a nation of as much civility that is possible in the times we're living in. Mount up and move out, people."

* * *

The Rebels made the run down to Great Falls in an hour and a half. Ben spread out his tanks, mortar carriers, and vehicle-drawn 105s facing the east. Planes carrying supplies from Lewistown had already begun landing at the airport by the time Ben arrived.

Standing on an overpass, Ben studied the city through binoculars for a long time. "A lot of history about to go up in flames," he was heard to mutter. He turned to Corrie. "Bring it down, Corrie."

She spoke into her mike and the relentless and destroying thunder erupted from the guns of the Rebels. The artillery dropped in WP, HE, and napalm. The gunners took the outer perimeters of the city first, setting it blazing. Then they began walking in rounds, from the outside of the circle inward, offering no creepie any avenue of escape.

The guns roared and spat and thunked their deadly rain all that morning. By noon, the city was a blazing valley of fire and smoke and destruction.

"Shut it down," Ben ordered. "Troops up to seal it off south and east."

The Missouri River prevented any escape north and west.

Small-arms fire began popping and cracking as Rebels brought down any creepies who had escaped the artillery barrage and now ran in sheer panic from the flames of the ravaged city. They did not run far.

By two o'clock that afternoon, there were only the sounds of the flames consuming the city, walls of buildings collapsing, and the occasional sounds of explosions as the flames hit pockets of gas or cached supplies of ammunition.

Ben had dispatched teams of Rebels to build fire

breaks around the city, to keep the flames from spreading into the countryside.

"We'll wait here until the fires have burned down to where they present no danger of spreading," Ben told his people. "Then we'll mount up and move south to Helena." He glanced at Buddy. "I want you to take your Rat Team and a platoon down to Helena. Take this route." He traced it with a finger. "That will take you down to a little place called Canyon Ferry. Cross over and work your way north from there up to the airport at Helena and secure it. Crush any resistance—any resistance—on your way there. Shove off in the morning. Considering the country you'll be going through, and the condition of the roads, it'll probably take you a good two days to reach your objective. We'll pull out on the morning of the second day. It's about a hundred-mile Interstate run for us. We'll be sitting on the outskirts of Helena when you make your first thrust at the airport. Any questions?"

"No, sir."

"Get supplied and ready to move."

"After Helena?" Ike asked.

"Butte and Bozeman. We bring them all down. And we do it in every state. I am not going to give the creepies a place to hide en masse. We'll make a complete circle and end the campaign back up at Conrad. We should be finished by mid-June. Then we strike at Malone's people in the wilderness area."

"When do we start flybys?" Colonel Rebet of Striganov's army asked.

"Not until we've finished this campaign and are geared up and ready to move into the area. Flybys will be a tip-off for Malone. And something else: we've still got those thousand or so outlaws roaming around this state, and then there is Matt Callahan to be reckoned with. We're going to have a very busy summer, people. It's going to be anything but a cakewalk."

"How about outposts in the western parts of Montana?" Ike asked.

"I don't know, Ike. It's rough country. I'm thinking that after we clean out Malone and his crud, I just may let the animals have it. All the way from the Canadian border down to Butte. We may try to set up something around Dillon. We'll just have to wait and see how things work out." He turned to Striganov. "How are things up in your part of Canada now that Malone has been, ah, relocated, so to speak?"

"Getting back to normal. I spoke with home base this morning. There's been no more trouble. Ben? We're in this to the finish. We're not going to go off and leave it half-done. My people are under your command. It's going to be a big, big job."

Ben folded his map case. "Well, let's get to it, then."

Beerbelly was unhappy and getting more so with each passing day. Pete Jones was getting delusions of grandeur and he was going to get them all killed if he followed through with his plans.

Beerbelly had not been an outlaw all his life, but he had a full decade of outlawing behind him. He'd been unhappy with it for some months . . . No, that

301

wasn't entirely the truth. He had, for some months, begun to realize that Ben Raines was not going to be stopped. Raines was going to bring law and order back to the battered nation. And he was, to put it quite simply, going to kill anybody who stood in his way. Ben Raines, Beerbelly knew, did not give a damn for constitutional rights. He was like an unstoppable steamroller, and if you were dumb enough to stand in his way, then, hell, you deserved what you got—and that was to be flattened like a damn pancake.

"What's the matter with you, Beer?" one of his cohorts in outlawing asked. "You been walkin' around with your lower lip draggin' the ground for two-three days."

"It's over, Hoss. It's all over."

"What's all over?" the man nicknamed Hoss asked, sitting down beside Beerbelly. Nobody knew Beerbelly's real name.

"Us."

Hoss looked at him. "What'd you been tokin' on, Beer? You sound plumb pro-found."

"Hoss . . . what'd you think about Pete's plans for us?"

"Well, I don't think too much of 'em, to tell the truth about it. I think Pete's done bit off more than he can chew. What about you?"

"I feel the same way. The other guys?"

"Oh, they all for it. They're gonna ride into Butte and strike a deal with those turrible cannibals and together they're gonna whup Ben Raines."

"So they think."

"Yeah. You got that right, man." He cut his eyes to

Beerbelly. "Beer, there ain't nobody never gonna whup Ben Raines."

"That's exactly my point, Hoss. Anybody with any sense knows it's over for guys like us. Oh, there's always gonna be people foolish enough to try Raines. People like Malone and that Ashley person. Raines will be fighting from now on out. But he ain't gonna be fightin' none of me."

"What are you gonna do, Beer?"

"I'm gettin' out, Hoss. I'm gonna check it all to them. I'm givin' it up. I'm gonna find me a woman that wants to settle down and raise me a garden and some hogs and chickens and so forth. I might have me some kids."

Hoss mulled that around for a few seconds. "You want some company, Beer?"

"Yeah. That'd be nice."

"I know a couple of ladies over in Central California. They ain't the best-lookin' women in the world, but then, good God, look at us. We sure ain't win no prizes neither."

"Tomorrow, we just sort of lay back and let the others get on around us. Then we cut west. Some miles behind us, we cut off our hair, shave, and find us some duds like normal people wear. We'll find us a pickup truck somewheres, get it runnin', and stash the bikes in the back. How's that sound?"

"Better and better, Beer."

The Rebels resupplied at Great Falls and rested for a day. They pulled out at dawn, heading for Helena on Interstate 15, for the most part, following the

Missouri River down south.

The Rebels spotted no one as they made their way south, but all could feel eyes on them. They were not hostile eyes, just curious and wary. By now, most in the state knew Ben Raines and his Rebels were working the area from top to bottom. But those watching just couldn't be sure this was Ben Raines and his army, for Malone's army looked pretty much as this one . . . and Malone was hostile to the core. Plus being a nut. So they would wait and see. Then they would step out and greet Ben Raines.

Ben pulled his people off the Interstate at a rest area about thirty miles north of Helena and stood them down for the rest of that day. Buddy had made better time than expected and was in position to strike at the airport located on the east side of the city.

"This won't be as easy as Great Falls," Ben admitted, once more studying maps spread over the hood of a vehicle. "We'll be coming in on the east side of the city; however, that will be a break for Buddy. If he runs into trouble, we'll be practically sitting in his lap. Ike, the next exit down the road leads to just west of the city. When we shove off in the morning, you take your battalion out about an hour earlier and head down there and get in place. Georgi, you and your bunch take this 453 and work on down south of the city. We'll start the bombardment at oh-eight-hundred."

"Are we heading straight for Butte after Helena?" Dan asked.

"No. I think we might be expected to do that, and I don't like to do the expected. We'll take Highway 12 over the Continental Divide and bring Missoula down. We'll be moving through some rough country, so make sure the tanks are boomed down tight. On the way back, we'll check out Anaconda and then strike Butte and Bozeman. We'll head on over to Matt Callahan's territory and put an end to him while we're at it, then head back to Conrad and prepare for the campaign in the wilderness."

"This is one state that's going to be nice and clean when we're through with it," Tina observed, then added, "In a manner of speaking, that is."

9

The attack came as no surprise to the Night People. They all knew that Ben Raines was driving hard to rid the earth of them; all knew, through a nationwide communications linkup, where Ben and the Rebels were, most of the time. But owing to the very nature of their miserable existence, the creepies had to band together to survive. They had to have adequate storage facilities for the human beings they feasted on, and had to have airport access, which meant they had to live in the larger towns. Their way of life had predoomed them . . . as long as Ben Raines lived. So the top priority of the Night People was finding out some way to get rid of Ben Raines. They would grab at any straw.

They accepted the offer of Pete Jones and his outlaws. Just as those trapped in the ravaged city of Helena now prepared to die under the guns of Ben Raines.

As Pete and his motley gathering—minus Beer-belly and Hoss and several others—were racing toward Butte to link up with the Night People there, to plan some skullduggery, Ben was giving the orders to destroy yet another bastion of the macabre, the hideous, and the Godless.

"Fire!" he ordered, and the guns thundered, just as Buddy and his Rat Team were striking hard at the defenders at the airport.

Butte began burning.

Ben kept up the pounding rain of death for two hours, using the same tactics he and the Rebels had perfected while destroying other cities. The outer limits of the city were set blazing and the artillery began walking in rounds toward the center, from all sides, effectively sealing the city from escape.

Buddy and his team faced much stiffer resistance this time, for the Night People knew they had but two options: live or die. They knew there was no hope of surrender; Rebels shot them on sight.

But slowly, with a curse on their lips, the creepies were forced back and out of the airport under the relentless advance of Buddy and his command.

Then the Rat Team began the dangerous job of clearing each room of each building of the airport complex. It was cautiously walking up and down darkened and stinking hallways, not knowing when or if a black-robed maniac would come hurling out of a room, foul-smelling with human blood still on their lips, screaming and cursing, with an automatci weapon in his or her hands, bent on killing a hated Rebel of Ben Raines's army.

It was slow and nerveracking and sweaty, deadly work. But Buddy and his team had worked it out to an art, and the airport was cleared and secure in an hour.

Over the pounding of artillery, Corrie informed Ben of the seizing of the airport and the clearing of it. He nodded his head in acknowledgment and once again lifted the binoculars, studying the rapidly destroying city from a vantage point on an overpass of the Interstate.

Ben continued the pounding of the city for another hour, until the city itself was obscured by the smoke from hundreds of fires.

"Cease firing," he told Corrie. "Sniper teams move closer and knock them down as they try to run."

"Dan reports that once again we have rescued Mr. Deason and some of his people," she said.

Ben looked at her. "Who?"

"The man from Billings. That one who headed the group called Peace Without Violence."

"Ahh, yes. That one. It didn't take him long to get his butt back in the stewpot again, did it? Is that loudmouth woman with him?"

"Yes, sir. Dan is bringing them up here now."

Ben sighed heavily. "How wonderful for me. I get another cussing. My day wouldn't be complete without that."

But it was a very different Sybil and Morris who once more stood in front of Ben.

"They were about to eat us," Sybil said. "We were scheduled to be devoured tomorrow."

"It was quite disheartening," Morris said. "Not to mention disgusting."

"I can imagine," Ben said, eyeballing the pair. "Were they going to serve you up as hors d'oeuvres or as the main course?"

"How crude!" Morris said.

"You're a vile, despicable man," Sybil told him.

"How can you joke at a time like this?"

"Because I'm looking at a couple of jokes. Where the goddamn hell do you people think you are? At a reception before a recital by a string quartet?"

Morris and Sybil and what remained of their little group stood in silence and glared at Ben.

Ben finally sighed and shook his head. "What the hell am I going to do with you people? I turn you loose and you end up right back in the hands of the creepies. Can any of you do anything?"

"I beg your pardon?" Morris asked.

"Can you do anything? You say you're scientists—what field?"

"We're from a great many fields."

"You want to go to work for me, down at Base Camp One?"

Striganov had wandered up, an amused look on his face.

"You!" Sybil shouted, staring bug-eyed at the Russian.

"In the flesh," Georgi replied.

"You know these people?" Ben asked.

Behind them, the city burned.

"Oh, yes. We've rescued them several times from the hands of outlaws and slave traders."

"You're just as bad as he is!" Sybil yelled, pointing at Ben.

"Thank you, madam," Georgi said. "I take that as quite a compliment."

"You would!"

"What the hell am I going to do with these people?" Ben pleaded.

"The Great God Blomm," Dan said with a straight face.

"What?" Georgi asked.

Ben smiled. Then the smile faded. "No, I couldn't do that to Emil. The little con artist fought his heart out in New York City."

"Do not feel obligated to do anything for us," Morris said. "We are perfectly capable of taking care of ourselves."

That brought a chuckle from all those standing around.

It's unfair, Ben thought. These people, naive as they might be, are attempting to live nonviolently in a world filled with violence . . . and we laugh at them. Have we all become so callous, so battle-hardened, that we have lost sight of one of the most important things that we're fighting for?

Ben looked at Dan. The Englishman's eyes were sad. He knew what Ben had been thinking.

Ben looked back to Morris and then at Sybil. They had lost their hostile expressions as they studied Ben's face; as if they, too, knew what Ben had been thinking. "You'll stay here with us until the birds . . . planes start arriving. That will be tomorrow. I'm sending you back to Base Camp One, down in Louisiana. If you want to stay and work for us there, that's fine."

"And live under your rules, General?" one of the women in the group spoke up.

"Under *our* rules," Ben said, waving his hand, indicating all the Rebels. "We live in more of a democratic society than you might think—or have been led to believe. We have only a few laws, but those few are quickly and very harshly enforced. We have a great deal of solar heating and cooling, so as not to pollute the skies any more than we have to. We will never have nuclear energy . . . we will never have nuclear weapons. We have zero crime in our outposts. That is very easy to accomplish, and it always has been: we just don't tolerate it. We don't have lawyers—practicing lawyers, that is. We do have courts; they are run by the people, and conducted in language that anyone can understand. So far as I know, we have the finest schools in all the world, and attendance is mandatory until age eighteen. We have adult education classes. We do not have illiteracy; there again, we don't tolerate it. We would appreciate your joining us as teachers. And yes, we have noncombatives in our ranks. How about it?"

Morris studied Ben for a moment, then smiled and stuck out his hand. "It would be a pleasure, General Raines. You paint quite a different picture of your way of living than we have been led to believe."

Ben took the offered hand with a smile. "Good to have you with us."

The Rebel column cut west, leaving the smoke of the ruined city, and the smell of death behind them. They drove over the Continental Divide, with Buddy and his Rat Team spearheading, and hooked up with Interstate 90, taking that northwest to the outskirts of Missoula.

"It's deserted," Buddy reported back to the column. "But only recently. I'd say the creepies bugged out until we leave."

"Hold what you have, son. I want to inspect the town."

It was disgusting to all of the Rebels. The stench of Night People clung over the small city. What was left of the bodies of human beings was found in several locations around the city. It was obvious to all that had the stomach to look at the human garbage heap that the men and women and kids had been carved on, the choice cuts taken for food.

"You think they might have bugged out for Kalispell?" Tina asked.

"I doubt it. That's right in the middle of Malone's territory. He hates the creepies nearly as bad as we do. If I had to guess, I'd say they joined others like them over in Spokane. It isn't that far from here. Destroy the airport and bring the town down with explosives. Georgi, what do you know about this Indian Reservation just north of here?"

"They've gone, Ben. Same with the Blackfeet tribe just to the east of them. And we don't know where they went. Danjou led an expedition down there a couple of years ago. Nothing. The place was deserted."

"They probably spread out in small bands all over the west. I'd like to have them as allies, but I damn sure don't blame the Indians for not trusting the white man, and I don't blame them for wanting to return to their own ways and cultures. It worked for them for hundreds of years. All right, let's take the town down, people."

This was something else the Rebels had become experts at: the destroying of buildings by explosives. Stress points were quickly located and the buildings

313

brought down with relatively small amounts of explosives. And with towns recently inhabited by creepies, the Rebels thoroughly enjoyed their work.

They worked fast and effectively. When they pulled out, they left behind them only a shell of a town, totally uninhabitable.

"It's not just the cities that are going to have to be destroyed, is it, General?" Beth asked on the drive down to Anaconda.

"I'm afraid not, Beth. But the bringing down of the small towns is something that the residents of the outposts will have to do—for the most part. We'll do it if we have the time." He lifted his map and studied it. "There's a dam just south of our present position. I'm curious as to how it—and all the others—are holding up. They've been years without maintenance. Beth—"

"I know," she interrupted with a smile. "Make a note. Right, sir."

For the next several miles, Ben rode in silence, thinking that there was just too goddamn much to worry about; far too much for one man to handle. No wonder the governing of a nation—any nation— almost invariably turned into a massive, ponderous bureaucracy. As well this one might again, Ben thought. But as long as I live, there won't be any deadheads in it.

And, he was forced to smile, no taxpayers' dollars being spent for foolishness. One advantage of not having any taxpayers.

And how long could they get away with that?

Just as long as possible, Ben answered his own question.

At a rest stop, Corrie said, "Fort Benton has intercepted radio transmissions, General. It was an open frequency. Pete Jones and a large force of outlaws have linked up with the creepies in Butte. They're going to dig in in the city and try to slug it out with us."

Ben thought about that open frequency business for a moment. "No, they're not," he finally said. "That's just a ruse to throw us off. They know they don't have a chance of winning by fighting us nose to nose."

"Anaconda?" Ike asked.

"I'd bet on it. They knew we seldom shell the smaller towns; especially if they're deserted. We go in, inspect, and then bring them down with explosives." He smiled grimly. "My, my. But are we going to have a surprise for Mr. Jones."

10

Ben split the column, sending Ike and his troops down Highway 1, while he continued on south toward Anaconda, using the Interstate. Buddy and his Rat Team, as usual, were ranging far in advance of the main party, sending scrambled messages back to both his father and Ike.

"If they're in there," Buddy reported to Ben, "they're well hidden." He was looking at the town, studying it through binoculars. "There is no movement, no smoke, no nothing to indicate any sign of life."

Ben had halted the column a few miles north of the town, waiting for Buddy's report. Now he was wondering if Pete Jones and the creepies were stupid enough to fortress themselves in Butte and actually attempt to hold the city.

No! He rejected that almost instantly. But if they were not in Anaconda, laying in ambush . . . then where were they? There were literally hundreds of places along the route where explosives could be used to bring down tons of rock on the column. But that was not the creepies' style and Ben doubted they would change tactics this late in the game.

Also Ben doubted any citizens trying to live out their lives in some degree of normalcy would attempt to do that so close to a creepie stronghold such as Butte.

He got his artillery in position and then radioed Ike, who was set up on the west side of the town. "What do you think, Ike?"

"Let's bring it down, Ben. I've got people in position on both sides of the Interstate about three miles southeast of the town. Any who try to escape that way will run slap into an ambush."

Ben turned to Corrie. "Commence firing."

When the first rounds began dropping in, shaking the earth and rattling the buildings right down to their foundations, a creepie turned to Pete Jones. "You son of a bitch!"

Pete had a sick look on his face. "Win some, lose some, my friend," he managed to be heard over the roaring of incoming.

The creepie shot Pete in the face just as Bruiser and Satan and several hundred other outlaws, who had managed to place themselves near a road leading to the east, cranked up and got the hell out of the town.

Pete Jones twitched once on the dirty floor and then died with his eyes open and with a very startled look on his face.

Injun Sam and Blackie and their outlaw following tore out of town, heading southeast on the Interstate. They rode right into the ambush set up by Dan Gray and Tina Raines and the Scouts.

It was like riding right through the gates of Hell, one biker who managed to escape the killing fire later told a group of outlaws. The Rebels would look you right in the eyes and then shoot you dead with no more emotion than opening a can of beans. It wasn't nothin' like the good ol' days, back when the cops had to read you rights and tend to your wounds and be careful how they spoke to you and you could stomp the snot out of a citizen and even a sorry lawyer could get you off with a slap on the wrist and a lecture from the judge.

But these damn Rebels were bad-asses, man!

While the town was being systematically destroyed, including everyone in it, the outlaws and bikers and other assorted crud who thought they had gotten away stone clear were dying in screaming and moaning and crying and begging piles of lower forms of life on the Interstate.

Dan and Tina took no prisoners. Ben had said that anyone who aligned himself with the Night People was to be shown no mercy.

No mercy was shown.

Bikers and outlaws tried to surrender from out of the bombarded town. A few tried. Those who watched them shot down resigned themselves to their fate with either a curse or a long-forgotten-until-now prayer for forgiveness from their Maker.

God's mercenary, Michael, mighty warrior that he is, probably got a good laugh out of that, for the skies over that area of the state suddenly began to darken from what had previously been a clear blue and a hard rain began to fall, accompanied by wicked lightning and rolling peals of thunder.

The relentless bombardment continued through the storm and the rain as mortars thunked and cannon howled and boomed, and snipers patiently waited for targets to bring down, all combining to hurl Rebel justice down upon the occupied town.

Several hundred escaped the ruined town, slipping out furtively, large humans emulating the disease-carrying and beady-eyed rats that they really were.

Ben ordered the bombardment shut down after an hour. The town lay smoking and silent.

"Do we go in?" Buddy asked.

"No," Ben said. "To hell with those in there. It's only about twenty miles to Butte. We take it down this day. There is no really effective way I can find on any map to get you and your team south of the city to the airport. You spearhead the column, stay on the Interstate, and start marking out artillery positions when you get there."

Deuce and a halves with scrapers on the front were used to shove aside the mess on the Interstate just south of the town. Bodies and vehicles were pushed unceremoniously into the ditches. No attempt was made to bury anyone.

Ben and his people had declared a no-holds-barred war on the crud that roamed the land, preying on those who were trying to rebuild from out of the ashes. The Rebels offered no mercy, no compassion, no sympathy . . . and no surrender.

"Jesus God!" MacNally whispered, watching from a brush-covered ridge as the Rebels mounted up and pulled out from the ravaged town, heading south toward Butte. "Them people ain't *human!*"

Bruiser sat in shock at the suddenness of the attack

and the harshness with which his friends had been dealt. Even Satan was having a hard time believing the ruthlessness of the Rebels. The big man finally shook himself out of his slight daze.

"They ain't gonna get away with it," he announced, standing up. "I'm gonna kill Ben Raines. I don't know how I'm gonna do it. But I'm gonna do it." He moved toward his motorcycle.

"Where you goin', Satan?" Mac called.

Satan turned around. "Ben Raines is makin' a big circle, clearin' this state of Night People and outlaws. It don't take no genius to figger that out. And I betya on the final leg, he's gonna go after Snake, over there where that soldier boy got hisself and all them men killed a hundred and some-odd years back. Puddin', custard . . . something like that."

"General Custer," Bass said.

"Yeah, that's him."

"So?"

"I'm gonna be there waitin' on Ben Raines, boys." He held out his massive hands. "And I'm gonna tear him apart with my bare hands."

"That'd be a sight to see, all right," Wanda allowed. "I think me and the girls will just ease over that way with you."

"You're welcome to ride along." He looked at the still-shaken gathering. "Anybody else?"

One by one, those remaining outlaws stood up and walked toward their motorcycles and cars and pickup trucks.

"We gotta do something, man," Morgan muttered. "It ain't no fun out here with Ben Raines on the prowl. Not to mention that it ain't safe neither."

Matt Callahan stood in the valley of the Little Big Horn, his horse picketed nearby. He felt it in his bones: Ol' Slim was a-comin'. He knowed it was gonna be thisaway all along. Ol' Slim and him would step out to face each other and they'd take that walk that would be a one-way stroll for one of them. And just about when fifty feet separated them, they'd both drag iron and commence to lettin' the hammers down and the lead flyin'.

Matt drew, cocked, and fired in one experienced and very fast move. He plugged a small tree.

Smiling with satisfaction, Snake punched out the empty brass and filled the cylinder up. He didn't twirl his guns; that was for tinhorns and punks.

He sat his Colt down in leather and walked over to the river, scooping up water in the palm of his hand and drinking. He suddenly whirled and drew his left-hand Colt and killed a piece of driftwood.

"Let Ol' Slim beat that," he muttered.

When the bombs came, the period that history would call the Great War, Matt Callahan had snapped. Already not too-tightly wrapped, Matt had spent the first few years tracking down and killing any writer of "dirty books" that he could find. Fortunately, he couldn't find too many of them; but he got a great deal of satisfaction out of killing those he could find. Especially those who write those dirty Westerns. Hard, tough, straight-shootin' cowboys in th real old West just didn't do the things that were so vividly and profanely outlined in the pages of those filthy books. Everybody knew that. Cowboys stood tall in the saddle and said "howdy" and "ma'am" and they didn't say bad words. And they especially didn't use their big toe in a manner like that cowboy did in one of those adult Western books. Matt knew that for a fact. He'd tried it with one of his girlfriends. Threw his back out of whack and couldn't walk for two weeks.

The only thing that Matt could say good about Ben Raines was that he hadn't written any really dirty books.

But that didn't make no difference. Snake was gonna gun him down like the low-down skunk he was.

Ashley and Sister Voleta had drifted down south. They had lost about half of their people and that had turned them very cautious. They had wound their way south, and were now camped just south of Crazy Peak in the Gallatin National Forest. They spent their time monitoring radio transmissions from the Night People and Ben Raines's Rebels.

And they knew Ben was winning.

"Damn him!" Voleta said. "And damn that bastard son of mine."

Ashley didn't pay her any attention. He was used to her rantings and ravings. He waited until she had wound down and said, "I think, my dear, that Montana has withdrawn the welcome mat for us. Rather rudely jerked it out from under our feet would be more like it."

"Then carry your ass," she bluntly told him.

"What do you hope to gain by staying?"

"A chance to kill Ben Raines."

"Voleta, I have been trying to kill that man for years. Our day will come, believe me. But it isn't in the cards this time around. Our armies have been halved. We simply don't have the manpower to fight the Rebels."

But the woman was unshakable. "I intend to stay right here, monitoring Ben Raines's moves. There is plenty of game to hunt, and we have water and shelter. We all need a rest and right here is as good a place as any."

"Might I suggest a better place?"

"Go ahead."

"Further south. On the Wyoming-Montana border. In the Custer National Forest."

"Why there?"

"Because the Rebels have already cleaned out Sheridan. They won't be expecting us to move in that close to a secure area."

Voleta thought about that for a moment. "All right. That sounds good to me."

The early summer campaign was winding down and Ben sensed its closing. It had been a brief campaign, but a highly successful one. For the most part, Montana was clear of human crud with outposts put securely in place. Ben was looking forward to a week's rest before tackling Malone and his bunch.

But, he thought with a barely audible sigh, there still remained some unfinished business.

Matt Callahan aka the Rattlesnake Kid.

Ben knew a lot of bikers and other outlaws had broken free of the assault on Anaconda. Had they retreated only to once more link up with Matt? It was a possibility that he had to consider. And how about Ashley and Voleta—where were they? Wherever they were, they were keeping their heads down and staying off the radio, for communications had heard nothing from them.

The ambush up north had cut deeply into the troops of Ashley and Voleta, but they still had enough men to be a problem. And it worried Ben because nothing had been heard from them. Ashley could be just as sneaky as Ben; there were lots of differences between the men, but the main difference was that Ashley was a coward.

Not so with Sister Voleta and her troops of the Ninth Order. She was a nut, but one with cunning and courage. Neither she nor Ashley could be discounted. Not yet.

And how in the hell was he going to flush Matt out of the Rosebuds without losing some people and wasting a lot of time?

Ben couldn't just turn his back on Matt, postponing the showdown until a later date—as much as he would like to do that—for the man would only rebuild his army and resume his warlord activities.

No, Matt had to be taken out during this sweep. With that done, Montana, from the Continental Divide over to Miles City, would be clean.

Ben smiled faintly, thinking: Only forty-nine states to go.

11

The Night People had pulled out of Butte. They had seen the futility of fighting Ben Raines on his own terms and had gathered their stinking robes about them and slithered away. The city lay silent and stinking under the sun.

"Check it out and bring it down," Ben ordered.

The Rebels spent the rest of that day and much of the night carefully going over the deserted city. No prisoners were found; obviously the creepies had taken their food supply with them as they bugged out.

The next morning, Ben's Rebels began destroying the city with explosvies while Georgi Striganov and his troops moved on over to Bozeman.

"Nothing," the Russian radioed back. "The town is as deserted as a grave."

"Interesting way of putting it, Georgi," Ben replied. "Start bringing it down, please."

Ben pulled his Rebels over and spent the night in a small town on the banks of the Missouri River, about halfway between Butte and Bozeman. His people were tired, and Ben was tired. They had circled the state in a very short time, with all of them pushing themselves hard. The Rebels had taken very few casualties, but they were, to a person, very weary. Ben made up his mind that after Bozeman was destroyed, they would travel the Interstate for a few more miles, and then stand down for a few days, doing routine maintenance on the vehicles, checking weapons, and resting. Then they would move against Matt Callahan and those still with him.

Ben felt he knew what Matt wanted him to do, but damned if he was going to oblige the man. Ben had no intentions of any such foolishness as standing up and quick-drawing like a scene out of some grade B Western movie.

At the airport in Bozeman, while the city burned, the Rebels checked out the aircraft the creepies had left behind them and found several planes in excellent shape. Ben radioed for pilots to be flown in to fly them out.

The Rebel convoy moved on. At a small town on the Yellowstone River, Ben halted the long column and told his people to relax and have some fun for a change. The Rebels were unaware that just south of them, the bikers and outlaws were gathering, and Ashley and Sister Voleta had joined them.

"We're still no match for them," Ashley warned. "I hate to keep harping on that, but Raines has, with the addition of the Russian's troops, about four battalions of troops."

Satan glared at him. "So what do you have in mind, pretty boy?"

"We pull this ragtag bunch of misfits into some sort of fighting force while we're waiting to see what Raines does. I have a hunch that he's going to launch a summer campaign against Malone up in the wilderness. Now while we're training, we add to our strength by pulling in all the smaller groups of . . . ah"—he looked around with some disdain—"outlaws and bikers. Then when Raines commits his troops into the wilderness, we go in behind him and box them in."

Satan squatted his bulk down and eyeballed—as best he could—Ashley. Finally he nodded his head. "All right," he said slowly. "I'll go along with that."

"Voleta?" Ashley asked.

The woman took her time in replying. "If I agree to go along with that—and I haven't said I would—the campaign is going to have to be very carefully worked out. Malone has to be notified, and not by radio. Raines would pinpoint us in a flash. We are going to have to be just as sophisticated in warfare as Ben Raines. And that means coming up with weapons that are on a par with his. Tanks are out of the question; they would be useless in the wilderness. But heavy machine guns and mortars—with people who know how to use them—will be essential. Discipline is something else. Your bunch of bikers and outlaws, Satan, have no discipline. You're going to have to put some steel in their backbones and make them understand that for this operation to succeed, they must follow orders and do so without question."

"Who gives the orders?" Satan rumbled.

"The mercenary, Kenny Parr, had a son. The boy is now a grown man and commanding a large group down in Florida."

"Who the hell is Kenny Parr?"

"A mercenary who used to work for President Hilton Logan. A man named Kasim killed him years ago. But not before Parr taught his son to hate Ben Raines and everything he stood for."

"How many men?" Ashley asked. Voleta was a constant source of amazement to him. It seemed that she knew every army of warlords and outlaws in what used to be the United States. And Ashley also knew that Voleta had more troops than she ever let him know about. She had Ninth Order people all over the country.

"About a thousand. But they are well trained and disciplined troops, skilled in the use of mortars and machine guns and rocket launchers."

"In other words," Satan said, a nasty tone to the question, "they're professionals and we're a bunch of bums and no-goods?"

There was no back-down in Voleta. She returned the glare and said, "Yes."

Satan smiled his horrible disfigured grin. "You a gutsy bitch, I'll give you that much." Then he shrugged. "All right, I'll take orders from this Parr." He looked at Ashley. "How about you, fancy pants?"

"I ran you out of Kansas once, you ugly bastard— remember?"

Satan smiled. "Yeah . . . so you did. That's when you was pimpin' for King Louie. So what about it?"

"Just keep it in mind. And also keep in mind that when you put a hand on me, probably twelve or fifteen of my men will shoot you so full of holes you'll be dead before you hit the ground."

Satan looked around him. True enough, about a dozen of Ashley's men were nearby, the muzzles of their guns ready to come up and blow him all to hell and gone.

"All right, Ashley," Satan verbally backed away. "You and me will work together. But when Ben Raines is dead, and we start splittin' up the country, you and me will stake our claims far apart."

"That suits me."

Satan walked away.

Voleta watched him go and said, "We will use the lout and his kind to achieve our goals, then we can dispose of him."

"And doing that will be a pleasure, Voleta. How do we get word to Parr?"

"I'll send some of my people. I'll dispatch them this afternoon. They'll go down into Colorado to one of my cells and send a coded message to the mercenary. He can be here in a week or ten days."

"It certainly would be a much nicer place to live without Ben Raines around," Ashley said wistfully. "I am so looking foward to the day."

"Not nearly as much as I am." Voleta spat the words like an angry snake.

There were dozens of questions that Ashley would have liked to ask, but each time he had tried to bring up the personal side of Voleta—such as her real name—she brusquely rebuffed him. And only once had he asked her about her son Buddy. The look she gave him silently warned him not to bring it up again.

"So you're in?" Ashley asked.

"All the way. Until either I am dead, or Ben Raines

is rotting in his grave."

Ben woke up that night bathed in sweat. He had worked his way through and out of the damnest nightmare he'd experienced in years. Someone had conked him on the head and tied him to a stake . . . then brush was piled all around his bare feet and the brush ignited.

He was being burned alive, and as he screamed while the flames licked at his flesh, Sister Voleta and her Ninth Order stood and grinned.

He awakened and flung the covers from him, his chest heaving, trying to catch his breath.

"Damn!" Ben whispered as he dressed and stepped outside for a breath of air.

A sentry was by his side almost instantly. "Something wrong, General?" she asked.

"Before he could answer, Buddy stepped out of the shadows and said, "My mother."

The sentry knew that Buddy was the son of Ben Raines through an affair with a Nashville woman years back, before the Great War, and father and son had been united only a few years back.

She knew that Buddy's mother was the leader of that strange and dangerous group called the Ninth Order. And she also knew that Buddy possessed some sort of mysticism about him . . . no doubt about that, his mother being a witch. The sentry moved away, sensing that family business was about to be discussed.

"What about your mother, son?" Ben asked.

"She is very close."

"How do you know these things, boy?"

"I don't know, Father. I just do. The Old One, my grandfather, once told me I was born marked, and could have gone either way; that being good or evil, I suppose."

"Marked . . . how?"

"I don't know, Father. He never brought it up after that one time."

"What's got your hackles up about your mother?"

"I had a dream. A nightmare. I was being burned at the stake. That is my mother's favorite way of punishing those who violate her rules. You should know."

"What do you mean by that?" Ben spoke more sharply than he intended. Goddamn! Did the boy actually know what he had been dreaming?

Buddy stared long at his father. When he spoke, his voice was soft. "I meant only that you encountered my mother, for the second time, after the Great War, while she was burning someone at the stake, did you not?"

"Yes. Over in Tennessee, I think it was." Ben sighed. "Did you know that I just awakened from a hellish nightmare?"

"No. But it doesn't surprise me. There is a little of my mother in me, and a lot of you in me."

Ben didn't know exactly how to take that statement. He minutely shook his head and then glanced at his watch. Nearly four o'clock. Time to get up anyway. "How close do you feel your mother to be?"

"Close enough for me to sense a great deal of danger."

"I ought to send you back to Base Camp One."

"No. I wouldn't want to disobey your orders, but on that one, I would."

"I'm going to have to kill her, Buddy."

"No, Father. I think not. I think my mother will meet her end at my hands. I think that is truth."

"I hope you're wrong, son."

Buddy shook his head. "I am correct in my thinking. But I believe that my mother will live a very long and very evil life before she meets her end."

"I'll certainly go along with th evil part of it," Ben said. "Will I be around to see her demise, son?"

"Yes," the young man replied. Then he turned and walked away.

"That's a weird kid, Dan." Ben had heard the Englishman come up, moving as silently as a wraith.

"Weird? Oh, I don't think so, General. I think he is simply blessed, or cursed, with the Insight, that's all. Considering the way he was raised, I think he turned out very well."

"Oh, I do too, Dan. No doubt about that. But he spooks me at times."

"Did you ever stand among the great rocks of Stonehenge, General?"

Ben smiled. "Oh, yes. Years ago, when I was visiting England. Yes, I know what you mean."

"Now *that's* spooky. I will be the first to admit that I got the hell away from there in a hurry."

Ben's smile broadened. "I rather enjoyed the sensation. I felt I was actually a part of those old ones who came and went long before us."

"And you call Buddy weird!"

*   *   *

It was a quiet time for the Rebels. A time that all of them had earned. They slept, they played, they swam, they gossiped, and they enjoyed just doing nothing.

All of them knew that it would probably be their last time for total relaxation for several long, hard, bitter, bloody months once the campaign against Malone was launched. That campaign, they knew, would be one where they could not rely on battle tanks and Dusters; it would be war in the deep forests, a very personal and, in many cases, one-on-one type of warfare. And while none of the Rebels were looking foward to it, they all knew it was something that had to be done.

Corrie came to Ben, several messages in her hand. "Base Camp One has picked up several coded transmissions, General. The first one originated in Colorado, they believe. The reply came out of Florida; they're pretty sure of that. They have not been able to break the code."

"Parr's bunch is the largest still operating in Florida," Ben said. "The young man is as tough as his father and twice as smart. He also hates me as much as Kenny did, thanks to his father. I've been wondering when he would break out and make his move. This may be the time. Go on, Corrie."

"Reports from Sheridan state that a large force is camped on the west side of the Bighorn River, around Fort Smith. The force has made no hostile moves and the Rebels garrisoned at Sheridan have no idea who they are. They are requesting orders."

"They could well be Ashley, Voleta, and the outlaws," Ben said. "The settlers in Sheridan are too small in number to tackle them . . . if they are

335

hostiles. Tell them to take no direct action until fly-bys have been done, Corrie."

"Yes, sir. Khamsin has been reinforced by foreign troops. Pilots flying recon state that several large ships have docked in ports along the coast of South Carolina. Several more ships are still at sea, enroute. We lost one plane and crew to what is believed to be a Stinger, or missile of that type fired from shipboard."

Georgi was studying maps. "Ships coming from *where?*" he questioned. "And carrying troops of what nationality?"

"Fair questions, Georgi," Ben said. "They could be from South America, West Africa, Europe. Son of a bitch!" Ben cussed. "About the time we think we're gaining ground, something like this sails in and sets us back."

"Ben," Georgi said, "if we strained every resource, using every man and woman and young person, say, over the age of sixteen, how many people could we field?"

"If we count the people at the outposts, oh, maybe five thousand tops. But I'd hate to think it could come to that."

Ike said, "The instant we start stripping and abandoning outposts to move troops east, the outlaws and crud would move in."

"And we'd have to do it all over again," Dan said with a disgusted look on his face.

"And we don't even know the nationality of the troops landing." That was put forth by Tina. "Could it be a multinational force?"

"It could be anything," Ben said softly. "But what keeps puzzling me is this: why are they leaving their homelands? What is pushing them toward America? We now know, through intercepted radio transmissions, that the death toll, worldwide, was not nearly as high as first thought. We now know there are millions of people who survived the Great War. What in the hell is going on in South America, Europe, China?"

"Night People," Buddy said.

"Probably," Dan agreed. "But the troops landing belong to Lan Villar." His voice was very soft. "Bet on it."

Ben shifted his eyes. "Lan is dead."

"That was never confirmed, friend," Georgi said. "Our overseas intelligence people could never autenticate his demise. And neither could your CIA operatives. As a matter of fact, our people swore they saw Lan in West Africa several times after his reported death."

That was fact and Ben knew it.

"Talk about a name from the past," Ike said. "I was on the SEAL team who was given the nod from the NSA to kill Villar back in '86. Then certain members of the House and Senate got wind of it and damn near pissed their lace drawers. Whole operation had to be scrapped."

"Dad," Tina looked at her father, "who is Lan Villar?"

"The most murderous, deadly, dangerous, despicable, and feared terrorist who ever lived."

12

"So they drove you out, too?" Khamsin, the Hot Wind, said to Lan Villar.

"Nobody has ever driven me out of anyplace," Lan corrected him. "But it looks like Ben Raines has sure done a dandy job of kicking your ass."

Khamsin offered no rebuttal to that. How can one rebut the truth? Instead, he said, "I cannot believe that you sailed only God knows how many thousands of miles just to pay me a social call."

One terrorist sat down across the table from the other terrorist. Lan Villar was a mixture of Scandinavian, Algerian, and Spanish. Back when such things were important, he had held dual citizenship between Algeria and Spain. Norway wanted nothing to do with the bastard. And said as much.

Lan had never felt any really allegiance to any country. He sold his skills to anybody, for the highest price. He would kill one, or a thousand. It made absolutely no difference to Lan whether they were men, women, or children.

Lan was now in his late forties, but still a very handsome man, and in the peak of physical conditioning. He had always been very vain about his looks, and with his black eyes and blond hair, Lan was a very striking-looking man. A big man, well over six feet, and a powerful man.

"So it's true, then: New York City is no more?"

"It's true. Ben Raines destroyed it, and almost destroyed me," the Hot Wind admitted.

"Ben Raines," Lan mused softly. "I met him a couple of times, in Africa, back in . . . ?" He shrugged his heavy shoulders. "I can't even remember when it was. He was there working for the Company. No matter. How many Rebels does Raines have under his command?"

"I would say he could field, and that would have to include the troops of the Russian, Georgi Striganov, between four and five thousand. But they are top troops. The black man, Cecil Jefferys, is in command of the base in Louisiana. The ex-SEAL, Ike McGown, is in command of another battalion; he's with Ben in the west. The mercenary, West, commands another battalion. And that damnable ex-SAS man, Dan Gray, commands the Scouts. They are nothing but ruthless thugs."

"I know Dan Gray. He tried to kill me twice, and almost succeeded the last time—when I was working for the IRA. If if had not been for the timidity of certain British politicians, Dan and his SAS men probably would have killed me."

"I heard you were badly wounded."

"I was. Came close to dying. Thanks to that British son of a bitch."

"It seems as though you despise Dan Gray almost as much as I do Ben Raines."

Lan locked gazes with the Libyan. Khamsin felt it was like looking into the eyes of a deadly snake. "More," Lan replied.

They all compared notes as to what they knew of the terrorist, Lan Villar. Only Dan seemed to hold back. Ben picked up on it.

"What's the matter, Dan?"

"There is something else you all should know about that bloody bastard, Villar. He despises me. I wounded him back in . . . oh, '85 or '86. I don't remember exactly. But he almost died from it." Dan smiled, and it was not pretty. "I hand-loaded my own ammo. Hollow-nose. But I sealed into the nose a liberal dose of cobra venom. I understand the terrorist son of a bitch hovered near death for months after that."

Everyone noticed the near-sadistic glint in Dan's eyes; and that was not like him. Dan was a professional soldier—he fought and killed the enemy because that seemed to be the only way to bring some sort of stability back to the earth—not because he was a person who took glee in inflicting pain on any living thing.

It appeared to all looking at Dan that Lan Villar was the exception to that.

"Tell it all, Dan," Ike said.

"Before I put lead into him, and poison, Lan Villar had kidnapped my sister. She was thirteen years old. He tape-recorded every . . . session of perversion with her. Took delight in passing her around to his men . . . and some of the women who fought with him. It took Marilyn a long and very painful time to die. Ben, compared to Lan Villar, Sam Hartline was a courtly English gentleman. And let me add this: If I ever get my hands on Villar, and take that rotten plague upon the earth alive, I assure all of you he will not die well."

The Englishman turned and put his back to the others for a moment, old memories heavy on his broad shoulders.

"Settle down, people," Ben said. "We don't know that it is Lan. Odds are that it is not."

"It's Villar," Dan said. "Before the Great War, he had settled in Angola and was fighting for the Communists there."

"That still doesn't prove anything, Dan," Georgi said.

"Oh, but it does." Dan turned to face the group. "Those communiques in several different languages we have been intercepting over the past couple of years, but all being spoken by the same man with the same strange accent, almost like a slur? The ones we believed originated in Africa? Well, Villar is multilingual and was born with a slight speech impediment. Add it up."

"I'd say you're getting warmer," Ben admitted. "But there still is a lot of room for doubt."

"In one way I hope you're right, General. But in another, I hope you're wrong." Dan nodded his head at the group, then turned and walked away.

"If it is Villar or isn't Villar," Ben said, "it still means that Malone and his bunch will probably have to be put on hold. Malone and his pack of screwballs represent only a fart in the wind compared to whoever is landing in South Carolina."

"Did you know Villar, Dad?" Tina asked.

"I met him twice in Africa years ago, when I was doing Company work. It was instant dislike from both sides. I knew who he was, but I was under no orders to kill him. I've already regretted that I let him walk away. Looks like I might regret it even more if Dan's suspicions are true."

"He certainly feels very strongly that he is correct," Georgi said.

"Do we head north, Father?" Buddy asked.

Ben shook his head. "No. We keep heading east on 94. I still want to finish up with Matt. We'll pull out in the morning."

"We have been sent help," Voleta said, walking up to Ashley. She was smiling, and that was something the woman did not do very often.

"Parr?" Ashley asked, rising as was his custom when a lady approached—even Voleta, whom he knew was the farthest thing from a lady.

She sat down on a log. "No. Are you familiar with a terrorist named Lan Villar?"

"I've heard the name. From newscasts years back. I thought he was dead."

"So did I. We were both wrong. He has landed in South Carolina with several thousand men and that many more on the way."

"He's linking up with what is left of Khamsin's people?"

"That is correct."

"I don't know whether that is a help or not, Voleta. Khamsin might not be too thrilled to see us after New York City."

"He will be after Ben Raines makes his move and we pull in behind them and get them in a box."

"Just us?"

"Don't be foolish. Parr will join us, I'm sure of that. Parr's father and Villar were old friends, when both of them were fighting in Africa. And I have other people I can commit."

"I thought as much," Ashley said drily. "Ben Raines's enemies are certainly popping out of the woodwork of late."

"It isn't Ben Raines that Villar is terribly interested in. It's Dan Gray. My people have just decoded messages they picked up sent from shipboard days ago."

"Villar came here solely to kill Dan Gray?"

"No. Europe and Africa are not safe. The Night People are worldwide—or at least in many countries. It seems they don't have a Ben Raines over there."

"Thank God for small favors. One of him is quite enough."

"We can't fail now," Voleta said, excitement in her voice. "Now I get my revenge against Ben Raines." Her eyes were wild with hate and fury.

Crazy bitch! Ashley thought.

Messages from Base Camp One confirmed Ben's worst suspicions: the army that was stepping ashore from the big ships was huge, several thousand more than Ben could ever hope to field. And according to citizens who still resided in South Carolina and spied for the Rebels, Dan had been correct. It was Lan Villar.

"We're in trouble, Ben," Cecil radioed from Base Camp One.

"We're in for a hell of a fight, that's for sure." Ben wanted to present a calm front, even though he knew he did not need to do that with Cecil. Someone once said, after watching Cecil Jefferys handle hours of a stressful combat situation, that if Cecil got any calmer, he'd go to sleep.

"Villar made any firm moves yet?"

"Negative. According to the people we have in the area, it's all pretty much in the staging status as of now. They report artillery, all the way up to 105s; but it's vehicle-drawn. I don't think Villar has any tanks."

"Probably hoping to pick up those over on this side of the waters. We'll disappoint him on that score."

Years back, the Rebels had gone to every military base and national guard and reserve facility in the nation, and had picked through what remained. They had hidden depots of everything from long-range 155s to BB guns.

"Uncork everything we've got, Cec. Get it operational. I want the self-propelled 155s ready to roll by the time I decide to commit."

"Eight inchers, Ben?"

"Everything, Cec. We've got to be able to give a hell of lot more than we receive."

"This Parr fellow is going to try an end-around,

345

Ben. He's moving now. Intel seems to think he'll attempt to link up with Ashley and Voleta. And some of her people have been coming out of their caves and holes around the country."

"That's ten-four. I expected it. How is West?"

"Able to hobble around and command from a Jeep."

"Tell him to get his people geared up and ready to go. We're going to need everybody on this operation."

"Thermopolis and his group?"

"If he wants to throw in with us, yes. I'm sure that Emil will want in."

"He's standing right here now, Ben, listening."

"At your service, General Raines," the unmistakable voice of Emil Hite traveled over the miles. "Always ready to assist the great General Raines, supreme commander of all allied forces on planet earth, great benefactor of—"

"Emil, for christ's sake!"

". . . the oppressed and the down-trodden. Protector of the aged and infirm—"

"Good God, Emil!"

Georgi Striganov and Ike and Dan, Tina, and Buddy stood around the communications truck, listening and laughing, mostly at the expression on Ben's face as Emil prattled on.

". . . the greatest military mind since Napoleon, with the possibly exception of Genghis Khan, and the man to whom Gods speak . . ."

Ben laid down the mike and rubbed his temples with his fingertips, knowing the only way to get

346

Emil to shut up was to let him run his course.

"I commit my small band of fearless warriors and warrioresses . . ."

"Warrioresses?" Dan questioned, a puzzled look on his face.

"We shall fight from the hedgerows and in the streets . . ."

"Oh, no!" Ben muttered, sensing that Emil was just getting wound up.

In the background, they could all hear Cecil's laughter.

"We shall never surrender! And ever with liberty be. We shall defend the Alamo until the last bit of shot and powder is gone . . ."

"I think he's getting confused," Buddy said.

Ben looked at his son. "*Getting* confused? I've never known him when he wasn't confused."

"I know how to shut him up, Dad," Tina said.

"Quick, tell me!"

"Is Michelle Jarnot still with Danjou's group?" she asked Georgi.

The Russian smiled. "Yes. Good thinking." He turned to an aide. "For God's man, get her over here immediately."

Emil had fallen elbows over ankles in love with the French-Canadian while helping Ben in the fight against the Night People in New York City.

Emil rattled on over the miles. "In the words of that great and immoral commander, Montgomery . . ."

"Immoral!" Dan blurted. "Oh, I say now! He's gone too far . . ."

"I have returned!" Emil shouted.

"I think he's got his generals confused," Georgi said.

"I think he's got everybody confused," Ben muttered.

Michelle ran into the truck.

Ben handed her the mike. "Here! Talk to Emil."

"Do I have to?" the woman asked. "I still have nightmares about that little man following me around New York City singing 'Bridge Over Troubled Waters.'"

"Speak," Ben said. "Please!"

"Emil," Michelle said softly.

"My poopsie whoopsie!" Emil shouted. "I feared I had lost you forever." Then he started singing.

Ben led the parade out of the huge truck, leaving Michelle with the mike. She dug in a pocket of her BDUs for aspirin . . . and silently cursed.

13

While Michelle was being treated by Dr. Ling's medics for a mild case of shock, brought about by Emil's singing—or attempting to sing—"Some Enchanted Evening," during which he lost his train of thought and slipped into "Shake, Rattle, and Roll," ending with a sermon given him, so he said, by the Great God Blomm, Ben was preparing to move against Matt Callahan and whatever forces he might still have.

Ben looked up as Danjou walked up. "How is Michelle?"

"The doctors sedated her. She drifted off muttering something about beware the frumious Bandersnatch and the Jubjub bird and the Jabberwock."

"A conversation with Emil can do that to people," Ike said. "That little con artist can drive you up the wall, but he'll stand and fight . . . I'll give him that much. When did he first wander into our lives, Ben?"

"Years ago," Ben said with a laugh. "He and his group once joined the Ninth Order, Emil thinking

Voleta was running a scam like his. Didn't take him log to discover that he had made a terrible mistake. He got the hell away from that group."

"Hours before my mother was to have him burned at the stake," Buddy said. "I remember that quite vividly. I never knew Emil could move so fast."

"All right, people," Ben said. "Listen up. Ike, you are to assume command and take the column on east. I'll be cutting south here"—he punched the map— "to deal with Callahan and what's left of, ah, HALFASS. It might take us a day, it might take a week or more. But I have a hunch it's all going to be settled very near where Custer and his men fell."

"And you want us to wait where for you?" Georgi asked.

"At the Mississippi River. You'll be angling south all the time, so let's make St. Louis our rendezvous point. Stay in contact with Cecil at all times. When Villar makes his move, it's going to be fast, and we don't want to be taken by surprise."

"You're going to be in trouble if Ashley and Voleta swing in behind you and box you in about where Custer was trapped," Georgi cautioned.

"You don't know Ashley," Ben said with a smile. "Before Ashley attacks, it's got to damn near be a sure thing. He has a yellow streak running right down the center of his back."

"There is one thing I have learned about a coward, my friend," the Russian said. "Corner him, and he'll kill you."

Ben and his column cut off the Interstate when they

reached 416. They cut south for a few miles, and then headed due east, traveling right through what had once been a Crow Indian Reservation. They saw no one. Ben halted the column on the Bighorn River at Saint Xavier and sent Buddy and his team south, to check out that a large force that had reportedly camped there.

Ben bivouacked his people along the river and waited.

"Nothing, Father," Buddy radioed. "There is evidence that there were men here, but no more."

"Any indications of when they pulled out?"

"Not more than twenty-four hours ago. If that long. Coals are still hot in cook fires. They headed north, Father."

"North?"

"Yes, sir. I would say we missed them by no more than a few hours."

"All right, Buddy. Watch yourself and head on back."

"Yes, sir."

Ben checked his maps. "Yeah," he said with sigh. "They could have done it. Probably took 313 and cut across to the old Crow Agency and picked up 212. That was chancy on their part, but just about the only route they could have taken to avoid our new outposts."

"They might be trying to stay south of the main column, but all the while parelleling them," Dan suggested.

"That's probably it. Ike will know soon enough." Ben turned toward the northeast, toward the Custer Battlefield National Monument and the Reno-

Benteen Battlefield Memorial. Matt was out there, waiting. Ben had been informed by the pilot who had spotted the group on horseback, some weeks back, after Sheridan had fallen, that it was no more than a hundred men. But those would be Matt's real hardcases, fighters all.

Ben had no intention of chasing Matt all over the Rosebuds. He had already ordered Scouts out to locate the man. He had ordered the PUFFs at Sheridan to stand by. He was not going to screw around with these HALFASS people, and certainly wasn't going to risk losing troops to Matt and his followers. He would locate them, then call PUFFs in to finish what he could not do with artillery.

He turned and headed back to his tent for an early supper. He had a hunch that tomorrow was going to be a busy day.

He was awakened at two o'clock in the morning.

"Scouts report a large number of campfires, sir. In the valley of the Little bighorn."

Ben shoved out of his sleeping bag. "That damn fool Callahan."

"Sir?"

"He's telling me where he is and to come and get him."

"That's rather stupid on his part, isn't it, sir?"

"Yes. It is. Radio the Scouts and ask if there is any possibility the fires could belong to Indians?"

"That's negative, sir. Colonel Gray already did that. According to Sarah, this reservation has been deserted for years."

"Corrie?"

"Here, sir."

"Advise Sheridan to get the PUFFs up. Have Dan give them the coordinates for the location of the hostiles. Tell them to cream that valley."

"Yes, sir."

An hour later, Ben and the Rebels, now all up and dressed and ready to go, heard the PUFFs drone overhead and to the east, heading north.

"Ask them if they can see the campfires," Ben said.

"That's ten-four, sir."

Ben shook his head. "Suicide. But why."

"He didn't think you'd play it this way, General," Dan said. "He is so far gone, he probably had delusions of you riding up on a horse and challenging him to a gunfight like in the Western movies."

"Then he damn sure didn't know me nearly as well as he thought."

When the PUFFs cut loose, the sight was visible for miles in any direction. From the Rebels' position, it was like a silent fireworks display as cannon and machine gun fire ripped the night.

To Matt Callahan, it was an act of betrayal—the code of the West had been ignored by Slim. When Matt had heard the planes coming, he guessed what they were and shouted for his men to hit the trail over to where their horses had been picketed.

The horses came through the deadly barrage alive; they had been picketed down near a creek. But very few of Matt's men made it off the ridges.

The Rebels waited until dawn before moving out. they took the two-lane highway over to the site of Custer's Last Stand and then followed the old road that wound through the entire battlefield. The carrion birds were already feasting on the dead, sprawled on and along the ridges.

Ben got out and walked among the silent and mangled dead. There was no one who even vaguely resembled Matt Callahan.

"What do we do with the horses, General? They're picketed down there along that creek, or river . . . whatever it is."

"Turn them loose. They'll join up with some of the wild herds we've seen out here."

It bothered Ben that Matt was not among the dead. For that meant that it was not over. And Ben wasn't about to go off and leave Matt alive to rebuild.

He walked back to the main building, which used to house artifacts of the battle and the era. It had long been looted. He sat down on the steps and rolled a cigarette, thinking and smoking. Ben guessed that if he sat there long enough, Matt would make an appearance.

"Rider coming," a Rebel called, pointing toward a ridge.

Ben didn't have to look up to know it was Matt Callahan.

"He's yelling something, General," another Rebel sid. "Sounds like Jim."

"Slim," Ben said, taking a final puff and grinding out the butt under the heel of his boot.

"You want me to shoot him out of the saddle?" a Rebel asked.

"No. That would be cutting against the grain of the code of the West."

The Rebel looked at Ben to see if he was serious.

Tina walked to her father's side. Matt was still on the ridge, sitting his saddle. "Dad, what cockamamie idea are you thinking of in dealing with that nut?"

"Cockamamie idea? Me? Daughter, you know me better than that. Get me a bull horn, will you. I'm not going to stand here and shout at that nitwit."

Bull horn in hand, Ben clicked it on and lifted it to his lips. "Matt! You think you're tough? I think you're as yellow as a damned sheepherder!"

"What's wrong with being a sheepherder?" Buddy asked.

"Cattlemen didn't like sheep on their range," an older Rebel said. "They were always fighting with each other."

"How strange," Buddy remarked.

"Strap on your hoglegs, you yellow coyote!" Matt hollered.

Ben lifted the bull horn. "Get off that horse and face me man to man, Snake! Let's settle this with fists, if you've got the guts for it."

The Rebels had all turned, standing quietly, listening to the strange exchange.

"Guns, Slim!" Matt yelled.

"I always knew you were a coward, Snake. Why don't you get you a sidesaddle?"

Matt screamed his outrage at this insult to his manhood.

"Come on, Snake," Ben taunted him. "Let's settle it man to man. You're afraid of me, aren't you? You damned yellow weasel!"

Matt slowly dismounted and untied the leather thongs that held his holsters to his legs. He unbuckled his gun belt and dropped the Colts to the ground. He started walking down the hill.

Ben laid his M14 aside and unhooked his web belt.

He took off his shirt and removed his restrictive body armor, put the shirt back on and rolled up the sleeves then started walking up the hill, all the Rebels following.

"I'm a-gonna clean your plow, Raines," Matt said as he approached Ben.

"I doubt it," Ben told him, and knocked the man sprawling with a hard right to the jaw.

Ben stepped back, allowing Matt to get to his boots, something that he ordinarily would not do. If he had been taking this fight seriously, he would have kicked Matt's face in while he had him on the ground.

Matt jumped at Ben, swinging. Ben blocked the punch and let him have five in the belly, following that with a short left hook to the jaw. Matt went down again.

He was slower getting up, but he got up, circling Ben warily. He snapped a couple of quick rights and then sneaked a left in, snapping Ben's head back and bloodying his mouth.

Ben shook his head to clear away the gathering cobwebs and chirping birdies and waded in, swinging both fists, standing toe to toe and slugging it out.

Ben was bigger and heavier and his punches held more power. He gradually drove Matt back.

"Time! Time!" Matt hollered.

"That's your ass!" Ben told him, and hit him in the mouth, busting his lips and loosening some teeth.

"Ungentlemanly!" Matt hollered, shaking his head and sending blood flying from his smashed mouth.

Ben hit him again and turned the man sideways.

Stepping in, Ben caught a left to the body and a right to the jaw that stopped him.

Falsely sensing victory, Matt closed with Ben and that move got him a boot to the knee that sent him to the ground. Rolling, he got to his feet and faced Ben, his fists held high and close.

Ben faked a left and Matt followed it, dropping his guard. Ben hit him with a solid right to the mouth and a tooth flew past bloody lips.

Screaming his rage, Matt charged, running into Ben and sending both men sprawling to the hot, dry earth, both of them panting for breath. They rolled on the grass, kicking up dust and cussing.

"Damn dirty book writer!" Matt panted.

"You're a liar, Callahan," Ben told him, all the while thinking: This is the most childish thing I've done in more years than I can remember.

Matt tried to knee Ben in the groin and Ben blocked the move and shoved him off, rolling to one side, getting to his boots and lifting his fists.

"Dirty book writer?" Dan questioned.

"Professional jealousy maybe," Beth said.

"I think it's demeaning," Corrie said. "The General shouldn't be rolling around on the ground like a common thug."

"It's stupid!" Jersey frowned.

"I think it's funny," Buddy said.

"Come on, Pops!" Tina yelled. "Give him hell!"

Matt knocked Ben down with a solid right to the jaw and then jumped on top of him, both fists flailing away.

Ben gouged Matt in the eye and that brought a roar of pain as the man twisted away from the painful fingers. On his knees, Ben clubbed the man on the side of the neck and got to his feet.

Matt tried to tackle Ben and Ben put a boot in the man's face. The sound of Matt's nose breaking was clearly heard over the panting and cussing.

With blood dripping from both their faces, the men circled each other, fists held high.

Matt closed and Ben hit him a combination, left and right, that jerked Matt's head back and glazed his eyes. Ben pressed on with a left to the windpipe and a right to the jaw. Matt's knees buckled and he almost went down, catching himself at the last moment.

He threw himself at Ben and again, both men went down, rolling in the dust.

Ben pinned Matt to the ground and started working on his face, both fists pile-driving. He stopped when he realized the man was unconscious, Matt's face a bloody smashed mask.

Slowly, Ben got to his boots, his chest heaving. "Clean him up, tie him up, and toss him in a truck. Let's get the hell out of here."

14

"What are we going to do with him, Father?" Buddy asked while Ben was washing his face and soaking his swollen hands.

"I don't know, son." Ben dried his face and hands and put on a clean shirt. "Nearly everything within me says we ought to shoot him. But I just can't bring myself to do that."

"He is a perverted, dangerous man," the son reminded the father. "And we do not have prison facilities."

"I am fully aware of that fact. But I do not believe in executing the mentally ill. I just don't know what to do with him."

Dr. Ling walked up and stood looking at Ben.

"Well?" Ben met the man's eyes.

"How are your hands?"

"Everything works without any crunching or grinding."

"You're lucky. The bare human hand was not meant to be used as a weapon."

"How is Matt?"

"He isn't going to make it."

"What!"

"He suffered a heart attack just after the fight. It's massive and there is nothing I can do for him. He probably will not last the hour. He's fading fast and he's asking to see you."

Ben walked over to where Matt lay, on a field cot, protected from the sun by a tarp. Under the swollen and bruised face, the man's color was awful. Ben pulled up a camp chair and sat down.

"Ben," he said weakly.

"I'm here, Matt."

"I've got a lucid moment; they come and go. Mostly go of late."

Ben said nothing.

"Tell me about Megan."

"She's working for Malone. She spun a pretty good yarn there for a time. She fooled me for a while."

"She tell you I sexually abused her as a child?"

"Yes."

"I did. I've been sick for a long time. Tried to get help when the world was still in one piece. But I guess I really didn't want it. I only went for a few sessions, under an assumed name."

Ben rolled a cigarette.

"Roll one for me, partner," Matt said. "Hell, I know I'm not going to make it. Feels like an elephant is sitting on my chest."

Ben lit the cigarette and placed it between the man's lips.

"You remember Luke Wynne, Ben?"

"Sure."

"I killed him."

Ben thought about that for a few seconds. "Why?"

"He wasn't a very good writer."

"Hell of a reason to kill somebody, Matt."

"It's as good a reason as any. You believe in life after death, Ben?"

"Yes. I do."

"I don't know whether I do or not. Is the light fading, Ben."

"Yes," Ben lied.

"You're lyin', ol' buddy."

"Yes. I am."

"Whole chest hurts, Ben." The cigarette fell from his lips. Ben picked it up and crushed it. "And my head feels like it's about to explode."

Dr. Ling came in and gave the man a shot.

"What's that for?" Matt asked.

"It'll make it easier for you."

"Dying, you mean?"

"Yes."

"You just induced dying, didn't you?" Matt asked, no malice or alarm in his voice.

"Yes. I did," Ling told him.

"How much time do I have?"

"About a minute."

"Powerful stuff," Matt murmured.

"Very."

Matt closed his eyes and let the lethal dose take him.

"Ben?"

"Right here, Matt."

"See you, Slim."

"Up in the High Lonesome, Snake."

Matt Callahan shuddered once and his head lolled to one side. When he spoke, the words were slurry. "I'm not going to bother to ask for forgiveness." He closed his eyes and died.

The Rebels buried Matt Callahan in a mass grave, piled in among his dead hardcases, and moved on, following Highway 212 east.

Even though Matt had been a no-good, and only God knew how much misery and grief he had caused over the years, his death bothered Ben for a brief time.

That night, camped in the Custer National Forest, Ben said to Tina, "You never know about a man. I always thought Matt was arrow-straight. He sure had a bunch of us fooled."

"If you could say anything about him, Father," Buddy asked, "what would it be?"

Ben smiled. "He was a good writer."

They pulled out at dawn and all were pleased to find that the old road was in surprisingly good shape. They would stay with 212 until just inside South Dakota. There they would cut south for a few miles and pick up Highway 79 south and follow it down to 385. That would take them south to Interstate 70. They would avoid the cities—not wanting to take the time to confront the Night People—and head as straight as they could for St. Louis.

"Do we check out the interior of any of the cities?" Buddy radioed to Ben.

"No. And we take action only if we are attacked. Spearhead us to St. Louis, Buddy."

And the highway, first in such good shape, soon

began deteriorating rapidly. A few bridges were out, some destroyed deliberately, others weakened by years of flash flooding and no maintenance. The Rebels were forced to detour many times and their advance became slowed to sometimes less than a hundred miles a day.

Buddy had approached Rapid City, on Interstate 90, and reported back that it was full of creepies. The awful stench of them and the remains of the rotting carcasses they had dined on was almost over-powering even without entering the city.

"Leave it, son," his dad told him. "Get back over to 385 and lead us down south. We'll deal with them later on."

None of the Rebels liked the idea of leaving cities filled with creepies. But they also knew that Lan Villar was the threat they had to crush first—if they could. And that thought was one they all had to entertain at some point.

Ike had taken the northern route—no particular reason, he just wanted to see the country—and was making good time. He had bypassed the cities full of Night People, even though it galled him to do so.

The Rebels were ready for a rest by the time they reached Sidney, Nebraska. What they got was a fight.

As fights go, it wasn't much of a fight, but it did slow them up for several hours.

Several hundred bikers, including Wanda and her Sisters of Lesbos, had broken away from Satan and his linking up with Ashley and Voleta and had struck out on their own. When they reached Sidney, they decided they liked it and were going to stay.

About four hundred people were occupying the

town when the bikers and other trash rolled in. And that was the only reason that Ben did not order the town blown off the map by artillery.

Scouts reported that prisoners were being held in the town.

"Orders, General?" Dan questioned.

"I guess we don't have a choice, Dan. Let's take the town. Swing your people around to the east side and I'll drive straight in from the west. I'm getting very weary of these types."

The Rebels took control of the town by using the same tactics of the bikers and outlaws: brute force. The Rebels tried not to shoot up the city, since people were living there and trying to carve something out of the ashes.

It was a sorry and bedraggled-looking bunch of misfits that finally lay down their arms and signaled frantically that they wanted to surrender.

Ben had them lined up, sitting on their butts on the concrete, with their hands behind their heads, while waiting for a report on how many townspeople had suffered from the actions of the outlaws.

"Rape, mostly," Dan reported back. "A half a dozen killings of townspeople when the bikers roared in."

"Have the people point out the guilty ones."

They did so.

"Take them out and shoot them," Ben ordered.

Several of the Sister of Lesbos and more than one biker pissed their dirty jeans at the emotionless-given execution order. But all of them knew that they had one chance of staying alive, and that was to keep their mouths shut tight.

The prisoners visibly flinched as the firing squads carried out Ben's orders.

"No more free rides, people," Ben told the group of about a hundred and fifty. "Those days are long past. How many of you were working for Matt Callahan? And don't even think about lying to me."

Most of the hands were raised.

"He's dead," Ben informed them. "I whipped his ass in a stand-up fistfight near where Custer is buried. His men were wiped out the night before by PUFFs. Most of you know what those are. Matt Callahan, aka the Rattlesnake Kid, died of a heart attack about fifteen minutes after the fight. That stupid HALFASS business just got put out of business."

Ben walked the lines of prisoners, glaring at them. And since they were already very badly shaken, Ben's cold stares did nothing to induce any feelings of immediate relief. "Now then, I have another problem: what in the hell to do with you people."

The bikers did a magnificent job of looking everywhere except at Ben.

"I have discussed this with Colonel Dan Gray." Ben pointed to Dan. "That rather imposing-looking gentlemen right over there."

They looked. They also knew that Colonel Gray was the man who had selected and led the firing squad. They shuddered.

"How would you people like to do something worthwhile just once in your miserable lives?"

The bikers blinked. All had but two thoughts on

their minds: what is it, and what's the catch?

Leadfoot was the first to speak. "We're listening, General."

"Join us," Ben said simply.

The bikers and outlaws and assorted other crud and crap blinked and looked at one another, not sure they had heard correctly.

"What's the catch?" Wanda was the first to speak.

"You fight with us and you obey the rules," Ben told her. "This is probably the last chance you'll ever have to turn your lives around and live decently."

"And if we don't join you," a biker asked, "you goin' to kill us?"

"No. You're free to ride on out of here. But if we ever meet again, and we will, bet on that, and you're not living a very quiet and law-abiding life, I'll kill you. And I think by now you all know that I mean that."

Leadfoot stood up, very carefully. A big man with a shaggy mop of hair and sharp, intelligent eyes. "Say we go along with you, General—what do we get out of it?"

"You mean as in pay?"

"Yes . . . sir," he added.

"Three meals a day, clothes, medical attention, weapons and ammo."

"That's it?"

"That's it."

The outlaws looked at each other; they'd never heard of such a whacky deal.

Wanda stood up. "Well . . . what do you people get out of doing"—she shrugged her shoulders—"all that you do?"

"A feeling that they're helping to restore some degree of civilization back to America," a biker said, standing up. "Pride in themselves. Intangible things. But very important things."

All the Rebels standing nearby, including Ben, turned to look at the well-spoken man.

"That is correct," Ben said. "Your name?"

"Frank."

"You sound as though you have some education."

"I got my degree from Stanford. Why I started outlawing is my business. Yours only if I decide to go back to it."

"That's fair enough. Are you in or out?"

"I'm in."

"Report to Colonel Gray." He once more faced the outlaws. "Make your decisions. I haven't got all day to waste."

"Oh, what the hell!" Wanda said. "Come on, girls. "We've been given a second chance—let's take it."

Leadfoot slowly nodded his head. "Might as well get on the winnin' side for a change."

"You might die on this side, too," Ben reminded him.

Leadfoot smiled and the smile changed his entire face. "That's a fact, General. But I haven't been real happy with myself the past few months. I think that's true for most of us. No one could really put into words why we pulled away from Satan and his bunch. We just did. Most of us here now was against takin' this town. But it's what we've been doin' for a long time. It's over, and I'm glad."

Leadfoot and his bunch formed a line, waiting to see Dan and the other Rebels who had joined him, taking names and blood types and other important personal history from the now ex-outlaws.

Buddy walked up to his father. "This just has to be the strangest army in the history of warfare," he observed.

Ben smiled. "I can hardly wait to see what happens when this bunch meets Emil and Thermopolis."

"Like I said: strange."

15

The Rebels pulled out the following morning, after seeing to the needs of the townspeople and having them flatly reject Ben's offer of becoming a part of the outpost chain.

"Then you're on your own," Ben told them. "Don't expect us to come to your rescue—not again. Because we won't."

"You're a hard man, General Raines," the spokesperson told him.

"I'm trying to rebuild a nation," Ben replied. "And you're either with me or against me. You've made your choice. Good day."

The Rebels crossed the South Platte with Buddy and his Rat Team spearheading some twenty-five miles in advance of the main column and they rolled eastward.

Ben had decided that the bikers who joined them could dress as they always had—after they bathed—and could carry weapons of their choice. But they would, like all the rest, wear body armor. Leadfoot was in command; the second in command was Frank. Ben had no idea how the bikers would work out; all he could do was hope for the best.

Buddy reported back that the Interstate was blocked at North Platte. The town seemed to be filled with outlaws. Ben told his son to stay put and out of sight. He halted the column and walked up to Leadfoot.

"You know these people in North Platte, Leadfoot?"

"I don't have any idea who they are, General," the biker said, "Most of us have mainly been working the northwest and southwest the past couple of years. Everything east of the Wyoming line is unknown to us."

Ben decided to put them to the test. "You think you can go in there and Size things up for us?"

"Damn right!"

"Well then, carry on, Leadfoot. I'll hold the column here."

With the column two miles behind them, Leadfoot pulled the bikers over. "This is our chance to prove ourselves, people. Let's don't screw it up. I kinda like being on the winnin' side for a change."

"It does feel sorta good, don't it?" Wanda said.

"All right, folks," Leadfoot began, "lock and load and get ready for war. And remember: we ain't outlaws no more; we're part of Ben Raines's Rebels. Let's roll."

The one hudnred and fifty bikers, Leadfoot in the front, rode brazenly around the roadblocks and right up the main street of North Platee. Wanda gunned her Harley and rode up alongside Leadfoot.

"I seen a bike that I know," she called. "This is Pistol's bunch."

"I heard of him. He's worser than we ever was. Him and his gang is people that even *we* could look down on. Piss on talkin', let's take the town!"

Frank took one group and Leadfoot took the other, and taking tactics from the Rebels, the bikers hit the town hard and fast and offered no mercy to the outlaws. They were all armed with Uzis and they knew how to use them. The fight was very short and very brutal. What was left of Pistol's gang, caught totally unaware by bikers they thought were going to be friendly, turned tail and hauled their butts out of town.

Using a walkie-talkie, Leadfoot radioed Ben. "Come on in, General. The town is yourn."

Smiling, Ben acknowledged the message and turned to Dan. "I believe we made the right choice, Dan."

"I believe we did, General."

Ben shook hands with every biker, complimenting them on a job well done. "From now on, you'll be known as the Wolfpack."

To a person, the bikers were grinning. Then they raised their Uzis in the air and cheered Ben . . . and another small but extremely loyal and hard-nosed unit had been added to the army of Rebels.

The Rebels spent a day in North Platte, seeing to the needs of the several hundred townspeople who had been virtual slaves of Pistol and his outlaw bikers. Unlike those a hundred miles back, this group was eager to become a part of the Rebel outpost system. Ben arranged for planes to start coming in, bringing much-needed supplies and weapons. Ben left a few of his own Rebels to oversee the training and setting-up of the new outpost and pulled out. Ike and General Striganov had reached St. Louis and were waiting for Ben.

Ben allowed a few of the Wolfpack members to ride with Buddy and his Rat Team spearheading the column. He wanted the bikers to learn military tactics concerning recon, and what Buddy couldn't teach them, Dan sure would.

Kearney was in the hands of outlaws and warlords and Grand Island belonged to the creepies. Ben ordered them both bypassed and said a silent prayer that both factions would end up killing each other.

Omaha had taken a nuke during the Great War and was hot; one of the few cities that had actually taken a nuclear strike. Lincoln was another stronghold of the Night People, so Ben ordered the column to cut south at York and took 81 down to 136. They would follow that all the way into Missouri.

They spent the night at a long-deserted town on the Missouri River and crossed over into what had once been the state of Missouri the following morning. Buddy cut the column southeast until linking up with Interstate 70. They would take that all the way across to St. Louis.

The Rebels found pockets of survivors all over the state, and stopped whenever they could to explain what was happening and why they could not linger any longer than to give medical attention to those needing it and radioing to Base Camp One with the locations.

And then there would be miles and miles of not sighting a living being. But all had the uncomfortable sensation of having unseen eyes on them.

"Just like in so many of the other states," Beth remarked. "They want to come out and meet us, but they're wary of us."

"We'll be back," Ben said. "God willing."

His team in the Blazer knew then just how serious conditions were, for Ben rarely invoked God's name.

"The Wood's Children live along this stretch," Ben said. "They range from North Dakota all the way over to the Illinois line." He reached for his mike, hesitated, and then picked it up. "Eagle to Rat."

"Go, Eagle."

"Start leaving messages for the Wood's Children, Rat. I told you about them. Wade and Ro and the others. Tell them to meet us in St. Louis. Theirs are the eyes that have been on us. They'll be there—bet on it."

"The people that worship you, General?" Jersey asked.

"Unfortunately, yes. But I think I got through to them the last time we met. We'll know in a few weeks." Ben was silent for a time, remembering his first face-to-face meeting with the Wood's Children, or the Orphans' Brigade, as Ike had named them.

"Here comes the Orphans' Brigade," Buck said,

sticking his head into Ben's quarters. "General, you have to see this to believe it."

"That bad?" Ben questioned, moving toward the door.

The columns of young people were still about a mile away from the HQ. They were marching steadily. Ragged and dirty, the kids marched with their heads held high.

Ben, with Gale by his side, watched the young people. One column was marching from the northwest, the other from the northeast.

"Damnest thing I believe I've ever seen," Ben remarked, lowering his binoculars.

"They're children!" Gale said. "Babies."

"Don't you believe that, Miss Roth," Buck said. "Those kids have been on their own for years. They're tough little guys and gals. And the way it was told to me, most of them would as soon kill you as look at you."

Gale's heart went out to the little ones in the column. "That's hard to believe, Buck."

"Believe it," Ben told her. "They've had no schooling, no parental or adult guidance, no discipline other that what they impose on themselves. A sort of tribal law, I imagine. They have had but one thought in all their waking years: to survive. Yet another sad postwar fact."

Gale wouldn't give it up. "But they look so helpless."

Ben said, "Bear in mind that those two columns of kids helped destroy four battalions of trained IPF personnel. And they took no prisoners."

Mary Macklin had joined the group. "Colonel Gray thought they looked helpless. He offered one little girl, about nine years old, a candy bar. She bit his hand to the bone. The colonel's Scouts said that Colonel Gray then became quite ineloquent."

"Poor little girl," Gale said.

Mary smiled. "Then that poor little girl grabbed the colonel's weapon, kicked him in the shins, and ran off into the woods."

Ike walked up and looked at the approaching young people, only a few hundred feet away. They marched forward, stopping a few yards from Ben and the group.

"Aw!" Ike said. "Look at them poor little kids. Makes your heart ache, don't it? Me and Sally got to take in a few of them to raise."

Ben had smiled.

Ike walked into the street and stood smiling down at the group. He felt his heart soften as he looked at a small girl, ragged and dirty. The stocky ex-SEAL knelt down in front of her.

"Howdy, honey," he said in his best Mississippi drawl. "My, but you sure are pretty. How'd you like to come live with me and my wife?"

The girl, about ten years old, pulled a pistol from a holster, cocked it, and stuck the muzzle in Ike's suddenly pale face. "How'd you like to eat some lead, fatso?"

Ben had to struggle to keep from laughing at the expression on Ike's face. It was very difficult to get anything over on Ike, and Ben knew this story would fly around the Rebel camps. Ike would never live it down.

"Now, darlin'," Ike said, very carefully getting to his feet. "There ain't no call for nothin' like this. I don't mean you no harm."

"Yeah?" the cute little girl asked belligerently. "That's what them other guys told me, too. I believed them. You know what they done to me?"

"I'd really rather not hear about it, if you don't mind," Ike said.

"I guess you and your wife is gonna love me and hug me and give me food and pretty clothes and all that shit?" The little girl demanded that Ike reply.

Ike winced at her language. "Well, ah, yeah, that's right."

"That's what them men told me, too. So I believed them. They took me to a house and did bad things to me. They hurt me real bad and left me to die. Then Wade and his people come along and him and his people killed them men who raped me. I believe Wade. I don't know you, so I don't believe you, and I don't trust you. I got my reasons, mister."

Ben stepped forward as the crowd began to swell with the arrival of more young people. "You can believe him," he told the girl. "Ike is sincere in wanting you to come live with his family. Ike and Sally are good people."

The ragged little girl with the pistol in her hand swung old/wise/young eyes to Ben. She holstered the pistol. "Maybe," she said, suspicion in her voice. "I don't know you neither, but you look familiar. Who you is, mister?"

"Ben Raines."

The girl reached into a leather pouch on her belt and removed a plastic-covered picture. She compared the picture to the man then turned to face the large group of young people, hundreds strong. "It's really him!" she yelled.

The little girl fell to her knees and every boy and girl in the crowd followed suit. Ben stood open-mouthed, astonishment on his face.

"What the hell?" he muttered.

Wade crawled toward Ben. Clearly embarrassed, Ben tried to motion the young man to his feet. But Wade would have none of that.

"Get up!" Ben whispered to him. "What do you think you're doing?"

With his eyes downcast, Wade called out, "All praise Ben Raines!"

"What!" Ben almost shouted the word. His own people were looking at him strangely.

"All praise Ben Raines!" the crowd of young people echoed.

Ben lost his temper. "Now just a damn minute!" he yelled. "All of you kids—get off your knees. Get up and face me."

Ben handed his old Thompson to Ike. The eyes of the young people followed the movement. They now viewed Ike in a different light. Ben, feeling awfully foolish, motioned the young people up from their prostration.

Reluctantly, and with fear on their faces, the kids rose to their feet.

"You young people do *not* worship *me!*" Ben told

them firmly. *"Nobody* worships me. I won't have it. It's silly. Where did you young people get such an idea?"

"It . . . is written," Wade stammered out in reply.

Ben looked hard at him. "Written? Where is it written that I am to be treated like some sort of god?"

"An old man told us that. I mean . . . he didn't exactly say it like that, but he talked real funny; old-time like. And he said that to worship a false god was a sin in the eyes of the Lord. I told him that maybe was so, but there was only one man I would ever bow down to, and that was Ben Raines."

Ben nodded, not knowing how the young people would interpret that nod. "Was the man's name the Prophet?" The old man with the long beard and robe and staff that sometimes popped up in several places at once. Ben had seen him; didn't know what to make of him.

At the mention of the old man's name, the young people drew back, as if very much afraid.

"Yes," Wade said, standing his ground but looking very much as if he would like to cut and run.

"What did the old man say and do when you told him that?"

"He said that perhaps you—Ben Raines—might be the man to do the job at hand. But that on your head would lie the . . . con-con . . ." He struggled with the word. "Consequences should you try but fail."

"What do you think the old man meant by that?"

A look of confusion passed over Wade's face. He finally shrugged his shoulders. That you are a god—

what else?"

"I am not a god. Not someone that you should worship."

"No, sir." The young man's reply was soft. "No, sir. I don't think so. And none of the people who travel with me think so neither. I been all over this land, from big water to big water, east to west. I been to Canada all the way down to Mexico. I have seen what some people have built in reverence to you."

Ben stirred. The rock and stone monuments that some had erected to him. But how to combat that was something that eluded Ben.

"You have many, many followers, Mr. Ben Raines. Some who live on the land, some who live under it, in tunnels and caves."

At that time Ben had only heard of the Underground People. He had never seen them.

Wade motioned to another young man and he stepped forward. "Ro," Wade said. "He leads the second group of young."

Ben extended his hand. Ro backed away from it.

"It is not permitted, Mr. Ben Raines."

"What is not permitted?" There was an edge to Ben's voice.

Ro looked at Ben and smiled. "It is as the Prophet said: you do not yet know who you are. But it still is not permitted."

Ben thought: I ask a question and get riddles.

Ro further irritated Ben by bowing to him. Ro turned to his people and said something that Ben could not understand. It sounded very much like Pidgin English.

Dear God! Ben thought. Have we reverted to this—already?

"And do they still worship you?" Cooper asked, after Ben had told them the story.

"I don't know. I hope not. We've only scratched the surface of what really lies out there." He pointed to the passing landscape. "And under it," he added softly.

16

A subterranean society did exist in what was once known as America, South America, Central America, Asia Minor, Africa, Asia—all around the globe. In Europe, the Night People were called Children of Darkness . . . they worshipped Satan. Their enemies, the People of Darkness, still worshipped a more kinder and caring God, a deity who had a face strangely like Ben Raines.

The people who lived in the caves and tunnels had long ago given up on modern technology and weapons and what was once considered the acceptable mode of dress and manner of living. They wore the skins of animals, and the soles of their feet were as tough as leather.

Some worldwide worshipped Satan, and all the horror that went with it. Others worshipped some form of higher entity, but for the most part they did not believe He was all-powerful. No true all-powerful God would have permitted the world to become as it now was.

Blind faith in the unseen was unacceptable to many survivors of the Great War.

But Ben Raines, now—he was real. Ben Raines was doing something to correct all this misery and awfulness. So, many of them reasoned, Ben Raines must be in touch with some higher power. And if that were true, then Ben Raines must be the man-God here on earth.

In a manner of speaking, the older and wiser of them cautioned.

Ben knew only too well that he was combatting much more than a tangible enemy.

That other enemy scared the crap out of him.

"This Wade and Ro," Jersey asked, "are they still alive?"

"I don't know. They would be older now, and perhaps no longer in the field. We'll just have to see. They live a hard and dangerous life. And they resist my efforts to bring them into our settlements."

The long column rolled on. They crossed the Missouri River at St. Charles and cut onto 270 just outside of St. Louis. All along the Interstate were mounds of equipment with more equipment being trucked and flown in daily from Base Camp One.

Cecil had brought his battalion up from Louisiana. West was there, the mercenary limping around with a cast on his ankle.

Ben stepped out of the Blazer and let the bad news hit him.

"Khamsin and Villar are massing for attack, Ben," Cecil told him. "They've already started moving units westward."

"Here we go again," West said, leaning on his cane.

Ben nodded his head. "And this time we'd better do it right the first time, or there won't be another time—for any of us."